Wings of the Wind

Novels by Marjorie Thelen

Mystery-in-Exotic Places
The Forty Column Castle
The Hieroglyphic Staircase

Fiona Marlow Novels
Designer Detective
High Desert Detective
Heroes in the End

Deovolante Space Opera Series
A Far Out Galaxy
The Next Universe Over
Hoodoo Canyon
Earth Rising

Historical Romance
Wings of the Wind

Wings of the Wind

*A historical romance
set in Galveston, Texas, 1850*

Marjorie Thelen

Cover and book design by Rachel Bostwick

Wings of the Wind
Copyright Marjorie Thelen 2019
This is a work of fiction. Names, characters, places and incidents are products of the author's imagination, or were used fictitiously and are not to be construed as real. All rights reserved. The republication or utilization of this work in whole or in part in any form by any electronic or mechanical or other means, not known or hereafter invented, including xerography, photocopying and recording, or in any information storage or retrieval system, is forbidden without the written permission of the author. The scanning, uploading, and distribution of this book via the Internet or via any other means without permission of the copyright owner is illegal and punishable by law.
ISBN: 9781089169451
www.marjoriethelen.com

*"You make the clouds your chariot;
You ride on the wings of the wind."
Psalm 104:3*

Chapter One

Galveston, Texas, 1850

"Jamie," Mercedes Lawless called to her younger brother, "someone's sent us a letter."

She waved it in the air as she sailed along an aisle of the Lavender Dry Goods Emporium, passing shelves of silk cloth and cotton prints on her way to her workroom in the back of the shop. She straightened a black mantilla here, a spool of creamy lace there, stopped in front of the soaps and scented water, took a quick visual inventory, and made a mental note to bring out more of the lavender water and soaps. They were good sellers. She inhaled deeply and smiled. The scent of lavender filled the air.

Jamie's dark, curly head popped up from behind a cabinet of tools where he was sorting a new shipment. "What?" he croaked from across the room in his uneven adolescent voice.

"I've just come from the post office. Someone's written to us and in a fine hand, too."

"What's it say?" he asked, following her to the back of the store mumbling to himself. He stuck his hand into a faceted glass jar sitting on Mercedes's work desk that always held fresh baked ginger cakes. He extracted one and took a bite.

Mercedes sat her shopping basket down on her neatly organized desk and smiled at him. "I haven't opened it yet. What were you mumbling about?"

"Thought maybe some long lost relative died, and we came into an inheritance. Then I wouldn't have to work."

Her laughter sparkled in the quiet of the room. "Don't you like the dry goods business?" She couldn't help teasing him because she knew what his answer would be. While she dreamed of a future for him in the store, he had different ideas.

He gave her an exasperated look. "You know what I want to do. I'd be a famous buccaneer like Captain Jean Lafitte. I'd be sailing the high seas, robbing Spanish galleons, stowing away treasure on Caribbean islands." He made grand sweeping gestures. "I'd be fighting other buccaneers. I'd . . ."

He grabbed an umbrella lying nearby and jumped up on a crate packed with washtubs. He battled an unseen enemy with the weapon, parrying back and forth. "I'd run them through with my sword. Take that," he shouted. "And that." He slashed and jabbed his phantom opponent.

"Oh, is it Jean Lafitte today? No matter that slaves were his treasure from the African trade?"

"That's not true!" He stopped parrying and jumped down to confront his sister. "Those are vicious lies that his enemies spread to discredit a noble buccaneer."

"Pirate, I'd call him and so have a lot of other people." Mercedes reached out to tousle his hair.

"Cut it out!" He jerked away. Displays of affection did not fit with his idea of how one treated a buccaneer.

"Let's see what's in this letter," she said. "Maybe it's an invitation to join a company of pirates. We could both go."

"Yeah," said Jamie with glee and then sobered. "But I'm not so sure about you. Women aren't cut out to be pirates."

"Mercedes," he said, drawing closer to her, "please see what you could do to get me a place on a ship. You know all the ship owners and captains. Talk to them. Please help me so I can go to sea." His deep blue eyes mirrored the eagerness in his words.

Mercedes reached out and pulled him to her in an enormous hug that said she never wanted to let him go. He was the rare jewel in her life since their parents had passed on. But she was running low on arguments to keep him. She knew that someday soon if she didn't help him get on a ship, he would disappear of his own accord.

He struggled to be free of her. "Please," he said. "I'm thirteen years old now."

"I'll . . ." she began as the bell over the front door of the shop jingled. She patted his shoulder reaching up to do so. He was already taller than she was. "I'll see to the customer. Then we'll talk."

She left the unopened letter lying on the desk and went to see who had come in. Jamie followed her, jabbing dispiritedly at the air with his umbrella rapier.

"Hello." Mercedes smiled at the short, round man who stood by the entrance. "Welcome to the Lavender Dry Goods Emporium. Are you looking for something special today?"

"Why, yes I am," said the man, tipping his top hat and mopping his forehead. "A wee bit warm out there," he said. He gazed about the shop, as if assessing the value of the neatly arranged displays and large variety of goods. "Not accustomed to such heat."

"Yes, it's warm but that's normal for Galveston,"

Mercedes said. "They say we have some of the finest resort weather anywhere. People come here to enjoy our sun and sea breezes."

"Is that so, lassie?" He gestured to the outside. "Aye, it is a lovely town."

"I don't believe you are from around here, are you?"

He chuckled. "That I'm not, lass. I hail from Scotland. I guess my accent gives me away. You've quite a shop. That's such a fancy sign with the name of the store in big purple letters over the door outside."

Mercedes beamed. "I'm glad you like the sign. I had it put up this last week." Several new customers had remarked on the sign so far. It had been expensive but it seemed to be doing its job of attracting more customers to the store.

"Someone has a real eye for business here," said the rotund gentleman. He looked around. "May I ask who the owner is?"

"Why, I am," said Mercedes, surprised, since it seemed logical to her who the owner was.

The visitor raised an eyebrow and glanced at a piece of paper in his hand. "I'm here looking for a Miss Mercedes Lawless. Would that be you then?"

"It would. I am Mercedes Lawless," she replied, wondering if he were a traveling salesman. He would be one of many that passed through trying to sell the latest in household goods and ladies fashions. She was always on the lookout for anything that might excite purchases from her large contingency of female customers.

Jamie came up behind her.

"This is my brother Jamie," Mercedes said, pleased when he responded with a polite bow to the stranger.

The man tipped his hat and returned the bow. "A

pleasure to make your acquaintance. My name is Duncan Carmichael. I represent the business interests of Captain Andre Lafitte."

"Lafitte?" Jamie said. He looked as though someone had set off a firecracker under him. "Is he related to Jean Lafitte, the great buccaneer?"

Mr. Carmichael cleared his throat like he had just swallowed something unpleasant. He found his voice and said, "That you would have to discuss with Captain Lafitte. He does not discuss his family with me."

"Jamie, please." Mercedes put a hand on his shoulder. "Try to remember your manners."

To Mr. Carmichael she said, "When Jamie's not helping at the store, he's over at the wharves pestering the seamen. They fill him with tales of the sea and the age of pirates. He's got quite an imagination. Please excuse him."

Mr. Carmichael's lips curved in an understanding smile as he looked at Jamie. "Probably, lad, you don't see many pirates around here any longer."

"Well, sir, no, we don't. We never see any," Jamie said. That did not deter him. He looked at Mr. Carmichael and said with a note of excitement in his voice, "Did you know that Jean Lafitte lived right here on Galveston Island? Soldiers made him leave but first he threw a pirate party and burned his big, red mansion to the ground. They say he buried treasure on the island, but it's never been found. Sometimes I go digging for it. Alls I found so far have been some broken whiskey bottles." Then hope brightened Jamie's face. "That was thirty years ago but he could still be alive. No one knows what happened to him."

"He could still be alive," Mr. Carmichael said, "or most assuredly his descendants would be. If the tales about him and his women are true, he would have a lot of them, but he'd be a mighty old man by now."

"Descendants, that's right." Jamie's face broke into a wide grin. "I bet they're living on a hidden Caribbean Island surrounded by treasure. By night they still sail the seas looking for loot, I betcha." His eyes glazed over at the thought.

"Enough of this, Jamie dear." Mercedes's voice intruded and pulled them back from their wanderings. She knew from past experience that Jamie's imagination could take them far away from the Lavender Dry Goods Emporium.

"You were saying, Mr. Carmichael, that you were looking for me? This is on some matter of business, I presume?" She wanted to get to the reason for his call. She had much to do each and everyday at the Lavender Dry Goods Emporium.

Mercedes smoothed out nonexistent wrinkles in the starched white ruffled apron she used in the store. She liked to look smart and well turned out for her customers. She wore her dark hair parted in the middle, pulled it into a chignon at the nape of her neck, and secured it with a lavender ribbon. A few recalcitrant curls escaped that she was forever trying to tame, but they wouldn't listen to her hairbrush. She wore a dress of a rich lavender print that she was vain enough to know brought out the lavender in her eyes. She liked to match and would have worn lavender shoes had she been able to find them.

"It's business of a sort, Miss Lawless," he said. "Captain Lafitte sent me to look for you on the matter of a relative of yours."

Mercedes shifted her attention back to the visitor, her interest engaged. "Relative?"

"Yes, an uncle to be exact."

Wings of the Wind

"That would be my uncle, Everett Lawless. I can send for him if you'd like. He is in our garden tending to his flowers."

"His name is not Everett Lawless."

Mercedes peered intently at the man. Until now she had had only mild business interest in this stranger. He must be mistaken. She had no other uncle. Not here, not anywhere.

He was mopping his brow again and sweat trickled down his reddening face. Alarmed at the sight of his face, Mercedes said, "Mr. Carmichael, please won't you have a seat and something cool to drink? I am forgetting my manners."

"Thank you. You are kind to offer." He cast a glance around him for something to sit on, and Jamie quickly pulled a straight back chair from behind the counter.

"Here, have a seat," Jamie said. "I'll get some fresh lemonade."

The man sank into the chair as the young man hurried off. He removed his top hat and used it to fan himself. She handed him a paper fan on a stick from the display behind him, took one herself and waved it vigorously over him, trying to cool him down.

Jamie raced back with three tall glasses of lemonade, balancing them expertly on a tray. One he handed to Mr. Carmichael, who took several gulps before coming up for air.

"That is quite refreshing," he said. "I'm afraid I am not used to this heat and humidity. There's usually a nice breeze on the ship, you know." He loosened his collar and burped. "Beg pardon," he said and finished the lemonade.

Mercedes stopped fanning but remained standing in front of him, wondering just what this gentleman was about. An uneasy feeling inched its way into her midsection.

"Mr. Carmichael," she said, as he continued to fan himself, "I'm sorry, but I confess I'm confused. I have no other uncle. My mother and father have passed on. The only living relatives I have besides my brother is my Uncle Everett and Cousin Julia."

Carefully Mr. Carmichael placed the glass on the counter. He cleared his throat. "Let me explain. As I said, I work for Andre Lafitte. He is the captain of the clipper ship, *Wings of the Wind*," he said, fanning himself slower now.

"What a beautiful name," said Mercedes. A soft smile spread across her face. "I saw her tall masts this morning on my way back from the post office. I wondered who the captain was. Your clipper is new to Galveston and a rare sight. Clippers these days are bound for San Francisco loaded with goods for the gold rush."

"Quite right," Mr. Carmichael said. "We're bound for San Francisco. However, we made a slight detour to New Orleans to pick up a special shipment of cotton and sugar to complement our cargo."

"And Galveston is another slight detour?" asked Mercedes.

Mr. Carmichael hesitated. "Yes. We have a consignment, some goods to pick up, and . . . " He tapped his chin. "Well, let me put it this way. Not long ago Captain Lafitte met this uncle of yours and had the opportunity to spend some leisure time with him. They passed the time playing cards."

Mercedes eyebrows arched as they had a way of doing when she was caught off guard. "Here in Galveston?"

"No, this man was a passenger on the *Wings of the*

Wind and sailed with us from Boston to New Orleans."

Mercedes slowly shook her head. "Mr. Carmichael, I have no relatives in Boston or New Orleans. Any relatives that I'd have that are not in the immediate vicinity of Galveston would be distant indeed. I am certainly not aware of them."

"This man indicated that he had not met you yet. But to lend credence to what I tell you, let me say that he knew your name, your whereabouts, that you had this store, and he knew your parents had passed away. He said he was on his way to meet you."

"What is this man's name, may I ask?"

"Jeffrey Norton."

It was Mercedes's turn to sit down. She eased onto a trunk across the aisle from her uninvited guest.

Norton was a name she had not heard in a years. Her hand covered her bosom, and she felt the blood drain from her face. She was going to faint.

Somewhere inside a door opened on childhood memories. Could it be possible that her mother had had a brother she didn't know anything about? Had her dear, sweet, kind mother have kept such a secret and why? This did not fit into Mercedes's neat, well-ordered life, and it rattled the walls she had constructed around her heart when her parents had died.

"Are you all right, Miss? You don't look well." Mr. Carmichael's voice deepened with concern. "Drink some of this lemonade. It's quite good." He offered her a glass from the tray Jamie had set on the trunk by Mercedes.

She waved the glass away, struggling for composure.

"Are you all right, lass?" Mr. Carmichael asked again.

Jamie grasped her shoulder in support. "Do you need the smelling salts?" he said.

Marjorie Thelen

She shook her head. She had never needed smelling salts in her life. She just needed a little time to absorb such a jolt. This man had to be wrong. She attempted to focus on Mr. Carmichael. Her mouth worked trying to form the words.

"It's just that . . . " Her voice trailed off. In a very small voice she said, "Norton was my mother's maiden name."

"I see," said Mr. Carmichael.

An awkward silence descended upon the three of them.

Mercedes took a deep breath to bolster her courage and looked Mr. Carmichael in the eye. Concern was evident on his face. Best to hear what he had to say. "Go on," she said.

"Well, lass, this man told Captain Lafitte that your mother had married a seaman against the wishes of her parents and ran off with him never to be seen again. The parents disowned their daughter and when they died they left a considerable estate that went in its entirety to this man, your mother's brother."

Jamie, standing quietly all the while, looked wide-eyed at his sister. "They'd be our grandparents, Mercedes, if what this caller says is true. But I thought they died before our parents settled in Galveston."

Mercedes nodded as she addressed Mr. Carmichael. "My mother said her parents had died back East before we were born, and she had come out here with our father to make a new beginning." This man had his story wrong.

Mr. Carmichael rubbed his chin. "Mr. Norton let on like they had died recently. He said he's been looking for you." He hesitated like he knew what he was about to say, Mercedes would not want to hear. "Your uncle said he owned the Lavender Dry Goods Emporium."

Wings of the Wind

Mercedes saw red, then brighter red, then stars. How could some non-existent relative own her store? This store was her lifeblood, her life, what she had worked hard to make a success.

"Impossible," she said. "I own this store." She thumped her breastbone for emphasis.

Mr. Carmichael shifted uncomfortably on his chair. "He said he was your legal guardian because you were a female, and he owned this store. He was concerned about your ability to handle finances and such."

Mercedes stood abruptly. Jamie stepped back, out of her way. "This is ludicrous," she said, hands fisted at her sides.

Mr. Carmichael eased his chair back, looking undecided about the menace before him. "Had he met you I'm sure he would have seen you had things well in hand." He gestured around the store. "But, lass, everyone knows women don't get involved in matters of finance and business."

"Well, obviously, I have. This is preposterous."

Mercedes seethed over the injustice of living in a world where men controlled the affairs of women. She had fought and struggled to keep her store out of the hands of men who thought she wasn't capable, didn't have a brain in her head, should be home making pies and babies. She would find this man and kill him. That's what she would like to do. But on second thought then they'd hang her, and she'd lose the store for sure.

"Where is this man who says he is my uncle?" she said, struggling to keep the anger from her voice.

Mr. Carmichael looked sheepish. "He disappeared when we docked in New Orleans."

Land sakes. He was a phantom uncle to boot. This

man must think she was an imbecile. "Why would he have done that?" she said, sweetly. "I thought he was on his way here to meet us?"

"He talked about some business in New Orleans to tend to first, and that he'd be coming over on a steamer later."

"Would that be later today or later next year? Am I supposed to wait docilely here for him to claim ownership of my store?" She narrowed her eyes at Carmichael. There was something suspicious about this. She leaned closer and saw little beads of sweat across his forehead. "Why are you here telling me all this?"

He blanched.

There was more to this awful, inconceivable story.

"Go on tell me. Out with it all." She tried to keep the hysteria out of her voice. Losing control was not like her. She was normally a calm, polite, gracious person.

Carmichael's words spilled out in a rush. "Because Jeffrey Norton put up your store on a bet in the last card game he and the Captain played before we reached New Orleans, and he lost. Captain Lafitte has a deed signed over to him that says he owns the Lavender Dry Goods Emporium."

"What?" Her stomach clenched into a knot. "What?" she said again. She could not possibly have heard the man right.

Carmichael scooted around back of his chair, as if it would protect him against the volcano about to explode. "I said Captain Lafitte is now owner of this store."

"That is outrageous." Her face took on a decidedly redder hue. Her hands jammed into her hips. She was trying hard not to spit and sputter. "Just who do you think you are coming in here and presenting me with such an outlandish scenario? A phantom uncle loses my store in a card game? Are you mad? It isn't even legal."

He stood hands wide open with an apologetic smile. "Lass, this is Texas. Men make their own laws out here. If they don't like the laws, they ignore them or side step them. Anything is possible."

"Not in my world," she said.

"Please, lass, calm yourself."

"Calm myself? You just told me someone else claims he owns my lifeblood, what I spent years building into a success. You think I'm going to be calm about that?"

She advanced with deliberate steps toward Carmichael who shrank away from her.

"You, sir, are a bold faced liar. I have the deed to this store, I can prove it, and you better tell your employer that I will fight this, and he will be sorry he ever heard the name Mercedes Lawless."

She flung out her hand toward the door. "Now get out, or I'll call the sheriff."

Normally she was a calm person. Gracious, polite.

He opened his mouth and put up a finger to protest.

"Out, out, out." Mercedes stabbed her finger toward the exit.

Mr. Carmichael popped his hat back onto his head, made a quick bow, and hurried from the Lavender Dry Goods Emporium.

"Gee, Mercedes, now what are you going to do?" asked Jamie his voice filled with awe, as they both stood looking at Carmichael's retreating figure.

What was she going to do? She was going to calm down. She was normally a calm, gracious, polite person. She was going to let her head clear. She was going to see her lawyer. She looked at Jamie.

Marjorie Thelen

"I am going to pay a call on Captain Andre Lafitte."

Chapter Two

"What the devil?" said Andre Lafitte. "What is that infernal noise?

Tito's huge bulk crashed through the door accompanied by Spike, a brilliant chartreuse green parrot, flapping to hold onto his shoulder. Tito wore a tight, sleeveless black jersey, wide leather belt and loose fitting brown pants. His bulging arms, feathered with scars, were deeply tanned.

"Mi Capitán, mi Capitán!" He gasped for breath. "Come, quick. A woman. In a boat. Come, quick!" He pointed then gestured toward the door as if the motion itself would propel Andre through it.

"Tito, how many times have I asked you to knock before you enter?" Fortunately, what the crew lacked in manners they made up for in sailing skills. Tito was a superb second-in-command but highly excitable. Usually the excitement blew over fast.

"Carry on and lower the shore boat, will you? We need to row into town. Carmichael tells me there's some difficulty with the shopkeeper of the store I won. I want to resolve the matter and be on our way to San Francisco."

"Capitán, I am sorry for not knocking," Tito said and saluted to help his apology carry more weight. "But did you not hear what I say? There is a woman coming alongside in a boat."

Andre's brows knit together. "What's a woman doing out here?" As far as he remembered, he hadn't arranged for a woman this evening. There must be some mistake. Besides, he wouldn't have ordered her out to his ship. He liked to entertain his women in a private fashion. Ships never lent themselves to privacy.

Tito threw up his hands. "Who knows what makes women to do these things?"

"Maybe one of the local madams saw my ship and sent along a little-pastime-for-the-evening." It had been over two weeks since he had been with one of his favorite girls at the Silver Slipper, the high-priced bordello in New Orleans that he owned. His mother had left it to him. Enjoying a female's company this evening appealed to him.

He recanted. "Ask her to stay till I return." He'd find a suitable place to entertain her when he went on shore.

"Oh, no, mi Capitán." Tito rushed over to confront his Capitán, stopping within a foot of him. "This is not a woman like that. She dresses pretty. She has a young man with her. An old man is rowing. She asks permission to come aboard. You must come quick. She is waiting in the boat for your permission. I said the Capitán would have to give the permission."

Spike squawked his agreement, stretched his left leg and wing, and settled into a parrot squat on Tito's shoulder.

Andre frowned. He didn't know any respectable woman in Galveston. Certainly none that would row out in a boat to board his ship without prior invitation. Wait, that wasn't true. He did know of a certain shopkeeper. He shook his head. It couldn't possibly be.

Wings of the Wind

"Very well." Too bad it wasn't a little-pastime-for-the-evening. "I'll have a look. Lead the way."

Andre emerged on deck and strode toward Tito, whose upper body was already hanging over the rail, Spike atop his back peering over with him. A small group of men leaned forward, intent on the water below. He ordered his men back and joined Tito at the rail.

He saw three figures in the boat, bobbing below in the green gray water of the harbor.

"Who goes there?" His voice boomed. "State your business."

The female rose and from where he stood he could see she wore dress of a lavender hue. A warning bell went off in his head. He remembered from his conversation with Carmichael that the disagreeable shopkeeper favored the color.

"Captain Lafitte," a clear, light voice rang out from below. "I request permission for my brother and me to board your ship to discuss with you a matter of some urgency. You can see we are not armed and are not dangerous."

"Dangerous? That hardly concerns me," Andre said. "You have not stated your business." He stood arms braced on the rail, assessing the trio below. That a woman and a boy could pose a threat to his crew was laughable, although a knife in the hands of the right woman in close quarters could do some damage.

"Would you keep me standing in a bouncing boat?" she said in a volume several decibels higher.

"I would. State your business."

"Very well. It concerns a man, an acquaintance of yours, who says he is a relative of mine. It has to do with the Lavender Dry Goods Emporium."

So it was the infamous niece and shopkeeper. Well, this would save him a trip to town. This female had nerve coming out to his ship on her own.

"Lower the rope ladder and help them aboard, Tito. It looks like we won't be going into town."

To the small company in the boat below he called, "All right you may come aboard. My men will help you up. Take care not to slip. The ropes are wet. We don't want to have to fish you out of the Gulf. None of my men can swim."

* * * * *

Mercedes arched her neck to better see the man behind the booming voice at the top of the ladder. He loomed over the men around him. His hair was dark. He wasn't the gray-whiskered, weathered seaman she'd expected.

That wasn't going to stop her. She would see this captain whoever he was. No one was going to threaten her livelihood. He had no right to claim her store. Anger rose in her again at the thought. She had her deed with her to prove it. She had stopped by to see Mr. Potts, her lawyer, and she knew her rights.

But fear wormed its way into her consciousness, the result of reading the letter that had arrived that day. After Mr. Carmichael departed, Jamie badgered her until she read the letter aloud. Jeffrey Norton signed it.

Mercedes looked back toward the shore, her resolve wavering. No, she had to go through with this. She had to get this mess straightened out. She had to find out who Jeffery Norton was and who better to ask than this Captain Lafitte?

She hoped her face was the picture of composure as

Wings of the Wind

she peered upward. The impressive bulge of the clipper ship filled her gaze, its lines long and lean. The sun glinted off its black shiny paint and gold trim. The scent of wet oak and cordage filled the air.

She would give anything to be owner of a ship like this beauty. Oh, to have wings like these. She would fly to famous cities, to exotic lands. Someday, if the shop did well enough maybe, just maybe she would be able to buy a share in a ship like this. If she still had the shop . . .

The boarding ladder dangled down the side of the ship. She sized it up for reliability. She had never boarded a ship by rope ladder before, let alone while wearing a dress. Jamie, the monkey, was already several rungs up.

She tried to prevent him from coming, not sure of who or what she would encounter. But attempting to keep Jamie away from a ship was like trying to keep the heat from a Galveston summer day. He was protection of sorts, though he had forgotten his umbrella rapier.

"Would it help ye, if we lowered the chair?" a creaky voice called from above.

Eyeing the ladder, she put her pride aside for the practicality of getting up on deck without drowning. "Yes, that would be very thoughtful of you. I don't seem to have brought my sea legs along."

A rusty chuckle answered from above as a rope chair-like contraption slowly lowered down the side of the ship.

"Sit on it and give a tug when you're settled," said the creaky voice.

Her Uncle Everett sat at the oars in the rowboat and struggled to steady it while Mercedes danced with the chair, trying to get a seat without success. Her dear Uncle was a superb gardener but a terrible seaman, and he was making a hash of it.

"Wait. I'll come down to help you, Miss."

"Thank you," Mercedes called up, relief at the offer obvious in her voice.

An apparition scrambled down the ladder and appeared beside her. He looked like someone Mercedes had only ever heard described as a pirate. He exuded a distinctive odor somewhere between stale tobacco and unwashed body.

"Here ye are, miss. Let me steady that for ye," said the creaky-voiced man.

Mercedes stared, her surprise blending with apprehension. Here was the gray, weathered seaman but he wasn't the captain of the ship. Her gaze glued to his face, she allowed him to lift, seat, and deftly rope her in while the boat continued its dance with the sea.

"Why you're nothing but a feather," he said. "There now. All in. Let's tug the line. Heave ho." He shouted to the men standing above.

The line tightened. Then Mercedes was dangling over the rowboat, inching upward on her journey to meet the captain of the *Wings of the Wind*. She clenched the chair ropes to still her trembling hands.

Sea gulls cried overhead and off the bow, the gleaming backs of a pair of porpoises cut the water. The bright sun brought out the aquamarine quality of the sea. It was heaven itself to Mercedes. She threw her head back and gazed up into the clipper's towering masts, pointing toward the heavens.

But the feeling of exhilaration at such a wondrous sight was replaced with a feeling of dread when she regarded the men standing above. What awaited her?

At the top a giant of a man with a squawking parrot atop his head helped her over the side and to her feet, but the captain was nowhere to be seen. The giant was most unusual in appearance and looked a trifle too much like a pirate for her taste. Was this really a den of pirates? Impossible. There hadn't been any in Galveston for thirty years.

Her stomach tightened another notch, but she followed with determined steps the giant with bobbing parrot headpiece who led the way to the Captain's cabin. He paused at a polished oak door and banged upon it.

"Enter," came the command from within.

Now or never, Mercedes thought. She smoothed her dress, squared her shoulders, took several discreet deep breaths to rid her belly of the fluttering creatures that seemed to have settled there, and tried to look properly stern and forbidding. The giant opened the door for her.

Captain Andre Lafitte loomed just inside. He stood arms folded across his chest. He was taller than she expected, towering a good head above her. Her first impression was mountain lion, lithe like a wild animal.

Their eyes met. His were whiskey brown fringed with dark lashes, like a lion's. For one brief instant he looked as startled as she. Maybe he was expecting someone much different also. Perhaps he was expecting an old crone with chin hairs.

Her mouth wanted to turn up into a smile, but she pressed her lips into a thin line. She did not want to be nice to this beast. Not someone who threatened her store.

"Come in," he said and stepped aside to allow her to pass. She swept by him her head held high. But the beast gave her little leeway, and she brushed his arm as she passed. She was not prepared for the jolt from that touch. It was only a dusting, the lightest of touch against his arm but it sent a shiver through her. Shiver of fear or . . . no, it was not fear.

He waved his hand toward a straight back chair in front of a large mahogany desk. "Have a seat. I take it you are Miss Lawless of the Lavender Dry Goods Emporium."

Good, he was getting right to the point.

"That I am." Mercedes took command of the chair, unnerved by her reaction to his touch, hoping he did not notice her flushed cheeks.

"I am Mercedes Lawless, proprietress," she emphasized the word, "of the Lavender Dry Goods Emporium."

She watched as he took a seat behind the desk on a magnificent dark leather chair buffed glossy with many sittings. Definite mountain lion. Smooth. Calculated. Deliberate.

She noticed the knife, the long, wide knife sheathed in the belt slung on his hips. Did pirates prefer knives?

He wore dark brown britches that hugged his muscular legs and a simple cream color cotton shirt open at the neck. Black boots encased his lower legs. Even dressed so simply he would stand out in a crowd.

She interlocked her fingers on her lap determined to maintain her composure.

"Please excuse my brother," she said. Annoyed to hear a quiver in her voice, she cleared her throat and tried to speak with a firmer note. "His passion is ships, and it was impossible to keep him at home when he learned that I was coming here."

"Not at all," he said. "My men will enjoy showing him around. Passion for ships I understand. I have the same passion myself."

Opening a richly tooled leather box, he extracted a cheroot, sat back and studied her. She found his gaze

Wings of the Wind

disconcerting.

"May I offer you tea? Or something stronger to drink? Sherry perhaps?"

"Thank you, no. Nothing."

She couldn't hold such a direct gaze. It seemed to strip her of all pretensions. What was he about? She glanced around the room, curious for some revelation about the man before her.

Brass trimmed the wood paneling and furnishings of the room. Bookshelves lined a section of the wall. Her eyebrows arched when she spotted Shakespeare among the nautical titles. The neat, trim quality of the space spoke of a well-ordered mind. She saw a bunk built into the wall to one side.

Her courage seeped away. She had hoped for someone she could intimidate into backing down from a claim on the Emporium. This was not a man to be intimidated.

His broad shoulders filled the chair. His big hands loosely gripped the arms. She noticed a long white scar across the back of one tanned hand. They were sculptured hands, worthy of Michelangelo, and spoke of someone different than what registered in his stern demeanor. She turned her gaze to his face and found him still studying her. The depths of those whiskey eyes were unreadable. He seemed to be waiting to see what she would do, like a lion with its prey in sight.

She took several discreet, calming breaths to try to quiet the fluttering in her stomach. Not only was he far from what she expected, he was more forbidding. Even worse, he hadn't smiled once and didn't look like a person who liked to smile.

"I must admit, Miss Lawless," he said at last, and the tension softened in the room, "that I was on my way to see you myself, when you. . . " he hesitated. . . "came calling." He struck a match, lit the cheroot, shook out the match and exhaled slowly, narrowing his eyes. "Wasn't this a bit risky for you, coming to call on me? After all, you don't know who I am, or what was waiting for you."

"I'm not known for my caution." She straightened her back to help with her courage. "I grew up on the wharves of Galveston, and ships, seaman and their owners do not frighten me. I know most all of the ships that call. I saw the masts of your clipper ship this morning and knew that this ship had never been to Galveston before. By the way," she added with a small smile to help warm the frigid atmosphere in the room, "she is a magnificent ship."

"Thank you. You have a good eye."

This man wasn't one for returning smiles. She tried another sally into polite conversation. Maybe if she asked a few questions, he would be less severe. "Where is your home port?"

He took a long drag on the cheroot and exhaled, his face unchanged.

"Boston."

"I understand you are bound for San Francisco."

He nodded. "We called at New Orleans to pick up sugar then here to pick up cotton, rope, some supplies. We brought a consignment."

"My pianoforte."

"Yes."

"I haven't seen it, but I'm excited about its arrival." She had saved for years to purchase a pianoforte. Little did she know that it would arrive on this ship carrying such disastrous news.

"I hear you are an accomplished musician."

Mercedes smiled to cover her discomfort at how fast

Mr. Carmichael had collected information about her. She wondered how detailed a report Mr. Carmichael gave him of their meeting. That he knew about her musical ability could only mean he had been talking to people in the community. She wondered if they had mentioned her scandalous reputation.

"I do enjoy playing. I'm not sure I am that accomplished." She played the pianoforte for church. Her repertory included hymns and a few classical pieces when she was able to acquire the sheet music.

"Chopin?"

That caught her by surprise. Mr. Carmichael had dug deeply to find who her favorite composer was. She maintained a stiff smile. "Do you enjoy him?"

"I heard that you particularly like Chopin."

"I do. His music is thrilling to hear, even more thrilling to perform." The melody of the Waltz in C# Minor drifted into her awareness. She shut her eyes and folded her hands up to her breast, momentarily transported from the difficult position in which she found herself.

* * * * *

Andre watched Mercedes, not interested in Chopin as much as he was in the ecstatic expression on her face. He had not expected an enticing young woman. Her lines were classic, like a well-built clipper, like the *Wings of the Wind*. He wondered what it would be like to have this tempting morsel under him with the same facial expression.

She opened her eyes, and he stared into lavender blue, deep lavender blue. Their eyes held a moment, then a breath longer before she lowered hers to study hands that she had dropped to her lap.

Andre sensed his body responding and adjusted his position. He definitely would have to look into a little-pastime-for-the- evening. He doubted this lovely creature would be able to fill the bill tonight.

He cleared his throat. "Miss Lawless, I understand you do not recognize my claim to your store." Since she hadn't brought up the subject, he would.

Mercedes frowned. It was the frown of a woman not pleased with the purpose of her visit. "That is correct. That is the reason I am here. I felt it was urgent that I speak to you."

He nodded once in an effort to encourage her to continue. He wanted her to reveal more of her hand.

"Well," she began, then paused. "First, I really must apologize for my behavior toward Mr. Carmichael. I was quite shocked and upset by what he told me. I'm afraid I lost my temper. But that is no excuse for behaving so uncivilly toward him, and I mean to apologize."

Andre considered her intent as he studied his cheroot. "I realize that the whole situation caused you distress. For that I am sorry." His gaze moved to engage hers again, adding weight to his words.

"It is good of you to say so, but we must address the underlying reasons for my bad behavior."

"And they are?"

She opened the slim leather pouch she had brought with her.

"The first and foremost reason is that I own the Lavender Dry Goods Emporium. I worked very hard to build the business, and no one will take it from me."

She gave him a pointed, narrow-eyed look. He read determination in every gesture.

Wings of the Wind

"Here is my deed to the store. It's all in order." She passed the document to him.

Andre studied it. He opened the side drawer of his desk, extracted another document, and handed it to Mercedes.

She scowled as she perused it. "This is exactly like mine except for the owner's name."

Andre nodded. "And the owner's name you see there is?"

"Jeffrey Norton."

"Turn it over and read what it says."

Mercedes did as requested and read aloud. "I, Jeffrey Norton, deed the Lavender Dry Goods Emporium to Andre Lafitte." She looked closer. Norton had signed and dated it.

She shook her head in bewilderment. "How very strange. How is it possible to have two renditions of the same deed?"

He shrugged in answer. It puzzled him but he had heard of more outlandish things in his life. In his world one had to be ever vigilant. Crooked deals and dishonest people abounded.

He waited. She seemed hesitant to launch her next barrage. The duplicate deed had given her pause.

At last she spoke. "This brings us to the second point of my visit. I've never heard of a man named Jeffrey Norton, let alone that he was my uncle. He is no relation of mine, and he had no right to gamble the Emporium away. He has no legal claim to me or to my store. My mother never spoke of any siblings. Her parents died young and left her adrift."

He pulled on the cheroot and exhaled a long plume of blue-gray smoke, giving him time to think. "Have you

Marjorie Thelen

considered the possibility that your mother never told you about her family for good reason?"

Her head inclined in a nod. "I have, but it is not in character with my mother. She was a sweet, honest, open person."

"Are you convinced that Jeffrey Norton is an imposter?"

She hesitated, chewed her lower lip. "Almost convinced."

He considered this, wearing his best poker face, something at which he excelled. He waited for the explanation of "almost convinced".

An awkward silence filled the room.

She looked as if she were trying to make a decision. Finally, she opened the leather pouch and brought out a letter.

"This is what gives me pause in the accusation of this man as an impostor. I cannot tell you how shocked I was when I read it. This is a letter from Jeffrey Norton addressed to me that arrived today. I didn't have a chance to read it until Mr. Carmichael had left."

Andre leaned forward and flicked ashes from his cheroot into a large conch shell on his desk. "May I see it?"

The soft clanking of the ship's rigging accompanied his request, the only reminder that the outer world existed.

Mercedes hesitated a moment longer before she handed the letter over to him.

He glanced at the outside and then opened it with care.

Boston
My dear Mercedes,

You will not know of me, I fear, as your mother, my sister, ran off with your father at a very young age. Lamentably, my parents could not accept your mother's choice, and so they considered their only daughter lost. They never heard from her again, nor did they attempt to communicate with her. Myself, I have faint memory of your mother, as I was only a very small child at the time.

Your grandparents have passed away. I don't know what your mother told you about our family and our trials and tribulations. Perhaps nothing, so this letter may come as a shock. I had to look long a long time for you and had almost given up. What a great joy to learn you have a brother! What sadness to learn that my sister, your mother, is gone.

Since we are alone in this world, I have taken it upon myself to see to your care and have appointed myself legal guardian of you and your brother. I'm sure you understand. As you are a mere female, any assets you have are now under my control. I see this as best for everyone concerned. I am sure you will be relieved, as such matters are not within the realm of female management.

I am now on my way to Galveston to make your acquaintance and hope that you look forward to a reunion as much as I.

*Your uncle affectionately,
Jeffrey Norton*

Andre finished the letter and passed it back. "This does not convince you?" It looked and sounded convincing to him.

Mercedes tucked the missive back into the pouch and rose to pace the room. "I don't want to believe it. I wouldn't mind an uncle, but not one who thinks mere females incapable of managing anything outside of a home. Certainly not one who thinks he can gamble away my livelihood."

His gaze caressed her figure as he watched her pace. Willowy was the word that came to his mind. She had an elegance and grace about her that would have made her a queen, had she been born in a royal family. Her dress was of simple fashion but so well fitted, it molded becomingly to her figure above the waist before it flared out into a full skirt.

She whirled to face him. "Very well, we both have deeds to the Emporium, but yours cannot be legal. The only way to clear this up is to find Jeffrey Norton to ascertain who he really is. Anyone can write a letter, but I need proof that he is, in fact, related to me."

She moved to the desk and leaned down to regard him with a level gaze. "Will you help me find him?"

She was so close he could see her irises were rimmed with deep blue that blended to lavender centers. He held her gaze, staring into eyes that echoed her question.

The corner of his mouth twitched with the beginning of a smile before he caught himself. The plea for help from the damsel in distress. How many men over the ages had fallen for that? She was a beauty, his body liked her, but he wasn't born yesterday. Damsels had a way of getting themselves into predicaments from which unwary men tried to rescue them only to be sucked into the morass. He was not among the unwary.

"Miss Lawless," he said, "may I remind you that Norton says he is on his way here. Why not wait for him to come to you?"

She lowered her head as she exhaled a long, low sigh,

Wings of the Wind

then walked away from him toward the open cabin window to stare at the sea floating outside.

"Why would he come here now?" she said, her voice edged with frustration. "He might run into you. I doubt he wants to meet up with you again."

She turned to face him, her arms folded under her breasts. "May I ask another question, Captain Lafitte?"

"By all means."

She walked to his desk and stood in front of him. "Do you find any resemblance between this man and me?"

He studied her as he gave the question due consideration. She was tall for a woman. Slender. Norton was slight for a man and of average height. Her straight nose, striking eyes, generous mouth had no equal in Norton. He gaze lingered on her lips then moved from her mouth to her eyes.

"I don't find a great resemblance." He stubbed out the cheroot in the conch shell. "If there is little family resemblance that leaves us where?"

"It leaves us that we don't have proof to satisfy me that this man is my real uncle and that you have any claim to my store. If we want to clear up the matter, we have to find the man."

She blessed him with a room-brightening smile. He watched that smile as he said, "We?"

"Will you help me?"

Andre leaned forward. "Help you? Miss Lawless, I'm already looking for him. I will find the man." He did not need a woman to help him with a man's task.

She leaned forward and spoke as if she had read his thought. "You need my help."

"Why?"

"Because I could be used as bait."

"Bait?"

"Bait," she said again with conviction.

"That may have merit," he said, but not willing to commit himself. It might bring out the prey faster but it could be risky. He didn't want to be tripping over her skirts in pursuit of the elusive relative. Besides, she would be too distracting. He had a business to run and a ship to sail to San Francisco. He would have to mull it over.

"I will give it some thought and let you know my answer tomorrow morning. By that time the rest of my business here should be concluded. I assume you have a well-thought out plan, Miss Lawless."

"Most certainly I do," she said, straightening. "But I will share that with you after I learn of your decision."

"I see," said Andre, leaning back into his chair. "One more point, Miss Lawless."

"Captain?"

"If I don't find your plan acceptable, I will take possession of your store."

Wings of the Wind

Chapter Three

"Now I know you have lost your mind," Julia said. "Mercedes Lawless how could you think of calling on a gentlemen alone, if in fact he is a gentleman? And on top of that propositioning him."

Mercedes's cousin stood in the family dining room gripping the back of an oak chair. Flower prints hung on the wall behind her and looked at odds with her stormy countenance.

"Julia, do not speak to me like that," said Mercedes, throwing down her reticule and whirling on Julia. She yanked open the ribbons to her bonnet, snatched it off, and threw it on the dining table. "You are not my mother. I did not proposition the man, and I didn't go alone. Jamie and Uncle Everett were with me."

"Well, I'm the closest thing you have to a mother," Julia said with a huff. "Someone has to be your conscience. You are reckless and headstrong, and you do the most outlandish things. That my father and your brother went with you demonstrates a lack of good sense on their part. I will speak to them both on that subject. If you didn't proposition him, what did you do?" Julia crossed her arms. Her face was so red it hid her freckles, and the scowl did no justice to her pretty features.

"I asked Captain Lafitte," Mercedes said in a very

controlled voice, enunciating each word, "to help me find the man that says he owns the Lavender Dry Goods Emporium." Her hands were on her hips, and although she didn't get as red-faced as Julia in an argument, her cheeks were rosy pink.

Jamie peeked around his sister.

"Cousin Julia, you should have seen that ship," he said, his face aglow from the excitement of the morning. He elected to ignore the bristling atmosphere in the room. "It was magnificent. Captain Lafitte's men showed me around the ship. They let me climb up the rigging. They showed me below decks and told me sea stories." He grinned in seeming delight that the seamen included him in their rollicking tales.

Julia focused her attention on her male cousin. "I know how much you love ships, Jamie dear. It must have been quite an adventure." She smiled a little in spite of her anger. Jamie's excitement was so genuine it was infectious, and Julia knew of his great love of the sea.

"Oh, Julia, it was. And I was there to protect my sister. Uncle Everett stayed in the boat so we could get away if anything bad happened."

"May the dear saints preserve us," Julia said, rolling her eyes. She pulled Jamie into a hug. "I know you are a strong young man, and you would have protected your sister. But sometimes you are a little too trusting of other people. You've lived a sheltered life and most of your adventures are in books."

"They are not," said Jamie, hotly. "I've had lots of adventures right here on the island looking for buried treasure."

"Very well, I concede on the adventure part." She sank into one of the high back chairs that framed the round dining table.

"Mercedes, why don't you sit down? Jamie, will you put on water for tea?" Julia asked, the strain telling in her voice.

"Aye, aye," said Jamie, saluting. He stepped jauntily out the open door into the garden and toward the kitchen enclosure off the dining and parlor rooms at the back of the store. Through the open window they heard him whistling a seaman's ditty as he set about his task.

Julia's color had lightened to pink. She wagged her head at Mercedes who eased into a seat at the table.

"Mercedes, it scared the life out of me when Mr. Potts came by and told me where you had gone. He said he had tried to talk you out of it, but you were dead set on your plan."

The set of Mercedes's jaw relaxed. "I'm sorry, Julia. I know you think I come up with hair brained schemes at times." She couldn't quite bring herself to look at Julia. She was not in the mood for more lecturing. They sat listening to Jamie busy himself with tea preparations.

"Mercedes will you please tell me what this is all about?" Julia said at last. Her breathing had quieted. She sat back in her chair. She wore a cornflower blue print that brought out the same color in her eyes.

Mercedes regarded her cousin. Julia was right. She was the closest thing she had to a mother, even though Julia was only a few years older than Mercedes.

She never meant to upset her, but she knew that if she had told Julia her plan to call upon Captain Lafitte she would have prevented her from going. Rightly so. It wasn't proper for a lady to call on a man the way she had. But the devil take it, she railed against convention and what women were supposed to do. She found it utterly stifling.

Mercedes searched for a way to start then said, "You know about the letter we received. I told Uncle Everett about it while you were helping out at church."

Julia nodded. "He was as shocked as you were at its message."

"A Mr. Duncan Carmichael visited us this morning in the store. That was before I read the letter. He told me that this man, Jeffrey Norton, claims to be my uncle, my mother's brother of all things, and to own the Emporium. He bet the store in a card game with Captain Lafitte and lost. The captain showed me the deed Norton signed over to him. It's exactly like mine. I was flabbergasted."

Jamie arrived with the tea tray and slid it in front of the two of them. He set out blue and white cups and saucers, put the matching teapot before them, grabbed his glass of milk and a large handful of biscuits from the cut glass plate on the tray and retreated to a wrought iron chair outside on the patio.

Julia poured for both of them. Mercedes helped herself to two spoonfuls of sugar for her tea, stirred, inhaled the comforting fragrance, and took a cautious sip. She glanced over at Julia who sat frowning, although now the freckles that went with her carrot red hair peppered her nose.

"Flabbergasted is a mild description for my reaction," said Julia. "How in the world did that happen? I bet it was someone in the town office where the deeds are recorded. But who would have done such a thing? It is unsettling to think someone is that interested in you and that we might know him.

"Do you have a plan to find this man," asked Julia, "and whatever would possess you to try to find him?

Captain Lafitte is dangerous. You need to let Mr. Potts handle this."

Mercedes concentrated on sipping her tea, electing to let Julia run on, trying to answer her own questions. She was not sure herself of the answers.

"I have a plan of sorts," Mercedes said. "Mr. Potts would do the legal end of it. But he said that a man with the reputation of Captain Lafitte might be difficult to deal with." She avoided mention of the part of the plan she had in mind that featured her as bait.

"Reputation? What reputation?" Julia's color began to rise again.

"Julia, please stay calm."

"Calm? How can I? Whatever have you gotten yourself into?"

"Me?" It was Mercedes's turn to exclaim. "Julia, need I remind you that I was minding my own business when this unwanted man shows up here and turns my life upside down in the space of ten minutes? I didn't get myself into anything."

Julia blew out a breath, looking around the room for the patience she didn't seem to have. "I'm sorry. You are right. This was not of your doing. But what concerns me is that you are going to take matters into your own hands, and, frankly, Mercedes that frightens me. I will add that I am justified in saying so based on your past actions."

Mercedes did not respond but sat upright, spine straight trying to rein in her temper. Julia was ever quick to offer an opinion, and this was not the first time Mercedes had heard this particular opinion. She toyed with the teaspoon on the table in front of her in an attempt to stay calm.

But Julia did not relent. "Mercedes, what scheme are

you cooking up this time and what reputation are we talking about? May I remind you that your own reputation doesn't need any more tarnish than it already has."

"My reputation?" Mercedes banged down the teaspoon. "Hogwash. Are you referring to the so-called scandal created when that great jackass, Derek Bragg, tried to coerce me into marrying him? It was his word against mine. He in no way compromised me." She pounded her fist on the table rattling cups and saucers.

"Mercedes, watch your language!"

Mercedes lowered her voice. "Let's not go over the circumstances again." She nodded in the direction of her brother on the patio.

"Very well," Julia said. "What about this man Lafitte? What did Mr. Potts mean when he made that statement about his reputation?"

Mercedes considered how much to tell Julia who had the uncanny ability to uncover the deep down secrets of anyone. It would be only a matter of time before word got round to her about Captain Lafitte. If that happened, she knew Julia would try to prevent her from searching for the mystery uncle.

She couldn't find this Norton person if she didn't have help, and Captain Lafitte had the ship she needed, the necessary connections, and the motive. But he appeared to be the kind of man that could drive a hard bargain. She would have to be careful.

"Mercedes, I can hear those wheels turning," Julia said. "Best be out with it. You know I will find out one way or another."

"Very well." Mercedes made up her mind to give minimal information and did her best to assume a nonchalant air. "Captain Lafitte, while he is a successful,

Wings of the Wind

commercial sea captain, had, it is rumored, in the early part of his career associations with some questionable gentlemen."

"Gentlemen, bah. You mean pirates. He was a pirate. Hah, for all we know he still is one."

"Yo-heave-ho," yelled Jamie from patio and jumped from his chair. "I knew it. I knew it."

He bounded in to face Mercedes. "Will you help me get a berth on his ship? We could sail off together, you on a quest to find our uncle, me, a seaman at last." He raised his arms high over his head in his exuberance.

Julia sprang up so fast her chair tilted over with a crash. "Mercedes, you cannot put that child on a ship like that and go yourself, too."

"Why not?" Mercedes leaped to her feet to confront her cousin. "Who else is in a better position to help us than the man who might want to get even for being duped?"

"Here now, what's all the shouting about?" Uncle Everett said, as he came into the dining room from the garden, wiping his face with a red handkerchief. He was tall, thin, and slightly stooped. His demeanor could bring calm to the stormiest of seas. "Who was duped?"

The cousins all talked at once.

"Hold on now, hold on. One at a time." He eyed their tea tray. "I wouldn't mind a cup of tea. It'd help me listen better." He straightened Julia's chair and sagged down into it. She poured him a cup of tea while she presented her case.

"Father, you must talk some sense into Mercedes. She is taking matters into her own hands again."

"Again? She never let go of those matters since she got a holt of them back when she came here to live. Isn't that right, Missy?" Uncle Everett shot Mercedes a smile.

"She is the most headstrong young woman on Galveston Island. Good thing she is," he said looking to Julia, "because we never could have made a go of the store, you and me, Julia. You know what I say is true." He patted his daughter's arm.

* * * * *

Julia smiled in spite of herself. She knew her father was right. When Mercedes had stepped in to help with the store she had saved them from certain ruin with her natural ability for business. She had all the brains, vivaciousness, and spunk that it took to run a business. She had an uncanny sense for investments. Her customers adored her. Their store blossomed from the first time Mercedes set foot in it. People were naturally drawn to her, her smile, her sense of what they needed and what they could afford.

She didn't begrudge Mercedes one bit of that. She did worry about her headstrong tendencies that were getting stronger every day, if that were possible. She had sensed a restlessness of late in her cousin that was worrisome. She loved Mercedes, loved her vitality. They had always been close and had shared secrets, triumphs, joys, defeats, and spats.

She took a deep breath and let it out slowly. "Right you are, Father."

She stepped over to Mercedes and took her hand. "Mercedes, you know I get upset because I am afraid for you." Tears glistened in her eyes.

Mercedes hugged her. "I know. You're like a sister to me." She held Julia at arm's length. "And, a mother, too." They both smiled. "I know you think me headstrong. I am, I guess."

Wings of the Wind

All three relatives nodded their heads in unison so fast, Mercedes laughed.

"So be it," she said. "The jury has decided." She continued on. "Captain Lafitte said he would make a decision tomorrow as to whether he would cooperate with the plan that I have, and he could say no. Then Mr. Potts will have to go into action."

Uncle Everett spoke up. "Missy, you know we have learned to trust in your judgment as harebrained as it may seem to us at times. Your schemes for the store have always paid off.

Julia broke in. "Mercedes, you say you don't have a definite plan, and you told Captain Lafitte that you did. What are you going to do?"

"I'll sleep on it," she said, yawning. "This has been a trying day. With your permission I will take my leave, look over the accounts, and retire to think this over. Will you trust me a little longer?" She looked round at them all.

Julia had her doubts but squeezed Mercedes's hand. Uncle Everett nodded. Jamie's grin was ear-to-ear.

"Good night, then." She looked at Jamie. "Bed time for you, too."

Jamie opened his month to protest, seemed to think better of it, and moved toward the parlor stairs, which lead upward to their bedrooms over the store.

After Mercedes and Jamie left, Julia pulled her father down to a seat at the table.

Uncle Everett nodded to Julia. "Tell me what you're thinking, daughter. I know it's weighing on your mind."

Julia smiled because her father knew her well. "Mercedes is so full of life and so boundless. There's nothing to stop her when her mind is made up. I've never had that. I envy her, I suppose."

Uncle Everett nodded. "It's not for all of us, daughter. You need to remember that. Because it works for her, it may not for you. Try not to worry too much. We'll be okay. I talked to Mr. Potts today."

"You did?"

"After Mercedes went to see him. He said that Captain Lafitte has no ground to stand on if that deed is not in order."

"I'm glad for that." Julia sighed. "It sounds like such a trumped up story. Someone out of nowhere gambles away a store he doesn't own in a card game."

Uncle Everett studied the tea leaves in the empty teacup, as if he could read the future. "That was the good of it. The other thing is Lafitte could make things right bad for her if he chooses. Potts says he used to keep some unscrupulous company. Hard to say if he still does."

He grinned, and it lit up the blue eyes his daughter inherited from him. "Kinda would like to be around when Lafitte tangles with Mercedes again. I'd a given a lot to be fly on the wall. Mercedes was not in good humor when she landed back in the boat with Jamie and me. Nor was the captain smiling as he looked down into the boat. The two of them might be a match for each other."

He raised his eyebrows at his daughter and placed a kindly hand on her shoulder. "We best call it a day. Tomorrow is shaping up to be real interesting."

Julia placed her hand over his and looked at him beseechingly. "Father, one more thing. What happens to us if Lafitte comes after the store?"

"Could be we'll be working for Andre Lafitte." He kissed her on the cheek, rose, and made his way to bed.

* * * * *

Wings of the Wind

Mercedes stripped to her shift and sat by the open window that overlooked the garden, trying to catch a breath of air. The heat of the hot, humid day had not left her small room even though the evening had cooled, and the stars twinkled in the night sky.

She felt the restlessness moving through her. It was more than the aftermath of spring this year. It was the bigger world. She was getting older and knew the chances for her to get away from Galveston were getting slimmer. A home and family of her own had never mattered to her like other young women of her age. Maybe it was the strain of being the main provider for her little family.

Uncle Everett, although the nicest man in the world, wasn't one to hold down a steady job. He was a gardener, botanist, and dreamer at heart, content to while away the days tending to his vegetable garden, which fed them well, and seeing to his remarkable flower garden that graced the walls and grounds to the back of the store.

It worked well for her since he didn't have fixed ideas of what women and men should do. So she was left to the management of the store and to everyone's surprised it prospered under her care. It wasn't enough. She had to see and experience something more than Galveston, Texas. It was small, and the rest of the world so large. The *Wings of the Wind* called to her from the harbor.

If she could just convince Captain Lafitte to take her with him to look for Jeffrey Norton . . .

She pulled the pins from her hair, brushed it out, braided it for the night, then lay on her narrow cot by the window. She hoped something miraculous would come of her dreams tonight. She needed something like a miracle to impress Andre Lafitte.

As she lay in the quiet of the late evening, she could

hear people walking along 20th street and caught snatches of conversation. But her thought were with Andre Lafitte.

Captain Andre Lafitte. He interested her. That was more than she could say of most men. She had expected an old sea captain she could strike a bargain with and found a virile Andre Lafitte who was not so easily convinced and who had challenged her natural ability to charm her way into anything.

She remembered how he had looked at her, studied her. She had felt his eyes on her even when she wasn't looking at him. He must be a superb poker player since he was so hard to read. But he wasn't to be toyed with. Her tactic of calling on him first, though brazen, had been to her advantage. It had caught him off guard.

She sighed at the word brazen. It would be all over Galveston by the time the sun rose on the morrow where she had been. Julia had the right of it. Her reputation was in sad shape since the Derek Bragg fiasco. People were still nice and gracious to her, but she knew they wondered what had transpired that night with Bragg. She could feel them thinking it. Bragg still fed people lies about her.

Captain Lafitte probably had that in his dossier on her. To propose that they set off together to find Norton, that she accompany him on his ship was outrageous. But why not? Her reputation couldn't suffer anymore that it already had and what did she care anyway about reputations? It hadn't hurt business.

She could not forget the jolt, the touch of him, and being keenly aware of his magnetism. The heat from his body seemed to pull her toward him, sucking her into him. He was like one of the dark gods she had read about in the tales of ancient Greece. What was it about him that attracted her? Was it a sense of having lived and experienced life? A man of the world. So unlike the local boys in Galveston, or Mr. Potts, who she knew adored her.

Potts was so predictable. That was it. Something about Andre Lafitte was unpredictable. He intrigued her. He was dangerous. She wondered about his pirate connections, and if the stories she had heard were true. Mr. Potts said he was the son of the infamous Jean. Could that be true? Anything was possible in this part of the world.

Jean Lafitte had a notorious reputation in New Orleans when he lived there and that reputation only got worse when he lived on Galveston Island. He had had many women. Who knows how many children he had sired?

Mr. Potts told her Andre Lafitte's past included smuggling. That he circulated in the nefarious underworld of smugglers who operated along the Gulf coast and up the Atlantic seaboard. There couldn't be much of that left. The real smuggler pirates had had their heyday in the last century.

Whoever he was, she knew that when she saw Andre Lafitte on the morrow, she would need a convincing plan featuring her as bait to lure the man that could set this whole ridiculous situation straight. Either that or a plan to remove Captain Lafitte from the picture until she could do some serious investigating of her own.

Chapter Four

Andre woke before daybreak to the sound of pounding on his door. He cursed, rolled over onto his back, and placed his arm over his eyes. How did one train grown men to respect their captain's sleep? Add to the pounding on the door, the bumping and scraping overhead of the men swabbing the deck, and he knew he wouldn't get anymore sleep this morning.

Curse it. He hadn't slept worth a damn. Toss and turn, toss and turn. Every time he started to drift off, a vision of lavender would appear in his mind. What was it with that girl anyway? You'd think he was a teenage pup the way his body was carrying on about her. To make matters worse, with all the work to be done on the ship, he hadn't been able to arrange a little-pastime-for-the-evening.

He yawned, stretched, rubbed his eyes. The pounding came again.

"Mi Capitán! Mi Capitán!" Tito's bass voice vibrated the door. "You gave strict orders to have you up by first light. Why I do not know, but there you have it. Are you awake?"

"I am now," Andre said, muttering to himself.

He threw off the sheet tangled around him and stalked to the door. His hair tumbled over his eyes. On the way he danced into the nearest pair of breeches.

Wings of the Wind

He yanked open the door. "I am awake!"

Tito sprang back. "I am only following orders, mi Capitán."

"Thank you," Andre said. "Have Mickey bring coffee."

"Si, Si, mi Capitán." Tito saluted and stomped off.

Andre slammed the door, walked back to the bunk, and lay down on his back. He laced his hands behind his head and blew out a breath.

He remembered why he wanted to be awake so early. He had a call to pay today on the lady he couldn't get out of his thoughts. What was it about her? He thought about their meeting yesterday. He had had trouble keeping his eyes off her. Good lines. Sleek with curves in the right places. There was a hunger in her eyes. What was that hunger? A man? Adventure? She had daring he liked.

If the rumors that Carmichael had gathered were true, she could have her pick of men and had. She didn't seem like a tease but then theirs had been a business meeting. It wasn't as though they had met on the dance floor.

Pounding on the door again.

"Enter!"

The door crashed open, and Andre's Chinese steward, Mickey Chinfatt, shuffled into the room on black slippered feet that matched his loose black pants, over blouse, and cap that perched on dull black hair braided into a skinny pigtail that hung down his back. A few strands of hair sprouted from his chin that were his face's answer to a beard. He carried a huge tankard of coffee and set it down on the small table to the side of the bunk.

"Coffee, boss. Somesing else?"

"Yes," he said as he sat up. "Bring the tub in and set up my bath."

47

Mickey's eyebrows flew up and his mouth open. "Ah, very special occasion, I see, boss. Right away." He slammed out of the cabin. Andre could hear him yelling to the kitchen boy at the top of his singsong voice to look lively and put the water on to boil for the captain's bath.

If he were going into town, he didn't want to smell like a wharf rat. Besides, he needed to think, and the bath was where he did his best thinking. He picked up the tankard and sipped the tar colored brew, walked over to the desk, sat down in the chair, and put his feet up.

He had decided on an early morning call to press the advantage with the lavender lady. He mused over which man to take with him. Carmichael, of course, since he was a solicitor, and Tito to look out for any trouble. He always liked to have a second pair of eyes to watch his back. It was probably one of the reasons he had lived this long.

There was the possibility he wasn't going to like what the lady proposed. There was the greater problem that he would. He chewed on his lower lip. She wanted to help find Norton, and what she had in mind entailed her as bait. That had merit, but it could be dangerous. He lit up a cheroot to help him think better and enjoy his coffee more. Finding Norton with a lure would be more exciting, and he was short on excitement these days. Being a commercial captain was rather staid compared to his early days of sailing in the Caribbean with the remnants of Jean Lafitte's band.

He had made enough money in his commercial venture to buy his way into respectability. He rather liked the respectable world. It paved the way into polite circles on the Atlantic and Gulf coast cities where he called on a regular basis. It wasn't risky like his old life but was much less exciting.

He missed the excitement. Enter Miss Mercedes Lawless. If he used her as some sort of bait, the Norton fish might be brought in much faster. Add to that the possibility that the sport would be carried out with an enticing female.

He got up, looked in the mirror on the wall, and rubbed over the dark stubble on his face. He would even shave.

Within the space of an hour Andre was scrubbed, shaved, and in the shore boat. In Galveston he made his way down the street toward the Lavender Dry Goods Emporium with Duncan Carmichael hurrying by his side, trying to keep up with Andre's strides. Duncan huffed and puffed with a sheen of sweat on his face while Andre seemed to be enjoying the chill of Alaska instead of the heat of Galveston.

"Carmichael," Andre said to his smaller companion as he pulled up short. Duncan stopped short of colliding into the back of the Captain. "Tell me again why you think we may have a legal problem."

"Well," Duncan said, fanning himself, "this revolves around a gentleman's agreement based on the uncle being the real uncle. The deed itself could be a fake, but I'll check into that today in the Records Office."

"I see." Andre watched a man unloading boxes of merchandise from a wagon across the street. The wagon was in front of the Lavender Dry Goods Emporium. "Do you think the lady knows this?"

Duncan pursed his lips. "I would say so. She did not appear to be representative of the uninformed segment of the female population."

Andre nodded. "My estimation also." The wagoner finished his unloading, and a young man carried the boxes inside.

The young man looked their way. He dropped the box he was lifting and shouted, "Captain Lafitte!" He bounded across the street to where the Andre stood, skidded to a stop in front of him, and snapped a salute.

Andre returned the salute solemnly and clapped the young man on the shoulder.

"How are you today, Jamie?"

"Just fine, sir, just fine. We got a shipment in early this morning and lucky for me that I was helping to unload, or I wouldn't have seen you. Are you here to see my sister?"

"That I am."

Jamie cleared his throat and leaned closer. In a low, confidential voice he said, "Might I have a word with you, sir, man-to-man?"

Andre put on his best man-to-man face. "What's on your mind?"

"Well, sir," Jamie began, as he pulled Andre a few steps away from Duncan. "I know you came about the Norton business but really, sir, we never knew about him. We are simple folk and law-abiding and all."

"I suspected as much."

"What I would like to know though, sir, is if my sister talked to you about me?"

Andre's brows knit together wondering where this was leading. "She said a few words about you. Was there something special she was supposed to say?"

Jamie sighed. "Didn't she say anything about me wanting to be a seaman?"

Andre looked more closely at the boy's uplifted face, the sincere countenance, the pleading in his eyes. His face had the leanness of beginning adolescent and the eyes of an intelligent youth growing toward manhood. Such yearning in those eyes.

Wings of the Wind

"A seaman, is it?"

"Oh, yes, sir."

"How does your sister feel about this?"

Jamie looked down at the ground and kicked the dust around. "She doesn't like it much. But I'm old enough to make my own decisions now, and, well sir, I'd like a position on your ship."

Andre didn't speak but studied the hopefulness in the boy's eyes. Even in the early morning the Texas sun was bright and hot and reflected in Jamie's deep blues. He waited for him to go on, sensed his struggle, watched the emotion on his face.

Jamie rushed on. "I'm twelve years old now, sir, almost thirteen. I'm getting too old to be a ship's boy. How will I ever gain a berth if I don't soon? Mercedes doesn't want me to go on just any ship, but I can't wait forever."

Andre considered. "Maybe you won't have to be a ship's boy. Do you help your sister with the sums in the store?"

"Yes, sir. I like helping customers, and I take their money and make change. I help keep the inventory of goods. You know, keeping track of what we get and what we sell. Mercedes taught me."

"That's a very useful skill, lad." Andre thought of his need for a reliable ship's clerk. "Can you read and write, too?"

"Yes, sir, I can. Mercedes taught me herself. We read bible and adventure stories. I like those the best. Sometimes I read the newspaper. I can sign my name, too."

Andre considered the boy looking up at him so hopefully. "I could use a boy who knows his sums and how to read and write. You would be a ship's clerk first while you are learning to be a seaman."

Marjorie Thelen

Jamie jumped up and down. "I could do it, sir. I could help you. Oh, I would do anything to ship out with you." He stopped jumping when he realized what he was doing. But he continued to twitch and jiggle, and the smile would not leave his face.

Andre knew the boy would do anything. He understood. He had been the same way. On a more calculating note he also knew that if young Jamie were with him it would be insurance in his dispute over the Lavender Dry Good Emporium. It might be insurance that he would see the lovely Miss Lawless again. He made his decision.

"All right you have the job. As soon as we finish the business with your sister, we sail."

"Yoweeee!" Jamie shouted, the dreams of his young life finally coming true. "I'll go tell Mercedes right away."

Andre grabbed Jamie's collar before he could go anywhere.

"Best we do that together." He sensed that the news might not be of the variety that would make Jamie's sister happy.

"Carmichael," he said to his perspiring solicitor.

"Young Jamie will be joining us on the ship. See to a berth for him."

"Yes, sir. Happy to have you on board, young man," he said to Jamie. "I'll do my best to make you feel welcome."

Jamie beamed and saluted, first Carmichael, then Andre. "You won't regret this, sir. Truly."

Andre returned the salute. "I don't believe I will."

Additional bargaining power never hurt, especially when dealing with the proprietress of the Lavender Dry Goods Emporium.

Wings of the Wind

* * * * *

The temperature dropped a few degrees as the threesome entered the Emporium. The overhang on the front porch dimmed the brightness from the street. Maybe the relative coolness would help Duncan, who Andre feared would succumb to heat exhaustion. If he would take off some of those infernal proper clothes he insisted on wearing, he might live longer.

Andre gazed about, surprised at the size and extent of the shop. The newly arrived boxes stood to the front of the store, and a woman with carrot red hair struggled to open one. She hacked with a knife on the cord that wrapped the box. The knife was obviously dull.

Andre stepped over and pulled out his knife. "May I help you with that, miss?"

Julia stared at the gleaming knife blade, and her eyes widened. She followed the proffered blade from the muscled hand, up a long, powerful arm clad in white muslin, and past the expanse of shoulder. She met the speaker's eyes. Her jaw dropped.

Jamie stepped in to fill the gap. "Captain Lafitte, may I introduce you to my cousin, Julia? Julia, meet Captain Andre Lafitte."

In one deft movement, Andre leaned over, slit the troublesome cord binding the box, and stowed the knife back in the sheath at his hip.

He bowed. "My pleasure, Miss Julia. This is my solicitor, Duncan Carmichael."

Duncan tipped his hat and bowed toward Julia. "My pleasure."

Regaining her voice, Julia dipped a curtsey and said,

"The pleasure is mine, gentlemen." Her hand covered her heart. "Forgive my manners. I was taken by surprise when I saw the blade. You certainly handle that knife with great skill, Captain Lafitte."

"An acquired skill. Forgive me, if I gave you pause."

"Boy-oh-boy," said Jamie, "will you teach me how to use a knife like that, sir?"

"We'll have to see first if you have any talent for it," Andre replied, smiling down at Jamie. "Shall we talk about this later?" He winked at Jamie, and Jamie winked back.

Andre returned his attention to Julia. "I've come to see Miss Lawless. She may be expecting me."

"I believe she is." Julia still stared wide-eyed at the stranger. "Let me tell her you're here. Excuse me." She hurried across the shop to the back of the store.

A customer came into the store. Jamie excused himself and went to help the matronly woman who announced she was looking for some of that fine lavender soap Miss Mercedes handled.

Andre and Duncan waited by the boxes. They watched a gentleman enter the store and walk to the building materials aisle. This was quite an operation. It impressed Andre that a young woman kept it going. Mercedes seemed so elegant, maybe the word was refined, to be involved in shop keeping, which seemed so coarse.

He thought about his claim on this store. He wouldn't mind having some claim to the woman's affections, too, like in mistress. Nothing permanent. A liaison. He'd take over her shop and leave her in charge or in some advisory role, take the profit, pay her a nice wage, and enjoy the fruits of her affection. He could visit from time to time to see how his investment and his paramour got on.

He wondered how to win her affection. Surely, she would be relieved to have the burden of the store removed from her shoulders. Duncan could stay on to oversee the operation. He would take Jamie with him. Yes, he could see this might work into a very satisfactory arrangement. He'd deal with Norton. He didn't need Mercedes's help. How could a woman possibly help in a matter like this anyway?

Then he saw her moving like a queen down the aisle toward him. This was her realm. In that instant, Andre realized his fantasy of a few moments before would not work with this woman. Today she had more of a contained air about her. Today she was in command. He was in her territory.

She was sleek, dressed in yet another variation of lavender with billowing skirts. The only deviation from the streamlined look was the curls that wisped around her face, curls too stubborn to submit to a chignon. She stopped before him rosy lips turned up into a smile, eyes twinkling.

"Captain Lafitte," she said, "so good to see you again." She dropped a polite curtsey. "I take it you met my cousin, Julia?" She gestured to Julia, who had stopped in another part of the store to help a small child with candy. Andre nodded without taking his eyes off Mercedes.

She bent around Andre to address Duncan, who hovered behind him. "Good day to you, Mr. Carmichael. I'm sorry I lost my temper yesterday when you were here. I hope you will forgive me. I was in a state of shock."

"Quite, quite." Duncan tipped his hat. "Not to worry. No harm done," he said.

"Might we go to a more private place to discuss business?" Andre asked, taking Mercedes by the arm. She did not pull away.

"Of course, please step this way," she said with a smile that dripped with sugar.

Her sweetness put Andre on the alert. What was she up to? The woman that had left his ship had not been happy. Maybe this was what they called southern graciousness.

She indicated an aisle that led to the rear of the store. Though reluctant to let go of the warmth and softness of her, Andre released her arm, as the aisle grew too narrow for them both to pass. He followed her at a short distance and watched her hips sway, took in the straight of her back and the curve of her neck. At the same time he stayed alert for any sign of trouble though he wasn't sure what form that might take. Something was up. She was being too nice.

To the back of the store, she entered a neat, organized office. A large, open window looked out onto a garden. A faint breeze stirred the curtains. She indicated a straight back chair for him, closed the door, and took a chair for herself in front of a pine desk.

Andre positioned his chair close to the window facing the door and lost no time in getting to the point. "Miss Lawless, I agreed yesterday to give you my decision this morning on the matter of your helping to find your uncle."

"Yes, Captain, you did."

"I wanted to hear what plan you had first."

"Yes."

Mercedes sat with what looked to Andre like a pasted on smile. Annoying. What kind of game was she playing?

"I'm here to hear what that plan may be. I don't have much time as we are sailing this evening." He hesitated then decided to introduce the icebreaker. "By the way, I have offered young Jamie a position on my ship, and he

Wings of the Wind

will sail with us."

The smile vanished replaced with an unbecoming scowl. "Did I hear that last part correctly? Would you repeat the part about my brother?"

Andre leaned back in his chair. "Yes, I said he will sail as a member of my crew."

Mercedes jumped up, hands on her hips before she was out of the chair.

"Over my dead body. San Francisco is too far, and your reputation is not the sort a young impressionable boy like Jamie needs for an influence." Her eyes blazed making them more strikingly lavender than before. "Moreover, I need him here."

Andre dropped his arm over the back of the chair. Now he was beginning to enjoy this. "No, I need him on my ship since Carmichael will be staying to help you and protect my interests. This is my store now, and I make the decisions on who and what is needed here."

"Your store? Carmichael?" Mercedes fumed and sputtered.

"I seem to have an echo." Andre searched round the room for cavernous enclaves.

"That does not fit into my plan," Mercedes said.

"The plan that features you as bait?" He hardly had the question out when the door to the office slammed open.

"You're under arrest, Captain Lafitte," said the man in the doorway with a growl.

Marjorie Thelen

Chapter Five

Andre peered into the barrels of two shooting irons and at a bright shiny star pinned to the vest of a short, stocky man with a droopy, gray mustache.

"Arrest, Sheriff?"

"For the murder of this young woman's uncle, Jeffrey Norton."

Andre flicked a sideways glance at Mercedes. "Interesting plan, but it won't work."

Mercedes narrowed her eyes. "Why not? You're the last person to see him alive, and he hasn't arrived here. You murdered and threw him overboard. Then you come here to me with that fake document and that ridiculous story."

No sound issued from Andre's direction.

"What do you got to say for yourself," said the Sheriff, "before I haul you away to jail?" He cocked the guns to show how serious he was.

Andre sighed and made as if to get up.

"Don't you move and keep your hands in front of you, so's I can put this here rope on them."

"I wouldn't be so hasty, Sheriff," Andre said. "How do you know you have the right man?"

"I do all right." The Sheriff aimed a spit of tobacco at the spittoon by the desk. "Miss Mercedes been worried to death about her uncle, seeing as how he hasn't showed up

Wings of the Wind

here."

"Worried to death, is it? Would that have been since yesterday when she received the letter?" Andre looked at Mercedes, who simulated a wan smile.

"What if I can prove that Mr. Norton is still alive?"

"You can't, and you know it," Mercedes said.

"Tito!"

Tito leaped into view behind the Sheriff.

"Now hold on there just a second," said the Sheriff. "You're making me nervous." With that he fired both guns but not before Tito threw his weight against the sheriff the split second before the guns went off, knocking him off balance. The pistols fired into the ceiling. Chunks of plaster rained down on them, one knocking Mercedes on the head. She slumped to the floor.

Tito hopped on top of the Sheriff, holding down his arms, while Andre, unscathed except for a sprinkling of plaster dust, relieved the sheriff of the guns. He dumped the bullets and threw the lot out the open window.

"Tito, use the rope to tie up the Sheriff."

He turned to help Mercedes. She was sprawled in a heap of lavender cotton print on the floor. He kneeled over her, searching for a pulse.

"Holy Smokes," Jamie said from the doorway, Julia behind him.

"Mercedes!" Julia screamed, peering around Jamie at her cousin on the floor. "You killed her."

"She's not dead, and it wasn't the Captain," Jamie said, coming into the room. "I saw what happened. The Sheriff shot wild and hit the ceiling. He was aiming at Captain Lafitte."

Julia rushed over to kneel by her cousin.

"Her pulse is steady," said Andre. "She'll come to in

a minute." He stood and hooked his hands on his hips.

"Get me the smelling salts, Jamie," said Julia. She gave Andre a withering glance.

Jamie disappeared from the room, shoving a few curious onlookers ahead of him. Gunshots were not out of the ordinary in Galveston, but curiosity reigned forever.

Tito had secured the Sheriff and turned him face down on the floor, where he muffled into the rag rug under his face.

"What now, mi Capitán?" Tito sat on the Sheriff's back to keep him from struggling. "If we are lucky, the Sheriff will suffocate to death."

Andre wagged his head slowly and surveyed the scene. They knew how to be melodramatic in this town. Murder? What could this young woman have been thinking? Naïve to tangle with him, but that might come from leading a sheltered life. But how sheltered could the life be of a woman who ran a store in Galveston, Texas, the not-so-long-ago pirate capital of the Gulf Coast? And she was rumored to have spent the night with one of the town's most infamous men.

Jamie arrived with salts for Mercedes, and Julia waved them under her cousin's dusty nose. Mercedes' eyes fluttered opened. The first person she saw was Andre Lafitte.

"Goodness gracious," she said. "Am I in hell?"

"More like Galveston, Texas in your own store to be exact," Andre said, as he nonchalantly brushed plaster dust off his sleeves and britches.

"Stay quiet, Mercedes," said Julia.

Mercedes turned her head to look at her cousin and winced. She reached up and picked a clump of plaster from her hair, then rubbed the spot where it had hit her.

Wings of the Wind

"I guess my plan didn't work so well."

"No, it didn't." Julia's response had a wistful note to it.

"What are you talking about?" said Jamie. "Did the two of you cook this up?" The set of his teeth and the tone of his voice had the quality of a cat that had just been dowsed with water.

"The Sheriff suggested this when I went to him with my concerns bright and early this morning," said Mercedes. "He was trying to help."

"Help?" Jamie's face burned crimson with what Andre judged to be embarrassment. "Since when has Sheriff McGreevy helped anyone more than to a bottle of whiskey?"

The Sheriff grunted on the floor. Mercedes shot her brother a disgusted look, then shifted up on one elbow and looked at the Sheriff. "It was worth a try." She looked to Andre. "What are you going to do now?"

All eyes focused on Andre except the Sheriff. He still mumbled into the floor.

"There wouldn't be anymore to this harebrained scheme, would there?" Andre's gaze rested on Mercedes lying in her dust bath on the floor.

"No." She looked somewhat contrite. "I thought that if I could get you behind bars . . . "

". . . or worse."

"I never thought they would hang you." Mercedes spit plaster bits off her lips.

"Murder is a hanging offense."

Jamie cut in. "Mercedes, how could you do such a thing to the Captain of my ship?"

"Jamie Lawless." She pointed at him. "You are not joining the crew of his ship." She sat up and tried to dust off.

"I am, too. Aren't I, Captain?"

Andre assessed the faces turned to him. Jamie's eager, hopeful one. Julia's puzzled one. Tito's impatient one. Mercedes lovely, dusty one. There was something about her disheveled hair that appealed to him. His pulse, which had just returned to normal, picked up again. Luckily, his mind still worked and was made up on the subject of Jamie. The lad was right. He needed to get away, especially from these crazy females. If it were the sea he wanted, the sea he would get.

"Yes, you are, Jamie. Miss Lawless, the wise choice would be to let him go with your blessing."

Mercedes sat upright, dust spiraling outward. Tears welled in her eyes and slid down her face turning the plaster dust to goo. "Jamie, tell me you don't want to do this."

"Mercedes, you know this is what I want. It's a good opportunity. The Captain is going to let me be his clerk and keep the books while I learn to be a seaman. Learn to use a knife, too."

Mercedes and Julia blanched.

"We'll see about the knife," Andre said.

* * * * *

Mercedes had meant Andre Lafitte no harm. But it would have been much better if he were in jail, instead of here in this room watching her. Better for her in more than one way. The way he looked at her was unnerving. In addition, she had the dreadful feeling she found him attractive, which would be a disaster. A man was not in her plans now or ever. A man would take control of everything she had worked so hard to build. Didn't Andre just talk

Wings of the Wind

about putting Carmichael here to oversee the operation? What was a lady to do? Of course, she still considered herself a lady, tarnished reputation or not.

It had been a matter of time for Jamie, so she might as well give over gracefully what she could no longer control. Jamie needed to learn to be a man, and she couldn't provide that education. Jamie wasn't cut from the same cloth as Uncle Everett. He was cut from the fabric of his father, who was gone. If she had to relinquish control of her brother's upbringing she wanted some guarantees, and she was going to bargain for a concession.

"All right, "she said at last. "Go with my blessing, dear brother."

Jamie whooped. Julia looked crestfallen. Andre watched her with skepticism written all over his face.

"But . . ." she said.

"But what?" asked Jamie.

"But I come, too. Together we look for Jeffrey Norton."

"Are we back to the united search for Mr. Norton, the one that features you as bait?" Andre folded his arms across his chest. "No."

"You haven't even heard the whole plan."

"I don't need to hear it. I understand already. The answer is no. You are trouble, and you will stay here." Andre looked around. "Where's Carmichael?"

Duncan stepped to Andre's side from his post at the door.

"Here I am, sir."

"We are taking over the Lavender Dry Goods Emporium. You will stay here and learn the business."

"Yes, sir."

To Mercedes he said, "I will let you know the financial

arrangements, as soon as Carmichael has sent his first monthly report to me."

"The legality of your claim is in question. You can't take over like this," said Mercedes, as she struggled to rise with Julia's help.

"I can and I am. I warned you that if I didn't like your plan, you would be hearing from my lawyer. Carmichael is my lawyer, and I did not like your plan."

"What about Norton?" Mercedes reached out and rested her fingers lightly on Andre's forearm. "You said something to the Sheriff about proving that Norton was still alive. Does that mean you know where he is?"

"Quick mind," said Andre, examining the fingers on his arm, "and excellent memory. I did say something to that effect before the Sheriff let go and blasted the ceiling."

They all looked up to the hole above them. Andre shook his head sympathetically. "Going to take some work to repair that hole. Why don't you ask the Sheriff to do it?"

"I am not amused, Captain. We'll get the ceiling and my head repaired after you tell me what you know about the whereabouts of Norton."

Andre ignored her demand. "Carmichael."

"Yes, sir."

"You will oversee the operation here, learn the business, help in anyway you can, and see to the legal papers, as we discussed. You will produce a detailed financial report of the state of the business. Am I clear?"

"Yes, sir."

"One other thing."

"Yes, sir?"

"I'd get rid of some of those clothes if I were you. You'll never survive in this heat."

"Yes, sir. Quite," said Duncan, appearing astonished

Wings of the Wind

at the idea.

Mercedes butted in. "You are avoiding the issue of Jeffrey Norton, Captain." Her grip on his arm tightened.

Andre raised a brow at the slim fingers clutching his arm. When their eyes met, his gaze was deadly serious. "That I am not, Miss Lawless. Mr. Norton remains upper most in my mind. However, you have proved yourself untrustworthy, so I will not share any information with you or the Sheriff on his whereabouts."

He glanced over at Tito. "Is the Sheriff still breathing?"

"Just barely." Tito's gold-rimmed white teeth glistened when he smiled.

"Better get off him then."

Tito jumped up and rolled the Sheriff over. He was out cold.

"Miss Lawless, I'm sure you can help the Sheriff back to the jail, when he comes around. Jamie, come lad, we need to be going."

Tito." Andre nodded toward the open window. "Let's be away. Carmichael, make yourself at home."

He turned to Mercedes. "Miss Lawless." Andre took her hand in his, dusted it off and kissed it. "We will meet again, I'm sure."

"Miss Julia, the pleasure was all mine." He bowed to her cousin.

Jamie waved goodbye, as he ducked out the window, followed by Tito, then Andre.

As she watched them disappear over the garden wall, Mercedes said in a low voice, "You will see me again, dear Captain Lafitte."

Chapter Six

Jamie gazed about the ship, wide-eyed with excitement. The deck was a flurry of activity, as all hands made ready to sail. He hugged the railing to stay out of the way. He couldn't believe his luck that he was on a real clipper ship, on the *Wings of the Wind*.

From his post at the rail he could see the Galveston wharves and the scene at the store came vividly back. He had waved good-bye to his sister. There was no time for anything else. Maybe he should have given her a hug. But he would see her again. She probably wouldn't miss him too much. She had looked pretty miserable though standing there with Julia.

He was glad no one had come looking for them. All that ruckus could have brought out half the city, but it had been early, and they were in the back of the store, so he guessed everything would just blow over like it usually did. The sheriff would recover okay. McGreevy was a tough old bird when he wasn't drinking, and meaner still when he was. Jamie couldn't fathom what Mercedes was thinking when she cooked up that plan. Women didn't make any sense to him.

Lost in his thoughts, he didn't hear the footsteps behind him. He jumped when a hand came down on his shoulder.

Wings of the Wind

"Enjoying the view?" Andre asked him.

"Yes, sir. I like looking at Galveston from the deck of a ship."

"Will you miss it?"

"I like Galveston all right. I have some nice friends there." Jamie looked thoughtful. "What I didn't like was being trapped in a store with two females. I wanted to be at sea, you see."

"I understand."

"You do?" Jamie brightened. "Were you surrounded by a bunch of females growing up?"

"Lot of females, more than you can imagine. I have a brother, and there was my mother, but I didn't see her that much. My brother and I were pretty wild. We had the run of New Orleans."

"What about you father?"

Andre shrugged. "I never knew him. My mother was very vague about who he was."

"Oh." Jamie furrowed his brow. "So you don't know if your father was Jean Lafitte?" Genuine disappointment showed in his eyes.

Andre smiled down at him. "No, but I doubt it. I don't know how my mother came by the name of Lafitte. She told my brother and I that she had been married, but with her I could never be certain of the truth. But Lafitte we are. You aren't the first person that asked me about my connections to Lafitte."

"Are you a pirate?" Jamie blurted it out.

Andre shook his head. "Sorry to disappoint you, but I'm merely a captain of a commercial ship."

"That's all? You don't do any pirating on the side?"

"Do you see any gun ports on this ship?"

Jamie peered up and down the deck. "No, sir, I don't."

67

"It's hard to be a pirate without guns on your ship."

"Gosh," replied Jamie, looking disappointed. "I never thought about that."

"I'm respectable now." Andre met the eyes of his new recruit. "I want to keep it that way."

"You mean you were disreputable at one time?"

"Let's just say, I kept some bad company. That's behind me now."

They watched a large boat nearing the ship rowed by two of the crew and stacked with provisions that Andre had ordered from town.

Activity on the deck centered on getting the winch and boom ready to help with the loading of the stores onto the ship. Barrels and boxes had to be lifted to the ship and into the hold before they could leave.

"That's too bad, Captain," said Jamie.

"What's too bad?"

"That you are respectable now. I was hoping for a little excitement. I wanted to fight some buccaneers."

* * * * *

Andre felt a stirring from his own childhood in those words. "Trust me, young man, we'll find plenty of excitement sailing this ship all the way down South America, through the Straits of Magellan and up the other side of the continent. I don't think you'll be bored."

Jamie grinned. "I can't wait until we sail."

"Come. I'll give you a tour of the ship, and then we shall have something to eat. We have an excellent cook on board, and we dine like kings."

They walked fore and aft, Andre showing Jamie the workings of the ship, Jamie admiring every inch of it.

Wings of the Wind

"Will I learn to sail and be part of the crew?" Jamie asked, as they made their way to Andre's cabin.

"I don't see why not. But right now I need someone to help me with the accounts. I lost a good one a while back when he decided he wanted to give up the sea, marry, and settle down. It isn't easy finding a good clerk that likes to travel most of the time. Carmichael filled in for him."

"Do you have any place you call home?" asked Jamie, as they entered the cabin. Andre gestured to him to take a seat at the table set for mid-day meal.

"I don't really. I've been on a ship since I ran away from home, and I was younger than you. The sea comes to me naturally."

"So you are always on the ship. This is your home?"

Andre nodded and rang for Mickey Chinfatt. "This is it. This is all I know. When New Orleans got too unbearable, I left. I shipped out with a captain friend of my mother, and I never looked back." He hesitated. "I did spend a little time on Galveston Island, as a small boy. I don't remember much."

Jamie's wandering gaze focused on Andre. "You were here when Lafitte was here, I betcha."

"Like I said I don't remember much. I ran wild then, too. Galveston wasn't built up like it is now. It was a flat piece of sand with a few shacks."

"What about Jean Lafitte's "maison rouge", his red mansion?"

"If he had a red mansion, it wasn't while I was in residence. We weren't here for long. My mother liked the refinements of a city, so we went back to New Orleans."

"Is your mother still in New Orleans?"

"She's dead now, but she lived there all her life."

"And your brother?"

"He's younger. He should be up north. He went on one of those expeditions up the Mississippi. He saw what he liked up north, and that's where he stopped. I think he's a guide but that could have changed. I don't hear from him."

Mickey Chinfatt banged into the room with a tray of steaming potatoes and meat and set it on the table in front of them. He came back with a bowl of fresh fruit.

"Somesing else, boss?"

Andre said to Jamie, "This is Mickey, my steward. You'll be working with him."

Mickey flashed a toothy grin at Jamie.

"We aren't organized like most ships," said Andre, "with a strict chain of command. I never liked a hierarchy like on military ships."

"Everybody more happy that way," Mickey piped in. "Okay, boss? You need some other sing?"

"That will be all. Please look over the stores to make sure the men got all the items on the list."

"Sure, boss." Mickey bowed out.

"I like the name *Wings of the Wind,*" said Jamie, around mouthfuls of food.

"It fits. We are two of a kind this ship and I. We both go where the wind blows us. Let me tell you, this ship can fly. We may establish a record to San Francisco."

They chatted on about the ship, the weather, how to sail, the chores Jamie would be doing, life on board the ship, the schedule of the day. Jamie brought up the subject of where they were going.

Andre sipped his coffee. "We're going to find Jeffrey Norton. Since I have good reason to believe he's in New Orleans that's where we're going. That wasn't on the schedule, and it will put us behind for San Francisco, but we have some leeway on the time. I want to get this matter

Wings of the Wind

cleared up."

"Boy-oh-boy, I get to see New Orleans. This is great." Jamie had not stopped smiling since he came aboard.

Andre stifled the urge to ruffle the boy's hair. The kid's enthusiasm was infectious. "Now, I have some matters to review with my first mate, so why don't you help Mickey with inventorying the stores? Be sure we have enough barrels of water on the manifest. There's nothing I hate more than to run out of fresh water."

"Aye, aye sir," Jamie sang out as he saluted and headed for the door. He turned back. "By the way, where would I find Mickey?"

"Follow the passage forward. You'll find his working quarters there."

"Yes, sir," Jamie saluted again and slammed the door.

Fits right in with the rest of the crew when it comes to closing doors, thought Andre. He poured himself another cup of coffee and took it to his desk. He sank into the big leather chair, put his head back, and closed his eyes. He wasn't accustomed to the endless questions and energy of a boy. He basked in the silence.

Thoughts of the disastrous scene with the sheriff elbowed their way into his head. Luck had it that no one was hurt. He wasn't sure he wanted to tangle with Miss Mercedes Lawless again. He was glad they left her behind in Galveston. She was too unpredictable . . . but captivating. He knew he didn't want to take on brother and sister at the same time. He'd rather take on Jean Lafitte's whole band of pirates. Those people he understood. This woman was too capricious . . . but fetching. What incredible energy the brother and sister had. Both had those same striking eyes, same expressions, same exuberance. If he had to keep looking at Jamie, he doubted he would be able to get his mind off the sister.

The problem was he needed a little-past-time-for-the-evening. Unfortunately, it didn't look like he was going to find a woman to ease his needs today, since they'd be sailing on the evening tide. When they got to New Orleans, he'd make a visit to his mother's former establishment. As bad a mother as she was, she had been an excellent businesswoman and madam of the most exclusive and profitable brothel in town, the one she had left to him. He would stop by the Silver Slipper and visit with his favorite girl, Beatrice. The thought cheered him.

Chapter Seven

Mercedes sat hunched in the stuffy, dark place and listened for sounds of movement. No one had passed by recently, and she needed to stand up and stretch. She feared her muscles would be permanently curled in a fetal position, if she didn't move soon. She removed the knothole in the side of the barrel and looked through it. She could see little, not only because the hole was so small, but also because the light was dim in the hold of the ship.

She pushed up on the lid of the barrel. It made a deep, popping sound as it lifted. She froze and listened. It would be a matter of time before she was discovered, but she wanted to make sure they were well away from Galveston before she was. She did not want them turning around to deposit her right back at the store. That would never do. Her plan was to stick with this beautiful clipper ship, the impossible captain, and her sea-crazed brother till they found the mystery uncle.

It took everything she had to convince Julia to help her get into the barrel and hide her. Of course, Julia had argued till she was red in the face, threatening to give her away to Duncan Carmichael. But Mercedes's reasoning had prevailed in the end. Julia had to concede that the only way to keep track of Jamie was to follow him, and the logical person to do that was Mercedes. Julia and her father would take care of the store. Duncan, who seemed pleasant enough, would help. Julia said she would make him comfortable in Jamie's room after *Wings of the Wind* was out to sea. Somehow they would manage.

So here she was constricted into a barrel in the hold of the ship. The barrel was supposed to hold beans, but they had to be left behind. Captain Lafitte would just have to do with fewer beans for this trip or get some in New Orleans, since she had heard the crew talk about sailing there first. She feared discovery when they came to inventory the boxes and barrels before sailing, but lucky for her, they only counted casks and not bothered to open any of them.

She poked her head up above the barrel top and scanned her surroundings. There was a coil of rope beside her barrel. She climbed out onto the coil, which was not easy in a dress, but she managed without tearing anything. She sat on the rope, massaging her tingling legs to get the circulation back. At least she had been able to clean up after all that plaster dust. Even with the risk of discovery, she had to get out of the barrel sometimes. It was boring in there and, though the scenery wasn't much better from the coil of rope, at least she could breathe better and feel the blood circulate in her legs again.

She took out a bit of the hard cheese she stashed into the small bundle she brought with her and nibbled away. She contemplated how she would present herself to Captain Lafitte. She could wait until discovery but that might not be until New Orleans. On the other hand, she could sneak up and announce herself to Captain Lafitte. Wouldn't he be surprised? She rather liked that idea, but it would be brazen. Wasn't what she was doing now brazen? She might as well live the role to the hilt. Andre Lafitte might be preferable to the critters that she heard scurrying

Wings of the Wind

in the corners down here.

She finished the cheese then sipped water from a small bottle. It seemed odd not having anything to do. Every day, every moment was a workday for her with never anytime off. This was a holiday in the hold of a ship. A better holiday would be in New Orleans. The thought had appeal. She had always wanted to visit New Orleans, but the demands of the store had kept her on Galveston Island.

She lay back on the coil of rope, snuggled into its interior coil, and shut her eyes. Sleep did not come. Thoughts swirled in her head. She thought of her brother and his perfidy in deserting her. Come Mercedes, she chided herself, he wanted to get on a ship. You knew it. There was nothing to stop him when someone like Captain Lafitte threw the opportunity right in his lap.

Captain Lafitte. Her thoughts turned to him like a sunflower to the sun. What kind of women did he like she wondered? Was he married? He didn't seem to be the marrying kind. Not that she was interested in something like that for herself. She liked her independence. She was never going to bow to the dictates of a man. That ruled out marriage.

She had many interests to keep her occupied. The Emporium was one, and the ship she hoped to invest in as soon as she had enough money saved was another. It was more than her brother that brought her on board this ship. She wanted to see close hand how one operated. Captain Lafitte seemed to be a good captain. He said he did commercial ventures, but she didn't rule out the possibility of a little smuggling mixed in. In this part of the world, just about anything went and did.

Footsteps overhead nudged her from her reverie, and she looked with regret toward her barrel. She dreaded getting back in and decided to take her chances in crouching in the darkness behind the barrels and boxes. She tapped the lid back in place and crept into the shadows.

The steps creaked. In the dim light she recognized the Chinese steward probably come to fetch supplies. He hung a small oil lamp on a hook overhead. Mercedes moved back further into the shadows to escape the light playing over the boxes and barrels. She moved one of the boxes and sucked in her breath.

Mickey did not turn around but busied himself opening one of the barrels. "That you Missy?"

Mercedes jumped. He couldn't be talking to her. Maybe he had a cat down here that he talked to, although she could not remember hearing or seeing one.

"Missy?" Mickey still sorted through a barrel, pulling out various parcels and bundles. "You get hungry yet?"

Mercedes made no sound but listened. Hungry? It must be a cat he was addressing, though such a beast could not be hungry with all the vermin that skittered around in this hold.

"Missy Mercedes. You come out. I know you there. You not afraid of me."

He said her name. She eased around the curve of the barrel to get a better look. Their eyes met.

"Missy, you okay?"

She swallowed hard. "Yes, thank you," she said, her voice barely above a whisper. "How did you know that I was here?"

Mickey turned back to continue his picking and sorting. He had some sort of a carrying canvas on which he stacked small bags of something.

"Barrel too light. Move too easy. Barrel make grunting noise."

"I could have been anybody stowing away."

"You only one with little brother on board. Besides, I know these things." He tapped his forehead then smiled the toothy smile that made his eyes disappear behind a sea of crinkles.

"Have you told the Captain?" she asked, reluctant to leave the shadows.

"No. Him know soon enough. You need food, water? I get for you."

"No, thank you, I'm not hungry. I bought food with me, and I've still got a bit of water."

"Okay, but get pretty dark down here." The Chinaman gathered up the handles on the canvas and lifted it up onto his shoulder. "You okay here. Nobody come much but me. I bring food soon. Water, too. You safe. But pretty dark here."

He shuffled to the stairs.

"Sir." Mercedes stood up, and he turned to look at her. "Thanks." She tried a small smile on him. "I could use a blanket, if you have any to spare."

His face brightened. "I bring soon."

"Thank you." She hesitated. "Maybe I could see the Captain when the time is right."

"Okay. I tell you when time is right."

"Thank you," said Mercedes. The light dimmed, as he moved away. He swayed up the narrow steps, and then his footsteps faded overhead.

Smug me, thinking I had everyone fooled. What a funny little man. Why didn't he tell the Captain I was here? She trudged to the coil of rope and plopped down. She dreaded spending the night in the barrel but was even more reluctant to face the Captain.

If she tipped the barrel over, she could lie down, and

with a blanket it would be more comfortable. She would pull the lid closed so the vermin would not be running over her during the night. It did get stuffy in that barrel though. Maybe she could sneak up on deck during the night to get some fresh air. She snapped her fingers. She should talk to Jamie. That was it. Maybe Mickey could come up with some pretense for him to come into the hold to help, and she could talk with him. He would help her.

She curled up into the coil of rope, pillowing her head against the hard braid of the rope. Her eyes drifted shut, only to fly open to the sound of footsteps overhead. She waited, listening. The footsteps descended, and she recognized the slippered sound of Mickey Chinfatt. She sat up.

He came to where he had left her and called her name.

"Here I am. Over here on the rope."

"Missy Mercedes, I bring blanket for you. You more comfortable with this." He moved closer to her and handed her a homespun cotton blanket, softened by many washings.

"Thank you. You are too kind. I am indebted to you for this and for not telling the Captain about me."

"Ah, so. Captain not like females on ship. Say bad luck for men." Mickey giggled. "We go to New Orleans. You get off there?"

"I'm not sure. I want to help find my uncle but the Captain said no, so that's why I had to smuggle myself on board. That and to protect my brother."

"You protect brother?" Mickey giggled again. "Very funny. He need to protect you. Not doing too good job so far."

Mercedes scowled. "Jamie's being difficult."

"No, him just being boy."

The scowl deepened. She tilted her head to one side and said, "Do you think it would be possible for my brother to come here to see me. I know he wouldn't tell the captain, and I would dearly love to see him."

"Brother get mad."

"Jamie? Get mad at me? Never. We've always gotten along well. He is at the age where he doesn't want a mother anymore." A heartfelt sigh escaped her lips. "I think I was suffocating him, but I meant well."

"Humph. Young boys same world over. Know it all. I same way. Look where I am." Mickey wagged his head. "I get boy here. We take inventory. I bring him."

"Thank you." Mercedes stood up, stepped over, and hugged him.

Mickey colored and pushed her gently away. "Not to worry, Missy. Mickey Chinfatt, good guy. He help you."

"Thanks again, Mr. Chinfatt," said Mercedes. "When do you think you can bring Jamie?"

"Maybe tomorrow, maybe next day. Must get to chores." He bowed and hurried up the stairs.

Mercedes called a soft thanks to his retreating back. She climbed back on the coil of rope and hugged the soft blanket to her. Her eyes adjusted to the dimness of the hold. She heard faint scrapings in the corners. Maybe she was daft to have taken on this mission. She wasn't sure what had gotten into her, but she had plenty of time to think about it down here in this dark, still hold. The ship sighed and groaned, as it pushed through the waves. From time to time, she heard the sounds of the crew at work two decks up. But in the hold it was still and silent, except for the critters.

This was her holiday, so she should enjoy it. It was nice not having to rush about the store, helping customers, arranging, inventorying, unloading, rearranging. It was peaceful here. Beyond the hull of the ship, she heard the whisper of the sea. She loved the sea as much as her brother but she could never aspire to a life like he wanted. Julia wanted her to aspire to be a wife. Instead she was a stowaway.

She didn't think she could lose making this trip. It was a welcomed adventure, it got her off Galveston Island, and it got her on board a ship. Maybe she could invest in this one. She had been saving money and had been eyeing every ship that sailed into Galveston harbor. She wanted to be a partial investor, but the opportunity had not presented itself yet. What would the Captain say if she offered to help back a venture for him?

If she hadn't brought the sheriff down on him, they might have been able to negotiate a business arrangement. In hindsight it was an ill thought move. But the sheriff had made it seem like such a good idea getting the Captain behind bars. That was the last time she would listen to Sheriff McGreevy.

Mercedes awoke in the barrel, stiff and grumpy. She had not slept well with all the skittering and scurrying outside her barrel. She popped open the top and hauled her complaining body out. She wanted to freshen up best she could before Jamie appeared. She hoped it would be today. She rummaged in her bundle, found water, brush and lavender eau de cologne that she wouldn't be without and set about brushing out her hair and fixing it back into a chignon. She rinsed her face with a handful of water, patted her neck with cologne, and made a mental note to ask Mickey for more water. A cup of tea would help get the day started. That might be asking too much, so she settled for a few sips of water and a few bites of bread and

Wings of the Wind

hard cheese.

Later in the morning Mickey made good on his promise to bring Jamie to the hold. Mercedes watched them, delighted, from the shadows. They talked about the inventory, and Mickey explained the need to check the barrels again, since they appeared to be missing the barrel of beans. Jamie nodded his agreement and looked at the inventory list on a clipboard. Mickey moved deeper into the hold, lifting barrel lids.

"Pssst, Jamie." Mercedes called hoarsely from the shadows. He kept scrutinizing the list. She moved from the shadows into the dim light and called again. This time he looked up from his work in puzzlement, as though listening to the song of a bird he didn't recognize. Then he turned in the direction of the sound and gasped.

"No, I am not a ghost." Mercedes laughed and ran to him.

"Oh, no," said Jamie. "Not you!"

Mercedes halted in surprise. Could this be the brother to whom she had just said good-bye? Horrified was not the look she expected. "Jamie?"

"How did you get here?" Jamie whirled and looked at Mickey, who came up behind him. "Did you know she was down here? Is that why you brought me down here to look for a lost barrel? If we are short on beans, it is because she was in the bean barrel."

Mickey smiled his big tooth grin.

"You did know." Jamie howled. "This is terrible!"

"Terrible?" asked Mercedes. "How could it be terrible? Aren't you glad to see me?" She stepped back at the thought that he might not be glad to see her.

"Of course, I'm not glad to see you." He reacted to the stricken look on her face. "I mean, I just saw you, I don't have to see you again so soon." He swiped his hand through his hair. "Mercedes, women are not allowed on this ship. Captain Lafitte will be angry if he knows you are here. You have to stay hidden here until we dock in New Orleans. Then I can help you get away to take a steamer back to Galveston."

Mercedes' hands were on her hips. "I will do nothing of the kind. I am going to go talk to Captain Lafitte before we get New Orleans. I am going to help look for Norton. I am going with this ship on this quest, and no one is going to stop me. Besides, someone has to watch out for you."

Jamie came over to stand toe-to-toe with her. She had to look up at him. Was that possible? Was he really taller than she was? Was that a hint of a mustache on his upper lip? My goodness, where have I been? Her hands fell to her sides.

For a long moment brother and sister studied each other, then Jamie broke the silence. "Mercedes, I appreciate your concern. It is touching, but I want to be free, I want to explore, I want to be with other men, learn their ways. I can't do that with you. I don't know how many different ways I have said this to you. I am not a child anymore."

Mercedes squeezed her eyes shut. He wasn't. Where had she been? She opened her eyes to gaze upon him. "Will you sit down with me?" She pulled him down onto the coil of rope. Mickey crouched across from them, listening, neither aware of their observer.

"I won't try to stop you," said Mercedes. "I know this is what you have longed for. How could I interfere with your dreams when I don't want anyone interfering with mine? I understand. I'll try not to embarrass you."

"That's a relief," said Jamie, not sounding like he

Wings of the Wind

believed her.

Mercedes shot him a look. "Jamie, I also came for me. I'm here because I have a big stake in this. I need your help with the Captain. I must see him, convince him to let me help, and explain the unfortunate incident back at the store."

Jamie winced. "That really was not well thought out. What possessed you?"

"I talked to the sheriff, and he convinced me that he could put the Captain behind bars until I could sort out the legality of that silly wager. It didn't work, and now the sheriff is mad at me. That was another good reason to leave Galveston. It will give McGreevy a chance to cool off."

"You could have at least given me some warning that you were going to bring in the sheriff," Jamie said with a grumble.

"Then you would have told the Captain, and I needed time to sort things out. Look, Jamie, if a man says it's legal then it is. A gentleman's agreement might make this bet legal. A female has little say, especially if the man is a relation. But if the uncle is an impostor and the deed is fake, that's different. That's what I have to prove. I've got to find Jeffrey Norton, and you have to help."

"No, I don't. The Captain left Duncan to help you. Mickey says he's an excellent businessman. He could improve your fortune at the store. The Captain didn't throw any of us out. He was civil. He offered me this position and has treated me well. What more help do you want?"

"I want my store, free and clear." She pressed her nose to his. "I need help reasoning with the Captain."

He pushed her away. "You're more charming than me. Use your charm. Why did you really come? It's not just the store. I know you. You want adventure."

83

Marjorie Thelen

Mercedes blew out a long, low sigh not willing to meet her brother's eyes. "Maybe. I hated being left behind. But I also want to find this uncle." She hesitated. "Has the Captain told you his plan to find this man?"

Jamie shook his head. "I know we're heading for New Orleans for that purpose."

Her face softened when she smiled. "I guess I did come for the adventure, too."

"You couldn't stand my having an adventure without you." He cast her a sideways glance but with a smile in it.

Mercedes sighed. "Jamie, you grew up, and I wasn't paying any attention."

"I've gotten out from under your apron strings, so now you can see me better. I've been grown up for awhile."

"It amazes me how wise you are for your age. Now you are living your pirate dream."

Jamie laughed. "Captain Lafitte says he's not a pirate. Leastways, not anymore."

"Not anymore?" Mercedes arched a brow. "What does that mean?"

Jamie shrugged a shoulder. "Don't go imagining things. He's respectable now. The rest is in the past."

Mercedes elected not to pursue the past. "Can you help me to meet with the Captain? Do you think he is going to be awfully mad about me being here?"

"After the way you treated him in Galveston, I don't know. But I saw the way he looked at you back at the store."

"What do you mean? Since when have you noticed things like that?"

He wiggled his eyebrows. "I wasn't always playing my pirate games. I'm an astute observer of my fellow human beings. His interest in you as a female might be your salvation."

"Well, I never."

He stood and looked down at her. "I'll see if I can find a way to talk to him. But you've put me in a difficult position."

Mercedes caught his hand. "Thank you."

"Don't thank me yet. Thank me if you don't get thrown overboard."

"What will you say to him? I don't want to be put off the ship and sent back to Galveston."

Jamie furrowed his brow and tapped his chin. "Simple. I'm going to tell him my sister is in a barrel in the hold of his ship and ask him what he wants to do with her."

Marjorie Thelen

Chapter Eight

Andre enjoyed supper with Jamie, Tito, and Spike, who sat atop Tito's shoulder, eyeing every bite of shrimp etouffee that went into his master's mouth and genteelly nibbling on tidbits of greens, when proffered.

Bruno, chief cook, rolled into the cabin with arms swinging wide at his sides, hands fisted. The crew referred to him as the whale. He kept his black hair slicked back with some kind of grease rumored to be the same he cooked with. For haircuts he whacked it off straight across at the back of his neck with a knife. A man of great appetites, his proficiency with a blade inside and outside the kitchen was renowned. He liked a good meal, a good woman and, most of all, a good fight.

"How's the food?" the whale asked.

"Nothing can beat Gulf shrimp," said Andre as he tossed his napkin on the table. "Bruno, you have outdone yourself again with the shrimp etouffee." He poured two glasses of Madeira, Malmsey 1806, and offered one to Bruno.

Andre marveled at his luck in finding Bruno in a dive of a restaurant in New Orleans called the Captain's Quarters. He had been so impressed with the fare that he offered his compliments to the chef, who came out of the kitchen to meet the complimentor. The two had gotten into a discussion on the need for fresh ingredients to make the best jambalaya, the qualities of fine Madeira, the skills one needed to handle a knife, which led to a discussion of great battles at sea. By the end of the conversation, Andre had offered him the position of cook on his ship, and Bruno accepted. They had sailed together ever since.

Bruno watched Tito chomp away on his second portion of shrimp etouffee.

"Excelente," Tito said, savoring a mouthful with his eyes closed.

"Avast, buckaroos, avast," Spike squawked, ending with several screeches for emphasis.

"Glad you boys are enjoying the meal," Bruno said. "This is the new recruit, I take it? Name's Bruno." He held out a scarred hand to Jamie.

"Glad to meet you, sir." Jamie's hand disappeared in Bruno's.

"You haven't eaten much, lad. Doesn't the food agree with you?" Bruno watched Jamie push his food from one side of the plate to the other.

"It's very tasty," he replied, placing his fork along side his plate.

"You aren't feeling seasick are you?" Andre asked, eyeing the young man.

"No, sir. I feel fine. I'm just not hungry."

Andre frowned. "You have not done justice to Bruno's cooking, I'm afraid."

Tito agreed. "He's the best cook in the Gulf of Mexico, maybe in all the seas. We are very fortunate to have him with us, so we treat him real good. You will get used to how delicious is the food, then other food will have no equal."

Spike squawked in agreement and crunched away on

Marjorie Thelen

square of green pepper.

"It's quite good," Jamie said in a low voice, his eyes on his plate.

"Come now," said Andre, "why so glum? You look like you've been asked to walk the plank. I thought you were happy to leave Galveston Island and sail on the high seas. You're not regretting leaving, are you?"

"No, sir. Nothing like that."

Jamie picked up his fork again and tapped it on the table. The sound filled the cabin. He looked up and realized the men were watching him, so he put the fork down.

Andre sipped his Madeira and considered his new clerk. Should he try to drag what was bothering out of him or let him come around in his own time?

He thoughts wandered to his own boyhood when he had lived on the streets of the French Quarter, while his mother worked her trade. He made his own decisions, going home to his mother's establishment for the night and reading by candlelight in the attic room he shared with his brother, removed from the noise of the floors below. He was a solitary lad, not given to strong emotions, withdrawn, inward looking. He would have had to come around in his own time. So Andre waited, sipping his Madeira.

Bruno sat his empty glass on the table. "I'll send Mickey in to clean up if you've finished." Looking at the new recruit he said, "Good to have you aboard, Jamie. I promise you a meal tomorrow that you will really like."

Jamie looked up at him and smiled. "I really do like it. It's not the food, sir."

Bruno waved a hand and rolled out the door.

Tito finished and rose to leave, Spike flapping his

Wings of the Wind

wings to keep his perch on the man's shoulder.

"Best I get back on deck. We have sails to mend while the light holds. The glass is dropping. Me bones tell me rain is on the way." Tito possessed the most reliable bones on board.

"On with you." Andre waved. The door slammed behind Tito, rattling the dishes on the table.

"Good man," said Andre, glancing over at Jamie. "But it's hard to get him to close a door soft like." He took another sip of Madeira, twirling the stem of the glass, admiring the ruby color of the liquid. He lit a cheroot, pulled deeply, and blew a long plume of smoke into the air.

Jamie finally spoke. "Captain?"

"Yes, Jamie."

"Have you ever had to tell someone something you knew they won't like, but it was important to tell them anyway?"

Andre looked thoughtful. "I believe I have."

"You have?" Jamie asked, incredulous.

"Sure. Every man has to do that sometime in his life."

"They do? Whew, I thought I was the only one." He sighed in relief.

"What's on your mind that needs to get off?"

The boy hesitated. "My sister."

"Your sister?" Maybe the boy missed her and needed to confide in someone.

Jamie nodded. "My sister." He paused, thinking. "Do you like my sister, Captain?"

Andre wondered where this conversation was going but didn't want to commit on such a loaded question. He pushed his chair back to consider his response and made a concentrated effort to clean the ash off the cheroot onto his plate.

"She seems like a nice sister to have. She seems to really care for you and goes to great lengths to protect you."

"She does, doesn't she? She doesn't like for us to be separated."

"So you want to go back to Galveston? You miss her?" Andre attempted to pinpoint the problem.

Jamie drew himself up. "No sir, it's not that. Actually, I don't miss her. I really did want to get away from her and Julia because they don't understand what's it's like to be a man."

Andre nodded in agreement. He could have added several pages on the subject but didn't want to deter Jamie from getting to what was bothering him.

"But sir, it's hard to get rid of my sister."

"Are you saying you haven't?"

"No, sir. I haven't gotten rid of her."

Andre ventured the question. "Where is she?"

"Here."

"On this ship?"

"Yes, sir. On this ship."

"How did she get here?"

"In a barrel, sir."

Andre shook his head and said, restraining a smile, "She smuggled herself on board." He had to admire her persistence. Then he did something unexpected. He laughed. Not a big laugh, but a discernable laugh nonetheless.

Jamie rushed on. "Yes, sir, she did, and she's here, and she wants to meet with you. But she's afraid you'll be mad and I was, too, so why are you laughing? That was a laugh, wasn't it?"

Wings of the Wind

Andre's face settled into a smile. His demeanor changed with the smile. The angles and planes of his face softened.

"Jamie, the first time I heard of your sister was in a card game. The first time I met her she had the nerve to come out to this ship to proposition me. The next time I saw her she had the sheriff come to haul me off to jail. So when you tell me she took to a barrel to get back on this ship again, it strikes me as funny. I've never met a woman quite like your sister."

Jamie looked like he should have chosen to walk the plank. "Gosh, sir. I am sorry, but she's always been rash like this, ever since I can remember. She gets an idea into her head, and there's no stopping her."

"Don't worry yourself, lad. It's not your fault. But she is entertaining." Andre stubbed the cheroot out on his plate. Poor kid. It must be a trial to have a sister like his. He could understand his need to get out from under her. He'd be okay after a few weeks at sea with the crew.

Andre sobered. But now what to do with her. He could send her off in the barrel she came in and hope she drifted back to Galveston. No, the Gulf Stream was easterly, and she would end up in Florida. He could dump her in New Orleans and let her fend for herself. No, that would be a mistake because she would probably try to find Norton and that was a frightening proposition. Better let her talk. He looked at Jamie.

"When would your sister like to see me? Would she like an immediate audience or would she prefer staying in the hold until we get to New Orleans? Is she still in the hold?"

Jamie spread his hands in supplication. "Yes sir, she's still in the hold. I only found out about this arrangement this morning. I was upset to see her and told her so. I told her that this was a man's ship, and she didn't belong here, and I would hide her until New Orleans then help her go back to Galveston on a steamer."

"What did she say to that?" Andre held up his hand. "No, let me tell you. She said she would have none of that that she was staying right here."

Jamie stared at Andre. "Yes, sir, she did. She said that she was going on the hunt to find Mr. Norton with us, and she was going to stay on this ship, and no one was going to stop her."

"Doesn't surprise me."

Jamie sighed and shook his head. "I should have known. Sir, my sister can be mighty stubborn."

Andre took pity on the sagging figure before him.

"Jamie, I'll handle this. You look to your chores, and don't worry. You'll be on the *Wings of the Wind* when we dock in San Francisco."

Jamie brightened considerably.

Andre pushed back his chair and stood up.

"Why don't you invite your sister to come by my cabin in one hour? Do you think that would be convenient for her?" Andre regretted the sarcasm in his voice, as soon as he had uttered the words.

"Yes, sir," Jamie said in a small voice, head lowered. "I really am sorry about this, Captain Lafitte."

"It's not your fault. Off with you now."

Jamie got up to leave.

"One other thing, Jamie."

"Yes, sir?"

"She's to come alone."

Chapter Nine

Mercedes stood outside Andre's cabin door for the second time since he had crashed into her life. Circumstances were different this time. She had played her first hand and lost, and her brother was not the staunch ally he once was. His loyalty had shifted. Standing alone outside the heavy oak door burnished to a rich golden hue, she questioned the wisdom of climbing into that barrel. Once more she was paying the price for her impulsive nature. What would the price be this time?

She hesitated. She wiped her sweaty palms on her skirt and tried to smooth the wrinkles. She hoped she looked presentable.

What was she going to say? She was glad to see him, wasn't it a lovely day, had he gotten over the sheriff's attack, would he mind if she went along on the hunt for Norton since she was already on the ship, and by the way, she hoped he wouldn't mind her freeloading like this. She was sorry about the empty barrel. She would make the beans up to him.

Mercedes felt her courage seep away. She had almost decided to turn around and go back, when the door jerked opened. Captain Lafitte loomed in the doorway.

"How long are you going to stand out here?" he asked. His voice had an edge to it, and he didn't look friendly. His mood seemed dangerous. She dropped her hand from her mouth, where it had flown after his sudden appearance.

She tried a tiny smile, testing the waters. "May I come in? I wanted to talk to you." She looked at her black booted toes, the polished plank flooring, the wood paneled walls, anywhere but into those forbidding eyes.

"I definitely want to talk to you, Miss Lawless. Do come in."

Andre stepped back to make room for her to pass by. The door clicked shut behind her. She was trapped in a room alone with this dangerous man. If she screamed who would care?

Mercedes turned around warily. Andre stood leaning against the door, arms crossed. His eyes traveled slowly over her. They lingered on her lips.

"Nice," he said.

She tucked errant curls back into her chignon. That only brought his gaze to watch her efforts, so she dropped her arms quickly.

"You look . . . " He stopped and seemed to change his mind. "You don't look like you spent some time in a barrel."

"I don't know what you mean," Mercedes said, searching her dress, as if there upon lay the answer to her dilemma. "I'm a little wrinkled, but I dress like this every day. I mean, this is my shop dress." She gave him a puzzled look.

"You should have dressed in pants. That would have made your exploits easier. Must be hard to maneuver in a barrel with a dress on."

"Never in life would I wear pants. Why, it's unseemly for a lady." Pants would have been much more practical. Why hadn't she thought of that?

"You would look good in pants. It would show more of your figure, although that dress does a nice job of showing off your upper half." His gaze wandered over her top half. "Pants would do more justice to your lower half." His gaze drifted lower.

Mercedes cleared her throat. "It's not for a lady to wear pants," she said. For that matter, what was a lady doing in a room alone with a man of questionable reputation? He liked watching her squirm. The nerve of him.

Then a little voice said, "Aren't you the one responsible for this? Let's not be a hypocrite, Mercedes Lawless. Traveling in a barrel isn't exactly ladylike."

She decided she best appear more humble. She was not sitting in the driver's seat. Drat.

He smiled a slow, lazy smile at her, a cat playing with a mouse.

"Here we are again, Miss Lawless. When I saw you last, you were covered with dust. I have the distinct recollection that I ordered you to stay in Galveston."

She cleared her throat again. She hoped she wasn't catching something. No doubt a case of Lafitte fever. "I want to apologize. I assure you, Captain Lafitte, that it was desperation that drove me to bringing in the sheriff."

"Desperation? Did desperation drive you into a barrel and onto my ship against my wishes?"

Mercedes fanned herself with her hand. She hoped she wasn't going to faint. "It was a desire to help my brother that drove me here. You, might I add, did not help the situation by taking him off so suddenly." She stopped the fanning when she realized he was watching her with a smirk on his face.

"I seem to recall the situation you placed us in

required a quick exit." He pushed away from the door and took a few steps toward her.

She wanted to back up, back away, retreat from the menace before her. But pride would not let her. She squared her shoulders and held her ground.

"I am truly sorry," she said. Her hands fluttered up to ask forgiveness. "The sheriff convinced me it was a good idea. He was trying to help me buy time so I could sort out the legality of your claim. Now he's mad at me. That's another reason I decided it was a good time to leave town."

"So we have two reasons you are on my ship. One, to help your brother and two, to avoid the sheriff. Anything else?"

"I want to find Jeffrey Norton. You seem to know where to find him. I took matters into my own hands and came aboard, since you had refused my offer of help."

"You certainly did take matters into your own hands. You like to be in control, don't you, Miss Lawless? Are you in control now?" He came to stand right in front of her.

"Oh, dear." She went back to tucking curls into place and looked around the room, anywhere but at the exceedingly male figure before her.

He caught hold of her hands. "Don't try to hide them. I like them."

"Hide what? Like what?"

"The curls. Here, let me help you." With exaggerated care Andre pulled the ribbon from her chignon, and let it drop to the floor. He ran his fingers into her hair, freeing the pins and combs that held her chignon together. One by one, he dropped them on the floor. He pulled her hair loose and curls cascaded around her shoulders.

"Yes, like that," he said in a husky voice.

The pleasure of it took Mercedes's breath away. How

could such a simple act evoke such a response in her?

"What were we saying?" He moved closer until he was only inches away. The heat of his body mingled with the heat of hers. She could hear his heart beating. Or was that hers?

"Saying?" She managed a hoarse whisper. She started to tremble.

"Cold?" He placed his strong, warm hands on her arms and rubbed gently, up and down.

"Yes. No. I don't know."

Their eyes met. She was trapped. The mouse was under both paws. She could not have moved, if she had wanted to. He gazed at her with a look that said she was not going to get out of this one.

He bent and brushed her lips with his. It was just a whisper but enough to make her want more. She had to stop this, but her feet wouldn't move. She stood on the spot like she was nailed to it. He put his hand under her chin and titled her head back. He kissed her lips. Sizzling sensations flashed along every sensory nerve in her body.

"Feeling any warmer?" he whispered in her ear, soft but unmistakable the words. Gone was the menace in his voice.

"Yes," she said, mesmerized by his touch.

"Do you want me to keep on?"

Not waiting for an answer, he pulled her to him and kissed her deeply. She sank into the moment of him and her and the kiss. On their own volition, her arms rose to encircle his neck. She responded to his kiss. Fire flared inside her.

His hands swept into her hair and pulled it back from her face. "I like it like this," he whispered against her lips.

"My hair?"

Marjorie Thelen

"Yes, it's beautiful. I love the richness of it."

His hands pushed deeper into her hair. He nibbled on her lower lip, her ear, her neck.

Delicious sensations flooded over Mercedes. Her body had a mind of its own, and it responded, pushing against him. Her mind told her to stop. Her body said no.

He moved them step-by-step, like a waltz, toward his bunk. Her mind finally communicated with her hands. They moved to his chest and pushed back.

"What?" he said, gazing into her eyes. "Do you want me to stop?" He traced kisses down her neck.

"My mind tells me to stop." A whispered moan escaped her lips.

"What does your body tell you?

"My body is behaving in a way I never dreamed possible. We must stop." But she made no move to stop him.

"Don't you like this?" Slowly his hands dropped to her breasts and held them.

A warning bell went off in the deep recesses of her mind. In a supreme effort of will, she placed her hands over his, pushed them down to her waist, and held them. She breathed deeply trying to clear her head so she could think. If she left this up to her body, she was doomed because he was like a magnet. She would not get unstuck from him.

He breathed into her hair. "Come, you aren't going to tell me, I'm your first."

Mercedes grew still then said, "The boy down the street tried to kiss me once in the alley behind the store. But that was a long time ago."

"That doesn't count."

He had heard the rumors. "Don't believe everything

you hear," she said.

He lifted her chin and searched her eyes perhaps for the truth. But the truth she masked, not willing to confirm or deny. He eased his hold. They still stood inches apart.

"Tell me," she said in a diversionary tactic, "is this the way you usually entertain women who visit you alone in your cabin?"

He frowned. "I don't entertain women in my cabin. It's bad for ship morale. The men get ideas that they need the same, and then we have litters of women aboard, no work gets done, and we lose our edge."

"What edge?"

"Our fighting edge."

"You fight? I thought you were a commercial ship?"

"I'm in commerce, but sometimes that entails fending off unwelcome pirates. Seamen need a fighting edge to sail a ship. It's hard work. The men need to be in top shape. Women have a way of dulling the blade."

She was so close she caught the faint twitch at the corners of his mouth.

"There aren't any pirates anymore," she said. At least that was what she used to tell Jamie.

"We must not travel in the same circles."

He outlined her lips with his finger. "But why are we speaking of this?"

Mercedes closed her eyes and savored the feel his touch on her lips. They tingled. His warm breath caressed her face. This felt natural and right, and she wanted the moment to last forever. She kissed his finger, as it traced her lips, opened her eyes and gazed into his. He seemed to be caught in the magic of the moment, too.

He played gently with the curls framing her face. "Tell me what I am to do with you?"

"Let me help find Norton."

"If I allow that, what will you do for me?"

"I will be the bait."

"I think you could do more than that for me."

"As in?"

He kissed her again. This time more deeply, more urgently, more honestly. Then he swept her up in his arms, carried her to his bunk, and laid her upon it, easing down beside her. He began to unbutton the tiny buttons on the bodice of her dress.

She caught his hand. "Andre."

He stopped at the sound of his name.

Mercedes studied the face so close to hers. The lean line of the jaw, the full curve of the lips, the dark lashes fringing those whiskey eyes. He wasn't like the men she knew in Galveston. He was contained, his own. He had nothing to explain or justify.

Her desire to lose herself in him was dangerous for a girl who wasn't ever going to marry, who championed her independence, who was wary of men.

"You want me," he said.

She looked away because she couldn't deny it.

He traced the line of her eyebrow. His fingers drift down her cheek. "I could make life sweet for you."

"In what way?" She looked back into those eyes that saw her desire.

Silence stretched between them, and in that silence they became aware of increased activity on deck. They both lifted their heads to the sound of footsteps pounding down the passageway. A fist hammered on the door.

"Capitán. Mi Capitán," Tito shouted. "We need you on deck."

Andre swore under his breath and rose. "All right," he

Wings of the Wind

called. "I'll be right there." He listened and looked out the cabin window. "Lightening. A storm is coming up." He swore again. "This is why I don't entertain women in my cabin. It keeps the captain from his duties."

He looked back at her, lying on the bunk, her curls playing across the pillow. "We are not finished. We will talk more about how I can make life sweet for you and what you owe me."

"What I owe you?"

Andre nodded.

"I'm not sure I can pay."

"We'll explore that later."

Andre rose and helped her to her feet. "I'll show you to your own cabin or do you want to stay here?"

Mercedes glanced at the bunk and then at him. "My own cabin would be better. I'll stay there till we get to New Orleans. No one will know."

He smiled. "Mercedes, the entire ship knows you're on board. Tito normally crashes in here to get me up on deck. He held back. Did you notice?"

"No, I didn't. I don't mean to be trouble."

"My dear, it's your middle name."

* * * * *

Mercedes didn't see the small, comfortable cabin to which Andre had shown her. She stumbled to the narrow bunk and collapsed. Her body still hummed from her encounter with Andre. She had called him Andre. He was Andre to her now. Not the austere Captain. Now he was flesh and blood.

She lay on her back with her arm over her eyes, as if darkness could give her perspective. What on God's Earth was she doing? She couldn't believe how she had behaved. She had to get a hold of herself and stop being so easily wooed. There was the trouble. Andre was a good wooer.

She listened to the sound of the wind, the crash of the waves. A great boom of thunder shook the ship, but it kept flying. *Wings of the Wind.* She knew clippers kept a full press of sail, no matter the time of day or the weather. It was as exhilarating as her interlude with Andre, the perfect accompaniment.

She gave a great yawn. She would rest a bit. It might quiet the storm raging inside her.

Fly, *Wings of the Wind*, fly. Let me sail with you forever.

Chapter Ten

A tap on the door awoke her.

"Mercedes, are you in there?"

She pushed herself up on an elbow. Light streamed through the slats in the door.

"Jamie?"

He let himself in and came over to perch on the edge of her narrow bunk. He tossed her small bundle on the bed.

"Are you going to sleep all day?" He peered around the cabin. "Say, this is a nice cabin you rated. Bet it was better than sleeping in a barrel."

"What time is it?" She was having trouble getting her bearings.

"Morning. Time to get up. We already picked up the ocean pilot for our approach to the mouth of the Mississippi, and we'll soon pick up the river pilot. The storm gave us an extra boost, and we're making fantastic time. It was a great storm, wasn't it?"

Mercedes sat up and combed her hands through her hair. She winced as her fingers caught in the tangles. She remembered how it had got tangled up and smiled. She wondered what the possibilities were for procuring a basin of water and a bar of soap for a nice wash.

She stretched. "I think I missed the best part of the storm. I closed my eyes and the next thing I know its morning."

Her brother fidgeted on his perch and gave her a sideways look. "What'd the Captain say to you?"

Mercedes avoided his eyes.

"You didn't . . . I mean, he didn't . . . ." His voice trailed off.

"No, he didn't, silly boy." She thought for a moment. "Besides, what *are* you talking about?"

"Hmmm."

"Hmmm, what? Don't look at me like that."

"Why's you hair all messed up?"

"From sleeping," she said in voice edged with irritation.

"You braid it to sleep." He didn't look convinced. "What's he going to do with you when we get to New Orleans?"

"We didn't get that far. I told him I wanted to help find Jeffrey Norton."

"That could take some time, since nobody knows where he is."

"Andre, I mean, the Captain says he is still in New Orleans."

Jamie's eyebrows rose at her referral to the Captain as Andre. But he didn't pursue it, because he wanted to regale her with stories of the men, how great the ship was, and what he did for Captain Lafitte. From the enthusiasm with which he told the stories, she knew he had fallen hopelessly in love with *Wings of the Wind*.

"I guess," she ventured, though she knew the answer, "there will be no enticing you back to the store."

Jamie shook his head. "Not a chance. I love this, and I want to learn all I can so that some day I can captain a ship of my own. I want to learn to sail. I've already spoken to the Captain about that."

Mercedes sighed. Well, she had tried. To put the best face on this adventure, she would concentrate her efforts on helping Andre find the phantom Mr. Norton.

Andre, there she had thought it again. She liked the sound of his name. She sighed again.

"What's all the sighing for?"

She heard the suspicion in her brother's voice and changed the subject. She asked if the Captain had spoken to him at all of Mr. Norton.

"Mr. Norton? Nope, we only talk about important stuff like ship stuff and sailing stuff."

Mercedes shoved her fist under her chin and shook her head at her brother. He was gone and irretrievable.

"I've got to get on deck," he said. "Shall I bring you anything?"

"A wash basin, water, soap, and a towel if it's not too much to ask. Please. That would be wonderful."

"Sure. Be back." He bounded out the door.

Uninvited, her thoughts drifted to Andre. The musky odor of his skin, the strength of his embrace, the touch of his lips on hers wove themselves into a tapestry that enfolded her.

Thoughts of her elusive uncle broke into the tapestry. She rummaged in her bundle, pulled out his letter, and studied the handwriting. The weak stems of the letters ended with flourishes and spoke of irresolution, a man who gambled with what was not his to give.

How could such a man be her mother's brother? Her mother had been kind, even-tempered, ready to give, and to please. She was in no way irresolute or greedy, never weak nor wanton of spirit. It distressed her that she, Mercedes Lawless, might be related to this man.

But in a corner of her heart Mercedes knew that she longed for this relation no matter how undesirable. She so loved her mother and father, the thought there might be someone yet alive connected to them, gave her the warmest of feelings. She resolved she would find Norton with or without Andre, but she hoped it would be with him.

She wanted to speak to Andre again about finding Norton. She had to convince him that she could help. Why wouldn't he take her seriously? Now that the storm was over, maybe he wouldn't be as busy. But then she considered the danger to her person and her betraying body. She had to see him to talk to him, but when she was near him she behaved like a fool.

She would have to enlist Jamie's aid. Much as she would like to see Andre, it was too dangerous. Jamie, it would have to be. She could feign seasickness for the rest of the voyage. Then she wouldn't have to confront Andre.

Jamie arrived with pitcher, basin, towel, and soap. He deposited the requested items on the nightstand, left and returned with a tray of tea and biscuits. Mercedes cleared space on the end of the bunk for the tea tray. She thanked him and dumped a healthy portion of sugar into a mug of black tea.

"Yum," she said, sipping the hot tea. "This is perfect."

"It's from Mickey Chinfatt's personal stock," Jamie said. "He made it special for you because he likes you. Men seem to fall for you, Mercedes. I've noticed that. Have you noticed that?"

Mercedes choked on her tea. "Me? Fall for me? Why Mickey is just being nice."

"In the store when men customers come in they always like when you wait on them."

"You're imagining things, Jamie."

Wings of the Wind

"Then what about the Captain?"

"The Captain? What about him?"

"I think he's kinda sweet on you. What did you talk about all the time that you were in there with him?"

"It was grown up stuff." Mercedes assumed an air of mystery as her defense. "We spoke of finding Mr. Norton, and that's where you come in."

"Me?"

"Yes. I thought since you are closer to the Captain than I am, maybe you could talk to him and find out more details about how he is going to find Norton."

"Why don't you ask him yourself? You're the charmer, remember?"

"I'm not feeling well and thought I should rest here in my cabin until we get to New Orleans. Anyway, he trusts you more than me."

"That's true. I wouldn't trust you either, considering how you've treated him so far. If I find out and tell you, what will you do?"

"If I know more about what he has planned then I'll see how I can help."

"Oh no, you won't. I know you, Mercedes Lawless. You'll go tearing off without thought or plan and ruin everything. Then we'd come running after you, and I want to be sailing and adventuring, not chasing after my sister off on some fool notion of hers."

He furrowed his brow when he observed Mercedes downcast face and threw up his hands. "I'll try to talk to the Captain, and see if he will tell me anything."

Mercedes smiled. That's what she wanted him to do.

"Very well, little brother, you handle this."

"All right but you have to promise me one thing."

"What's that?"

"That you won't go tearing off on your own."
"It's a deal."

*****

"When we arrive in New Orleans, we'll anchor off shore and take the boat in. I want you two to head for this address." Andre shoved a wrinkled piece of paper printed with block letters across the desk. The black letters were smudged from being stowed in a sweaty pocket too long.

Steam rose from three mugs of coffee on the table, adding to the humidity of the early morning.

Tito slurped his coffee and glanced at the address. His bushy eyebrows went skyward running into the sweat beading on his forehead.

"Rough side of town, mi Capitán. What do we do when we get there?"

Spike picked at the calluses on the hand that Tito used to stroke the silky feathers of the bird's head.

Andre reached for his mug, felt the heat from the drink, reconsidered, and put it aside. "Ask for Remy Thibodeaux. Tell him I sent you. He's expecting me to contact him. He'll tell you what he's found."

Bruno cut in. "What's this about, Captain?"

"It's about finding Jeffrey Norton. He's in the cotton brokering business, and so is Remy. Remy owes me a favor, and I asked him to make some inquiries for me when we docked in New Orleans last time. He'll tell you where Norton operates and what his set up is. Find the place and check it out. Report back to me. Keep your wits about you and your knives at the ready."

Bruno pulled out one of his knives to test the cutting edge. The sound of it leaving its sheath, amplified in the still air of the cabin, made a gritting, metallic sound. Andre and Tito watched Bruno run his finger up the flat of the long blade, the gleam alone revealing the sharpness of the edge.

"A beauty, ain't she?" He swiveled and parried the knife with his wrist.

"I like the pearl handle," said Tito. "I hope you will leave me that one, if you die before I do."

Bruno glanced over. "I will, the Captain as my witness."

"Thanks, co-padre," said Tito, one gold tooth glinting in his smile.

"What about pistols?" Bruno asked. He re-sheathed the knife and stowed it back in his waistband.

"No pistols," said Andre. "You are at your best with knives."

The two mates grinned and nudged each other.

"Mickey, you'll accompany me. I have business at the Silver Slipper and at the lawyer's office."

Mickey Chinfatt smiled at Andre over the rim of a delicate, gold-rimmed china teacup decorated with flaming dragons, poised over a matching saucer. He ignored the fallen faces of his two mates squinting in his direction, who were left out of a trip to the Silver Slipper.

"We'll all meet at Fabienne's shop later in the day. Bruno and Tito, if you run into trouble, get a message to me there."

"We help missy girl?" asked Mickey Chinfatt. "She nice person. You think so, too, boss."

Andre looked at three big smiles across the desk from him. Nothing escaped these men. That could work for him and against him.

Andre crossed his arms and pretended not to hear.

"Miss Lawless will accompany me to Fabienne's and wait there while I see to business. Fabienne is good at entertaining. She will be able to show Miss Lawless the sights of New Orleans."

"Missy girl like that," said Mickey, undeterred. "Girl not related to Norton."

Andre paused, his coffee mug suspended halfway on its journey to his mouth. He set it down again. "What makes you say that?"

"Not look anything alike."

"That don't mean nothing," said Bruno. "He don't have to look like the girl."

Mickey set his teacup and saucer on the desk, shaking his head. "Not act alike either. He not related. He try to pull big one over on Captain. Mickey Chinfatt know these things." He tapped his forehead for emphasis.

Andre gazed at some far point over Mickey's shoulder. "I don't think he's related either. But how did he know so much about her family?"

"He run into someone know girl or family," Mickey said.

Andre focused back on Mickey. "That's a long shot. What I need are facts, and that is where Remy Thibodeaux comes in. Tito and Bruno, find out what you can, be discreet, and don't get sidetracked in any whorehouses."

Chapter Eleven

Mercedes layered on shift, corset, petticoats, and dress, wrinkled but brushed. The cool water of the bath and the creamy French-milled soap restored her spirits. She wondered where Jamie had found a bar of French-milled soap. Perhaps from Mickey Chinfatt's stores. She had brushed out her hair and recaptured it in a braided chignon and ribbon.

The entire time she bathed the memories of her time with Andre replayed in her thoughts. The feeling and sensation of him played over and over again in her mind. Over and over. The kisses, the caresses, the sensations. She sighed, rummaged in her bundle, and drew out a small bottle of lavender water, a necessity even when stowing away in a barrel. She gave herself a liberal sprinkle and the soft scent filled the air. She checked her creation in a small mirror from the bundle. It would have to do.

She studied the small cabin and knew she wouldn't be able to remain in it for the duration of the trip. She had to go up on deck. She'd go up and catch a breath of sea air. She'd be careful no one saw her. Just five minutes. Throwing open the door, sunlight streamed down the stairs from the main deck. She tiptoed up and at the top took a cautious look around. When she felt the sun and breeze, she knew she would not be able to feign sickness and stay confined to her cabin.

Sunlight sparkled on the sea, a fine mist sprayed over the deck from the bow waves, and the sails were filled with ocean breezes. The day was washed brilliant from the passage of the storm. She looked up into the sails and turned in a circle, taking in the vastness of them. Beautiful. More than beautiful. They were riding the wings of the wind.

Mercedes was familiar with the verse from the Psalms, "You ride on the wings of the wind". She loved the psalmists. Oh, that she could express herself like they had. This ship was surely the embodiment of that passage from long ago. She wondered about the owners of the ship and how they had named her. She would ask Andre about them and the story behind the naming of this the most beautiful and most perfect of ships. She ventured to the rail and took several deep breaths. She wanted to throw her arms out, throw her head back, and call out, laughing at the world and her good fortune to be alive on this day. But she didn't. She didn't want to call attention to herself.

Movement overhead caught her eye and she looked up to see men working aloft in the rigging. They jumped about their tasks to the calls of command by one of the men below. She contented herself for a while watching them, then the surge of the sea in the deck beneath her feet brought her gaze back again to the horizon.

She tried to avoid thinking about Andre, about what he was doing, and where he might be. Then she caught sight of him out of the corner of her eye. She looked toward the stern of the ship and there he stood at the wheel, legs braced. And here came her dear brother, hurrying toward her.

"Mercedes," he said with a hiss, halting in front of her.

"You said you weren't feeling well and were going to stay in the cabin till we got to New Orleans."

"Yes, I said that but now I feel better. I couldn't bear to stay below and miss all this." She made a wide gesture with her arm. She leaned closer to him and said in a loud whisper, "You don't suppose I could go up there with the Captain while he's at the wheel, do you?"

"I wish you had stayed at home," he said, ignoring her question.

"What kind of thing is that to say to your sister?"

"You have the whole crew and the Captain distracted. Everyone is watching you."

"They are?" She glanced around. Curious glances indeed darted in her direction.

Jamie fisted his hands. "Females. I was hoping to get away from them."

"Jamie . . ."

He backed out of striking distance. "Don't tousle my hair in front of the crew."

"I wasn't going to tousle your hair. I won't touch you from now on. No hugs either."

"Fine with me. I'm a seaman now. All that stuff is over."

Ha, thought Mercedes. Wait till you meet up with your first girlfriend.

"I will treat you with the respect a seaman deserves."

"Really? Promise?"

"Yes, I promise. Now tell me. Anything from the Captain about Mr. Norton?"

"Not from the Captain because I haven't had time to talk to him. But my mates say he's going into New Orleans with Tito, Bruno and Mickey."

"Oh, dear." Mercedes couldn't keep the

disappointment from her voice.

Jamie grimaced. "They say that he's taking you, too."

Her eyes lit up. "Really?"

"Yeah, and he wants you to join him at the wheel," said Jamie with a look of disgust. He marched off across the deck toward the bow.

Mercedes stifled a desire to go after him. Poor kid. She knew someday she would have to do penance for making him miserable.

Magically, her feet were already moving in the opposite direction, toward Andre at the wheel. At least, if they were meeting out in front of everyone, and he had his hands on the wheel, there was no danger.

She smiled at the men she went by, and they doffed their hats and returned her smile. Heads turned to follow her. Eyes said they approved of the figure outlined by the wind against her dress, of the willowy way she walked, of the twinkle in her eyes.

* * * * *

From his post at the wheel Andre watched Mercedes' progress then motioned for Tito to take over. When she arrived before him, he took command of her elbow and steered her toward the rail, affording them a view of the ship's wake and a panorama of where they had been.

Mercedes cheeks glowed pink from the breeze, and her hair glistened in the sunlight. Because he would have preferred resuming where they had left off yesterday in his cabin, Andre grasped the rail to keep his hands from wandering. He struggled to keep his eyes on the horizon, gave up the struggle, and caught her gaze.

"Feeling better?" he asked.

Wings of the Wind

"Much, thank you. I slept well." The smile on her face hid no secrets.

"I'm glad to hear that. The storm did not disturb you then?"

"No. I fell asleep to the boom of thunder and awoke to the sun on my door."

"Good." He paused. "When we get to New Orleans, I'll take you into town. Would you like that?"

"Of all things, yes. I'd love to see the city." She hesitated. "What about Mr. Norton?"

"My men and I will attend to that. I will drop you by the shop of a long time friend, Fabienne Beluche. She is a dressmaker, and she may be able to outfit you with a new frock, if you'd like."

He caught the raise of her brows. He did not elaborate on what terms the dress was offered. Instead he squinted into the sun on the waves.

"My friend will, no doubt, want to take you sightseeing."

"I'd like that of all things," she said, clasping her hands together. "I've always wanted to visit New Orleans." She frowned. "I'd hoped to accompany you to find Mr. Norton."

"First, we have to establish that he is in town. That will take some inquiries. I have personal business to attend to, so it's best if you spend time with Fabienne. By then we may know Mr. Norton's whereabouts."

"Very well," she said. Andre took her easy acquiescence to signal she understood that stowaways didn't have much bargaining power.

"Might I spend some time on deck? It is so lovely, and this ship is so beautiful." Mercedes peered skyward into the sails.

115

Andre followed her gaze. Her face told him she felt the same way about the ship he did. For any seaman *Wings of the Wind* was love at first sight.

He looked down at Mercedes and wished he hadn't because she had a look of ecstasy on her face. His gaze drew hers, and their eyes held. He wished she hadn't done that either. He forced his gaze back to the sea and sanity.

"You may enjoy yourself here on deck. Stay out of the way and try not to be a distraction."

He inclined his head toward the strip of land in the horizon. "We approach the entrance to the Mississippi River. This entrance and the river itself are treacherous sailing. That's why we have the ocean pilot on aboard now. He'll pass us off to a river pilot further up river at a place called Head of Passes."

"How long will it be till we arrive in New Orleans?"

"Depends on the river and the sailing conditions. With any luck a few days, sometimes it's eight to ten days, but my guess now is three or four. My crew and I know this river well. We've been up and down it many times. I'll be on deck for the duration of the voyage. She's unpredictable the Mississippi, and we don't want to sit for two weeks on a sandbar because the Captain neglected his duties."

* * * * *

Mercedes waved to the passengers of yet another steamship that slapped its way past them up river to New Orleans. It might be a faster way of travel she thought but it wasn't as romantic as a sailing ship, especially not one with a Captain like Andre Lafitte.

Lady Luck blessed them. Andre had just informed her they would anchor at New Orleans in the morning. A little

Wings of the Wind

over three days had passed on the river since they had left Head of Passes with their river pilot. The pilot, a skilled crew, and a vigilant Captain helped them avoid the sandbars, snags, and shifting currents that ensnared unwary ships on the river.

Mercedes had passed the mornings watching the mud brown river slide by, observing herons skim the shoreline, admiring the crew's sailing skills, as they tacked back and forth against the current. Throughout the day she had stolen glimpses of Andre.

He had assigned Jamie to the old salt that had helped Mercedes onto the ship the first time. Her brother split his duties between learning to swab the decks and keeping accounts, so Mercedes saw little of him. Andre she admired from afar, not wanting to distract his attention and be the cause of a river disaster. At least her good sense had returned. She kept to her cabin during the heat of the day, enjoying a new book of poems by Henry Wadsworth Longfellow that Andre lent to her. The soft river evenings drew her on deck. The sighs and whispers of the river reminded her of the interlude with Andre in his cabin and that tapestry gently enfolded her in dreams through the gentle river nights.

* * * * *

Andre strode about his cabin, collecting the things he would take with him into New Orleans. He strapped on his knife and inserted another into the sheath inside his boot. He checked his pistol and slipped it into the leather pouch he was taking with him. New Orleans looked civil on the surface, but underneath it was a city of intrigue and violence. He should know. He had lived there long enough.

Marjorie Thelen

His business would take him by the Silver Slipper to check on the enterprise and then on to meet his lawyer to discuss selling it. But first, he'd set Mercedes down with Fabienne Beluche, who would keep her out of harm's way for an afternoon.

He heard a soft knock at the door. That couldn't be one of the men. Soft was not in their vocabulary.

"Enter."

Mercedes stepped into the room and stopped.

"You sent for me?"

Andre's eyes played over her, allowing himself a respite after three days of holding himself in check. Three long, painful days of unfulfilled desire. He sincerely hoped Beatrice was on duty at the Silver Slipper. He was tired of pretending this infuriating female was not on his ship. He had to get into New Orleans, find Norton, resolve the ownership of the store, put this lovely lady on a steamer back to Galveston, and sail on to San Francisco. He was spending entirely too much time thinking unholy thoughts of Mercedes Lawless.

He continued stuffing legal papers into the leather pouch. "We are going ashore," he said, more gruffly than he intended.

"I'm ready."

She looked so soft and pliable standing there, but he knew that underneath that pretty exterior lurked a mess of trouble.

He walked to a wall cabinet, opened the door, and drew out a bonnet, shawl, and parasol. "Here, you might need these." He handed them to her.

Andre watched a smile light her eyes. She received the gifts with reverence. Delicate yellow flowers trimmed the creamy bonnet. A ruffled trim decorated the edge of the

Wings of the Wind

cream colored parasol. The shawl was of Irish lace. She had enough discretion not to ask him how he came to have them. Thank you was all she said.

"Mercedes."

Their eyes met as she pulled on the bonnet and started to tie the ribbon beneath her chin. Even that small act endeared her to him.

"We need to come to an understanding."

He held her gaze as she waited for him to continue, suspended in the act of tying the bonnet ribbons.

"You will accompany me as far as the shop of Fabienne Beluche. You will stay with her until I return. New Orleans can be a dangerous city and is not a place for a woman alone. Do not, I repeat, do not try to take matters into your own hands. Do not look for Norton on you own. Do not get into any trouble. Am I clear?"

"Yes," she said without hesitation, "I won't be any trouble. I promise." Her wide, luminous eyes echoed the promise.

Her willingness made him almost believe her, but he knew it would be unwise to trust her given past experience.

"I'll keep you to your promise." Unable to resist the temptation of her parted lips, he bent and kissed them. Her wispy intake of breath encouraged him to linger into the kiss, but Tito's cry to lower the shore boat cut into their stolen interlude. He reluctantly released her, and they both sighed as one.

"We need to go."

He picked up the leather pouch and guided her from the room, his hand resting firmly on her back.

Chapter Twelve

New Orleans was alive. Alive!

As the open carriage rolled through the streets of the French Quarter, Mercedes drank in the strolling ladies attired in elegant outfits, ragged children playing stick ball in the streets, wagon after wagon loaded with cotton, produce, boxes, commercial goods of all description. She tried not to blink for fear she might miss something.

She sat beside Andre, holding the open parasol over her head. Mickey Chinfatt sat dozing across from them. Bruno and Tito had taken off on foot after a short conversation with Andre on the dock. Andre pointed out sights of interest and answered her endless questions. Many were of the commerce she witnessed whirling about them. Soon the carriage turned into a district of more simply appointed buildings.

"Are we soon there?" Mercedes asked, as the scene changed from the elegance of Jackson Square to the monotony of trade shops and warehouses.

"Almost. In the next block is the shop of my friend." He lowered his voice. "Remember my warning, Mercedes."

She nodded once but did not meet his gaze.

"Mercedes." He caught her chin lightly with his finger and turned her head toward him. "Do not take matters into your own hands. Promise me."

A smile danced across her lips. "I promise. I'll enjoy the day."

He searched her face then dropped his finger and simply said, "Yes, enjoy the day."

They drew along side a well-kept shop. The shop window displayed the headless form of a woman dressed in a creation of pale yellow silk. Articles of matching accessories, a shawl, bonnet, parasol, and reticule, fanned out around the dress. Neatly lettered in gold across the bottom of the window was the name of the shop, La Femme Extraordinaire, and below in smaller black letters Fabienne Beluche, Proprietress.

Andre helped his charge from the carriage and instructed Mickey and the driver to wait for them. He guided Mercedes by the elbow to the shop door where he rang for admittance. A bell tinkled from the depths of the shop. After a few moments a small girl peered out the window at them. Her face broke into a smile. She flung open the door and jumped into Andre's arms.

"Uncle Andre, Uncle Andre." She planted tiny smooches on his cheeks. "Oh, it's you. How wonderful you've come. Auntie Fabienne said you might. It is so good to see you." Her slender arms wrapped around his neck.

Andre gave her bear hug and kissed her cheek. "Hello, Claudette, my little one who is not so little anymore. Here let me see you." He put her down then stepped back. "How you have grown. How long has it been since I've seen you? Over a year? Can that be possible?" The little girl's face dimpled. "What a pretty girl you are growing up to be. But then you always were very pretty." He pinched her cheek gently, and she slipped a small, trusting hand into his big one.

Marjorie Thelen

Mercedes regarded Andre with surprise and new appreciation. Gone the austere Captain Lafitte. In his place stood a man at ease with a child. Andre stood talking quietly to the girl, asking her about her friends, her music lessons. As a woman measures a man as a sire for her children, so Mercedes now measured Andre.

The child had a history with Andre she realized. An odd feeling of jealousy squeezed Mercedes' heart. Could she be jealous of a child? No, not of their affection for each other, she decided, but of their history together. Mercedes understood then that she wanted a history with Andre.

Andre smiled in her direction. "Claudette, let me introduce, Miss Mercedes Lawless. She is from Galveston Island and is here to meet Fabienne and spend the afternoon."

"Pleased to make your acquaintance, mademoiselle." Claudette dipped a little curtsy.

To whom did this lovely little girl belong Mercedes wondered.

"I'm please to make your acquaintance also, Claudette. Are you from New Orleans?"

"Oui, mademoiselle," said the child shyly, looking up at Mercedes through white blond lashes that fanned in spiky points across her eyelids. Matching hair wisped to her shoulders, and pixie point ears completed her gamin look.

"Shall we find Aunt Fabienne, little miss?" asked Andre.

"Please follow me," said the child.

He stepped aside to allow the girls to enter the shop before him. They passed through a hallway with rooms opening to the left. A show room was first. It opened onto

Wings of the Wind

a sitting room where a woman sat, needlework in hand. The woman rose to greet Andre and his guest. She was as tall as Mercedes and wore a dress of dark green silk cut low across the bodice. Her figure filled out the dress handsomely.

"Andre." She held out her arms to him. They embraced and kissed on both cheeks in the French fashion.

"Is it possible you are here?" said Fabienne Bcluche. She spoke in the French accented English of Creole New Orleans.

She clasped his arms and stood back to look at him. "As handsome as ever, maybe even more, if that is possible." Her eyes swept over him not missing an inch. She nodded her approval and blessed him with a wicked smile.

"You are as beautiful as ever," Andre said, ignoring her assessment.

Fabienne threw back her head and laughed. "In my younger days, mon cher, but this creature doesn't turn heads like she used to."

Andre shook his head. "That's not what I've heard."

Fabienne's laughter ended in a smile, her face alive with the compliment and the joy of seeing Andre. Her honey brown complexion glowed, set off by ebony curls piled high on her head. Her jade green eyes danced and not a wrinkle troubled her face. High cheekbones revealed more of her mixed race ancestry.

"Please sit down." She indicated chairs behind them. "Let me have something cool brought in to drink. Claudette, please ask Lucy to fix refreshments for us."

"Mais, oui," the child said, skipping from the room.

Fabienne turned her assessing glance to Mercedes.

"Who do we have here, Andre? You didn't tell me you

had a sweetheart. She's a pretty thing."

Ignoring the mention of sweetheart, Andre said, "This is Miss Mercedes Lawless, proprietress of the Lavender Dry Goods Emporium in Galveston, Texas. She is here with me on a brief visit to New Orleans."

"Is she now?" Fabienne flashed Andre an I-know-these-things smile. To Mercedes she said, "The Lavender Emporium, you say. Would that be a ladies shop?"

Mercedes smiled in return. "The Emporium is a dry goods store and includes cloth and notions for ladies' wear, patterns and such. Several seamstresses on the Island buy from me. I give them a good discount and offer quality goods. They are excellent customers."

"Are they? You look too young to be a proprietress. You mean you help your daddy with the store?"

"No," said Mercedes. "It's my store. My uncle started it. When my folks died, my brother and I went to live with him and my cousin. I gradually worked my way into managing the store. It wasn't hard. My uncle has no head for business. He prefers tending his gardens, and I seem to have a knack for trade."

"Is that so? I'm glad to meet another woman with a head for business. There are not so many of us around."

Mercedes nodded her agreement, wanting to ask Fabienne more about her business after Andre left.

"Sit down, sit down." Fabienne said again, as they still stood.

Mercedes sat in a straight back chair beside Fabienne. Andre pulled up another straight back chair across from them. Claudette wheeled in a tea tray and positioned it before them. She presented frosty classes of lemonade topped with mint.

"Can I get you anything stronger, Andre?" asked

Wings of the Wind

Fabienne.

"Not at the moment, thank you. This will do. The boat ride in from the ship got hotter the closer we got to land. The ride here was the usual New Orleans summer ordeal."

"Surely our lovely tree-lined streets gave you relief from the sun, and I see that your friend brought her parasol. A wise woman."

Andre and Mercedes exchanged glasses, and she smiled a silent thank you for the parasol.

"It wasn't so bad," Mercedes said. "It's like Galveston here, only grander."

"I have not been to your island paradise, but I hear it is a nice resort. You have lovely beaches, they say."

"Yes, we do," said Mercedes. "Perhaps sometime you can come for a visit, and I will show you our island."

Andre seemed to choke on his lemonade, and Mercedes looked at him with a puzzled frown. Fabienne thanked Mercedes for her kind invitation and changed the subject.

"How is your new ship, Andre? How is she called? *Wings of the Wind*? She is a fast one, no? I imagine business will be excellent with her. They tell me you are on your first voyage to San Francisco, a town I would love to visit. Good business opportunities abound there, they say, for an enterprising woman." She gave him a devilish smile.

"Let's pursue that topic another time, Fabienne," Andre said with a censorious look in her direction that made Mercedes wonder what was going on. "As for *Wings of the Wind* she is a superb ship. She is everything I thought she would be. The men are especially pleased with her speed and how she handles. We sail day, night, and storms."

Fabienne laughed her infectious laugh. "Those boys would love anything that they could push to its limits. That ship is just as wild as they are, I think. Are they behaving?"

"Behaving? Not a word to be associated with my crew. Not one of them takes well to rules and limits. But we share a love of the sea and sailing. What more do I need?"

Fabienne smiled. "You fit perfectly together. That is why you all have been together for so long. I'd certainly would want your crew on my side in a fight."

"I agree," said Andre. "That's why they are in my employ." He drank deeply of his lemonade.

Mercedes declined the teacakes that Claudette offered her. She didn't want to be distracted and miss one word of this enlightening conversation.

* * * * *

"Fabienne," Andre said, after finishing his drink and setting it aside, "I'd like if Mercedes could spend a few hours with you. I thought she would find your shop and company interesting. Mercedes has never been in New Orleans, so perhaps you could take a drive through the city while I'm gone."

"I would be delighted to do that."

Fabienne focused her attention on Mercedes. "Would you like to see more of New Orleans? We could drive to the French Quarter to see the sights."

"Yes, I would love to see more of the city and chat while we do that. I'd like to compare notes with you on your business."

"The dress shop business, Fabienne," Andre said.

"Of course." She gave him a wink. "Excellent. We

Wings of the Wind

will take a drive and stop for refreshment at my favorite outdoor cafe."

"Perfect," said Mercedes.

"It's done then," Andre said. "I'll take my leave and continue on my calls."

Andre stood to leave. "Thank you, Fabienne. Please keep a close watch on Mercedes and make sure that she doesn't get lost. I leave Mickey Chinfatt to accompany you. He's waiting outside."

"How thoughtful. Mickey is a favorite of mine. It will be nice to have him along. He knows a lot about New Orleans."

Andre cast a glance at Mercedes. "I'll see you here later this afternoon."

He knew that Mercedes didn't need an interpreter to understand his meaning.

He bent to give Claudette a kiss on the cheek. "See you later, sweetheart."

Fabienne accompanied Andre into the hallway to the door. As they kissed farewell, Andre murmured into Fabienne's ear to please behave.

Fabienne patted his cheek and assured him she would.

"Mercedes doesn't know about my mother," Andre said.

Fabienne drew back and looked at him with raised eyebrows. "Don't you want your sweetheart to know about the family?" She was teasing him.

"She's not my sweetheart."

"Looks like one to me. Feels like that, too." She tapped his heart. "You should see the way you look at her. Like you want to devour her."

Andre gave her a twitchy smile. "Devour I would like but I'm not sure I'm ready for the commitment of a sweetheart. Would you do me a favor?"

Fabienne nodded.

"Do you think you could find a nice frock for her to wear to see New Orleans?"

"Of course. I noticed her gown looks travel worn. This will happen on ocean voyages. She will be elegant, I promise you."

"Not too elegant," said Andre, glancing down at Fabienne's cleavage.

She laughed. "You be off, and I will attend to mademoiselle."

* * * * *

Fabienne walked slowly back into the salon. "That is quite a man," she said. "Too bad I am old enough to be his mama."

Mercedes looked startled. "You can't be that old."

"Oh, yes I can."

Mercedes wondered about their relationship. Maybe on their outing the older woman would open up to her. If she could rein in her impatience, she hoped the loquacious Fabienne would give her more details. Details like why the fair Claudette called them Aunt and Uncle.

"Claudette, would you carry out the tea things while I help Mademoiselle Mercedes? Then we shall all go on a little outing."

The child clapped her hands eagerly and busied herself collecting cups and saucers.

Fabienne studied Mercedes with pursed lips. "Andre says you are to have a new gown, and I think I have just the thing. It is for a customer, but we will make another. The customer will have to wait."

She bustled into the next room before Mercedes could protest and soon returned with a filmy yellow, pink, and white creation. Mercedes melted when she saw it. Fabienne helped Mercedes out of her traveling dress and into the walking-out costume. Fabienne pulled and tugged, shifted and arranged the dress until she was satisfied. She finished the ensemble with a shawl of white silk lace and led Mercedes to a mirror.

Fabienne stood behind her and measured the effect. "Very pretty. I knew it would fit you. They are marvelous colors for you."

The dress floated around Mercedes. She turned this way and that, admired the swishing skirts, white filmy voile over white cotton. The sleeves fitted close to the elbow then opened to a pagoda-flared sleeve with white lawn undersleeves. The bodice formed a V to her waist and was accented with small pink and yellow flowers. The scoop neckline showed off her slender neck and elegant shoulders.

"Do you like it?" asked Fabienne.

Mercedes stopped swishing and smiled. "It's like nothing I have ever experienced. It's cool and light on my skin. The colors are delicate. Is it a Paris design?"

"Of course. No beautiful designs exist outside of those from Paris." Fabienne tempered her haughty look with a smile.

She studied Mercedes' hair. "We will re-work your braid loops into sometime a little more elegant, and then we shall go." She indicated a chair for Mercedes to sit upon.

Claudette, finished with her task, approached shyly. She watched as Fabienne deftly brushed out Mercedes's hair and re-worked it.

"You look lovely, mademoiselle," she said in her soft child voice. "Uncle Andre will like you very much in the pretty dress." She reached out to touch the skirt of the dress.

"I don't think he will notice," she said, hoping in her heart that he would.

"Cherie, not only Andre will notice you, but all of New Orleans," Fabienne said, as she finished dressing her hair. "We are ready now."

Fabienne turned her creation for a last look in the glass. She had pulled Mercedes hair into a cascade of curls at the back of her head, finishing with long curls to frame her face. Mercedes's smile and wistful look told Fabienne she had succeeded in her transformation.

"Claudette, please ask Henri to bring round the carriage."

The little girl bobbed and ran from the room.

Mercedes, emboldened by the dress, ventured a question about the child. "Claudette is such a pretty little girl. Is she your sister's child?"

"My sister?" Fabienne turned away from the mirror, seemingly caught off guard. "I have no sister. I have no brother." She hesitated. "Claudette is an orphan, the child of a friend who died too early in her young life. She has been with me since a baby. Andre helps to support her. He knew her mother."

Without thinking, Mercedes asked, "Is he the father?" Then pressed her fingers to her lips, when she realized her boldness.

Understanding moved Fabienne's lips into a soft smile. "I don't know. I don't think so."

She produced a bonnet and parasol to match Mercedes's dress and fetched hers.

Wings of the Wind

"Shall we go?"

She helped Mercedes with her bonnet and slipped a small beaded purse over her wrist. Finally, giving her creation one last critical look, she nodded her approval, held out a hand for Mercedes, and arm-in-arm they left the land of makeover.

Mickey awaited them on the steps of the shop. He bowed low when he saw Fabienne, and his mouth edged up into a smile when looked at Mercedes. "Good day, lovely ladies. Nice to see Missy Fabienne."

He amazed Mercedes when he took Fabienne's hand and kissed it.

"The same debonair Mickey Chinfatt," Fabienne said. "How good to see you again, sir."

"Pleasure is mine," said Mickey, and he bowed again. "Ladies." He indicated the open carriage where Claudette was already perched upon the seat.

The carriage was deep glossy brown with gold trim and appointed in gold velvet seats. Mickey helped Mercedes and Fabienne in and took a seat by the driver. Mercedes wondered about the wealth of Fabienne Beluche. She didn't think that a seamstress made enough money to keep a carriage, let alone such a fine one. She wondered if Andre supported her, too.

They proceeded along the route they had come earlier toward Jackson Square with slight detours for sights of interest. The horse trotted along briskly, and the breeze from the ride refreshed them. The ladies chatted gaily beneath their parasols.

Fabienne regaled them with history, pointed out the homes and businesses of the rich, famous, and infamous, and kept up a running commentary on the flowers and trees they saw. They passed into the French Quarter where

Mercedes admired the buildings with ironwork and balconies. Trees, flowering shrubs, and flowers framed the picture they gazed upon.

After several circuits of the French Quarter, they pulled up beside Fabienne's favorite outdoor café called La Fleur De Lis. Mickey helped them down then returned to his seat by the driver to await their return. The café had an outside garden decorated with small black wrought iron tables and matching chairs. Live oaks trimmed in Spanish moss shaded the sitting area. They took a seat at a table where they could watch the steady stream of passers-by and carriage traffic.

Fabienne pointed out the ladies with the latest Paris fashions. Some strolled past on the arms of men in top hats.

It must be nice to have a life of such leisure, thought Mercedes. Galveston had their share of the leisure class but not in these numbers.

Fabienne took it all in stride, not the least concerned a ride in the city might take her away from her work. Mercedes recalled how hard she worked at the store in Galveston. Even on Sundays after church, she retired to the store to review the accounts. The work never ended for her. Here the wealthy enjoyed their leisure. She couldn't imagine such a life for herself.

"How do you like New Orleans?" asked Fabienne.

"Incredible."

Young Claudette piped up, "It is a very pretty place, don't you think?"

"Yes," said Mercedes. "The flowers and trees are lovely. I like the houses and the balconies. The outsides of some are austere, though. Could they be more beautiful inside?"

"Exactement," said Fabienne. "Those homes are

Spanish style and built around an interior courtyard with flowers, trees, and shrubs. Some have fountains. They have rooms with tall doors and windows facing the interior courtyard. High ceilings and many doors and windows allow the air to circulate."

"We use lots of doors and windows in Galveston, too. We build houses on low stilts, which help avoid flooding and catch more breeze."

"We call them plantation-style houses," Fabienne said. "They have raised basements and steep roofs. The rooms have wide verandas front and back. Canvas flaps roll down to keep out hot sun and bad weather. It is a good style for a city like this."

"Tell me, Fabienne, what do these people do for a living? How can they be out here during the day strolling? Do they not work? How do they earn their money?"

"These are the creme de la crème in New Orleans," said Fabienne. "They do not have to work. They have people to do their work for them. They are plantation owners, who come here to do business. They have slaves and servants. The trades people are in the commercial district. By not having anything to do these people tell us how wealthy they are. It is all a show. Many of these ladies are my customers."

"Really? You must do very well indeed," Mercedes said, but stopped short of asking how she afforded her own carriage.

"I do well. This city has been good to me, and I have been good for it." But Fabienne did not elaborate, and Mercedes wondered at her remark.

A waiter came to the table with menus. Fabienne suggested they order a light meal and some lemonade. She picked out an assortment of cheese, chilled soup, greens, and pastries for dessert. The waiter collected their menus and left.

While they waited, four men came into the restaurant garden and took a table not far from them. They all wore top hats and lightweight coats even though the day was hot and humid. Mercedes judged them to be businessmen, as their attire was more somber than the strollers on the street.

One man nodded his head in their direction, his eyes sweeping Fabienne, the girl, and lingering on Mercedes.

"That man seems to know you," said Mercedes to Fabienne.

"He knows me very well," said Fabienne who, after acknowledging the man with a smile, turned toward Mercedes. Fabienne saw her puzzlement. "I see you do not understand. This man is my benefactor. He looks after me. It is the reason I can keep a carriage and the style of life I now command."

"I see," said Mercedes and fell silent. She had never met a woman with a benefactor. This, indeed, was a world much different than her own.

Their lunch arrived, and they enjoyed the simple fare with tall glasses of lemonade. The café had filled now with mid-day trade. The clientele was mostly men with a sprinkling of elegantly attired ladies.

When they finished, Mercedes excused herself to look for the powder room Fabienne said lay to the rear of the establishment off a courtyard. Mercedes followed a narrow, dimly lit corridor that led to the shaded, bricked courtyard. She stopped to admire a small, tinkling fountain surrounded by ferns. Gold fish darted back and forth in the clear pool.

Charming, she thought, watching the antics of the goldfish. This city is truly enchanting.

Wings of the Wind

She heard footsteps behind her and turned to glance over her shoulder to see who might be joining her. She was not fast enough. The blow came from behind. She crumbled to the brick pavement and into darkness.

Chapter Thirteen

Fabienne met Andre at the door upon his return to her shop. She told him what had happened, spilling the story out in a jumble, her eyes glistening with tears.

"Do you have any idea where she went?" asked Andre, trying to remain calm, trying to remain rational.

"She said she was going to the powder room at the cafe," said Fabienne, her voice breaking. "She didn't return after ten minutes or so, and I went to look for her. I thought maybe someone had engaged her in conversation. You never know in the city. People are friendly, and Mercedes is an attractive young woman."

Andre wondered whether Mercedes was foolish enough to do the very thing he warned her not to do. Curse the woman. Trouble again. "Was she enjoying herself?" he asked. He was having trouble believing Mercedes had disappeared after all his warnings.

"Oui, oui, oui. You should have seen her watching the fashionable people parade by us. She asked many questions and had comments on everything. She did not look to be unhappy."

Andre frowned. "Was your friend, Jack Lormand, of any help?"

"He did what he could under the circumstances. He questioned the cafe staff. No one saw her go into the powder room, which is just off the courtyard. Mickey was with the carriage, but he didn't see her. No one saw her leave."

No one saw her leave, Andre thought. Two possibilities. One, she sneaked out to do some sleuthing on her own, which she promised not to do. Two, she didn't leave of her own accord but was smuggled out somehow. Who would know who she was? Why would they want her? He didn't like the feeling in his gut.

"Where can I find Lormand?"

"He's at his club. He said he was going back there when he left the café."

"The one off Jackson Square?"

"That's the one. Mon dieu, I feel so awful about this. I do not know how this could happen." Tears streamed down Fabienne's cheeks. "She is a lovely girl. I am afraid for her. Who would have done such a thing?"

"I'm not sure, but it's not your fault. You were doing me a favor." Andre pulled her into a comforting embrace. "I'm going to see Lormand. I suspect he might know more about this than he lets on. Tito and Bruno are to meet me here. When they arrive, tell them to wait here. I won't be long."

"Please be careful. Lormand is not the easiest of men to deal with."

"That I know," said Andre. He turned to go then swiveled back. "What was Mercedes wearing? Did you find a new dress for her?"

"Oui, She had on a stunning white dress trimmed in pink and yellow flowers. She looked so beautiful." Fabienne's voice trailed off.

Andre strode down the walk to the carriage in front of Fabienne's shop. He leapt in, gave the driver the address, and they sped away.

His thoughts were in turmoil. He went over the endless possibilities of what had happened to Mercedes. The one that niggled most in his mind was that Norton had found out that she was in New Orleans. If his suspicions were correct, Jeffrey Norton wanted desperately to see his niece, enough to kidnap her.

* * * * *

Andre jumped from the carriage before the wide, marble steps of a stately building off Jackson Square. He took the steps two at a time and entered through tall, open doors into a foyer. An unassuming brass plaque to the right of the door read "Jackson Square Club". Andre handed his card to the uniformed doorman.

"Jack Lormand, please."

The doorman perused the card.

"Is he expecting you, Captain Lafitte?"

"I expect so. Would you tell him it's a matter of urgent business?"

The doorman nodded and disappeared into the cool interior of the building. He reappeared shortly and indicated to Andre to follow him.

They walked down a long, dim hallway. Murmurs of conversation floated out from behind the closed doors of the rooms they passed. The doorman stopped before a high-ceilinged room and motioned for Andre to enter.

Jack Lormand stood before a fireplace with a brass fan screen, arms folded across his chest. He wasn't a tall man, but his barrel chest and wide shoulders gave the impression of power.

"Lormand," Andre said without a smile. He stopped

Wings of the Wind

just inside the door.

"Lafitte."

"I wish I could say it is good to see you again but that would be a lie." Andre stepped further into the room.

"I could say the same."

Andre said, "I'll come right to the point. I thought you might help locate Mercedes Lawless, the young woman who disappeared this afternoon from the café."

"I don't know what happened to her. I don't know if she was abducted or not."

Andre studied the man opposite him. Lormand held himself like he owned the world and probably did own half of New Orleans. The gray at his temples added a distinguished look that softened the hard lines of his face.

Andre knew him from his mother's establishment where Lormand had been a regular client for years. His mother had been Lormand's favorite, and after her passing, it had been Fabienne.

"Why don't you have a seat?" Lormand unfolded his arms and walked over to a mahogany sideboard where cut glass decanters stood in shades of amber brown, gold, and deep red. "Sherry? Whiskey?"

"Whiskey," said Andre, who remained standing.

"You've seen Claudette, I take it? A pretty thing, isn't she?" said Lormand. He offered a cheroot from a carved wood box to Andre, which he accepted. Lormand took one himself then lit both. He handed Andre the whiskey.

Andre exhaled and studied the cheroot. "She is far too beautiful for a child so young. She is innocent." He leveled a hard look at Lormand. "I trust she will stay that way."

"Yes," Lormand said, making the word two syllables. "She's in good hands with Fabienne for now." He changed the subject. "How's that new clipper of yours?"

"Superb craft. Excellent response," replied Andre. "I didn't come here to talk about clipper ships."

Impatient to find Mercedes, he was not in the mood to be gracious. He detested this man his mother had favored. The man with whom she had preferred to spend her time and not with her sons, who had run wild in the streets of New Orleans.

"Do you know where Mercedes Lawless is or don't you?"

Lormand examined his drink and made a show of sampling both it and the cheroot before he spoke. "At Fabienne's request, I made some inquiries."

Andre clenched his jaw and waited, not wanting the older man to see his frustration nor his fury. Lormand knew everything that went on in New Orleans, and if anyone knew where Mercedes might be, he would. Another matter was whether he would be willing to share the information with Andre.

"Someone saw a woman being helped into a closed carriage after the disappearance of Miss Lawless. It was in the alley behind the restaurant. They said the woman appeared to be stumbling. They couldn't see the face for her bonnet but she had on white dress. A large man was helping her."

The twitch in Andre's jaw was imperceptible. He willed himself to remain calm.

"Did this person," he said, "see which way the carriage went?"

"At the end of the alley the carriage made a turn toward the dock area."

"Who would the large man be?"

"The person didn't get a good look at him. Could be any large man in New Orleans." Lormand made a vague

Wings of the Wind

hand gesture and shrugged his shoulders.

Andre stubbed out his smoke in the marble ashtray on the table. He set down his untouched drink. Lormand knew the large man, but he wasn't saying. Andre knew he would get nowhere with a cross-examination.

"Anything else?" asked Andre, as he turned to go. With Lormand there was always a price to pay.

Lormand smiled, but it didn't reach his eyes. "I heard you are selling your mother's establishment. I'd be interested in buying."

Andre's smile matched Lormand's. "I'll keep you in mind," he said and left without a backward glance. He brushed past the doorman on his way out, who flattened against the wall so not to be trampled.

He strode out of the club that Lormand had founded and jumped into the carriage, calling to the driver to take him back to Fabienne's shop. If he were going to the dock area, it wouldn't hurt to take his men, and he needed to know what they had found.

He didn't want to think about what might be happening to Mercedes, but Lormand's words played over and over again in his head. A stumbling woman in a white dress. A large man helping her.

A large man helping her. Was it possible that Mercedes had found someone in the restaurant to help her find her uncle? He was almost sure that she didn't know a soul in New Orleans. She had promised him not to go off on her own. But she wasn't a woman to be trusted, as he had found out in Galveston.

A stumbling woman. Stumbling sounded more like she was being forced to do something she didn't want to do or that she was hurt. He knew Mercedes was a resourceful woman, but his gut instinct told him he should be worried.

But worrying about someone implied vulnerability, and vulnerable was something he couldn't afford. It was not a part of him. It had never been. He didn't want to care about anyone too much. It was one thing to have a beautiful woman as a plaything that he could enjoy and then walk away. It was another to care for her.

He also was angry. If the man had hurt her, Andre had in mind various unpleasant lessons he would impress on the man. He hoped the other disquieting feeling swirling in his chest was not jealousy. It couldn't be. He was not a jealous man. He had never cared enough to be jealous. But the thought that some other man had his hands on Mercedes made his blood boil. He wanted to punch someone, and he hoped that someone would be a large man.

The carriage pulled up in front of Fabienne's shop where three unscrupulous looking men loitered outside her door. It was Bruno, Tito, and Mickey. Andre motioned them into the carriage. Fabienne appeared at the door and ran to the carriage.

"What did he say?" she asked, the concern in her voice mirrored in her face.

"She may be somewhere in the dock area," he said, as his men climbed into the carriage. "We're going there now."

She reached for his hand and squeezed. "Be careful, cher."

Andre returned the squeeze and told her to take care of herself and Claudette. He would get word to her when he could.

As they took off at a trot, Andre shifted his attention to Bruno. "What'd you find?"

Bruno leaned his big frame forward in the seat,

squeezing little Mickey Chinfatt against the side of the carriage.

"Remy Thibodeaux has a cousin," Bruno said, talking as if he were sharing a secret with Andre. "This cousin is kinda crazy. He don't live here. He operates out of Galveston. Name is Bragg. He's a big guy."

"A big guy," Andre repeated. "Mercedes was linked to a scandal with a man by the name of Bragg. Are we talking about the same person?"

"Might be," said Bruno.

Tito and Mickey looked back and forth between speakers, intent as Andre on what Bruno said.

The driver's whip snaked out over the top of the horse's head, as he urged him faster down the tree-lined street.

"Do we know where the Galveston Bragg is now?" Andre asked.

Tito cut in. "Remy told us he's in New Orleans."

Andre blew out a breath. That bastard. "What is he doing here?"

"Looking for Miss Mercedes. That's what Remy told us. Somehow he knows she's in New Orleans," said Tito. "Not only that. Remy says where you find his cousin you'll find Norton."

While Andre considered the implications, Bruno and Tito turned their attention to two well-dressed and well-endowed young ladies strolling by.

"Anything else?" Andre asked.

With great effort Bruno and Tito pulled their attention back to Andre.

Bruno nodded. "He said his cousin is involved in the slave trade."

Andre grimaced. "Is Norton involved in the slave

Marjorie Thelen

trade?"

"Financing," Bruno said. "Norton is involved in financing the trade. He's been down on his luck though and has been hard put to raise the capital he needs. He's taken to gambling, which you already know, and he's been losing, which you already know. He is getting into shadier deals to raise money. That's where Bragg comes in. Bragg got connected with Norton when he lent him money. Now he wants the money back. Norton can't pay so he is on the hook to Bragg. Bragg does under the table deals in just about anything that involves cotton, sugar, and human flesh. Bragg isn't as clever as he is ruthless. Norton is clever but facing financial ruin. They're a team. Now they are into extortion. Enter Mercedes."

"So Norton wants to extort money from Mercedes?" asked Andre.

"Looks like it."

"That would mean that Norton might not be related to Mercedes."

"Right."

"Norton might not be his real name."

"Right. Remy says there is a growing extortion ring in New Orleans that feeds off the weak. Unprotected females, widows, unmarried women with fortunes are groups they particularly like. They also have victimized widowers, old people. They appear to be getting quite good at it. There's little to stop them because they threaten their victims with harm, if they try to tell the authorities. As if it would do any good in this town to ask the law to protect you. This has been a nice source of capital for them."

"Where do they get the names and financial information for their victims that they go after?" Andre asked.

Wings of the Wind

"Remy says that it comes from obituaries, tips from cronies, talk around town. From what he can tell they are operating mostly in New Orleans but now it looks like they've moved into Galveston. Mercedes is a target because Bragg knows her." Bruno hesitated. "Most important, he wants her. He wants her so bad he wants to ruin her financially so she'll come begging to him."

"What do you mean wants her?" Andre eyes narrowed. His blood started to simmer.

Bruno took an extra deep breath. "Remy says gossip has it that the man tried to put Mercedes in a compromising position back in Galveston to force her to marry him. It created the scandal that he wanted, but he misjudged the lady. She refused to marry him which made her name mud in Galveston but it didn't make it Bragg."

"What kind of compromise are we talking about here?" Andre sat forward in his seat. He needed it spelled out.

"Bragg swears he spent the night in bed with her."

"Spent the night in bed with her," Andre repeated. He was going to do more than just punch Bragg.

"He kidnapped her in Galveston and took her to his place on the far west end of the island. It was morning before she showed up in town in a buckboard she stole from Bragg."

"She has an amazing ability to get herself in and out of difficult situations," said Andre.

Bruno nodded. "Appears she wasn't worse the wear. Somehow Bragg ended up with a broken nose that had to be tended by the doc in town."

"Not many women have that much gumption," said Andre with admiration in his voice.

"However," Bruno continued on, "the story

circulating is that Mercedes had been compromised."

"What does the lady say?" Andre asked.

"She denies it."

Bruno watched Andre's face. He had a dangerous set to his jaw.

"It looks like the bastard got her again," Andre said. He made a fist and pounded his leg. "He needs to be taught a lesson."

The three men watched Andre's fist, looking glad they weren't going to be on the receiving end of whatever he had in mind.

The carriage rolled to a stop. They jumped out and stood watching the dock activity.

"Did Remy give you the address where Norton can be found?"Andre asked. His eyes flashed back and forth over the area assessing the situation.

Bruno nodded. "Yep. It's right here in the dock area. The Wholesale Traders Warehouse." He pointed to a building in the distance along the water's edge. "Should be right down there. According to Remy its right off the main loading area."

"What about Bragg's operation?"

"In the same building."

"That makes things easier," Andre said then looked at each of them in turn as he gave out instructions.

"Bruno, you and I are going to call on Mr. Norton. Tito, I want you to ask around about what ships and steamers are leaving today and see if anyone has seen a big man with a lady in a white dress in the area. They travel in a closed carriage. A pair like that would stand out here."

"Mickey will stay with the carriage. If we aren't back in an hour or so, come looking for us at the Wholesale Traders Warehouse." He nodded in the direction of the

Wings of the Wind

warehouses.

"Si, Si, mi Capitán." Tito saluted.

Mickey bowed.

"C'mon, Bruno," Andre said.

They strode through the crowded dock area dodging carts, piles of horse dung, puddles of sewage, and groups of rough looking men.

"What happens if we find Norton?" asked Bruno. "He must know you are here and looking for him. You think it will be that easy to find him?"

"I doubt it. But I want to make sure he knows I'm looking for him. He's already in difficulty if he owes a lot of money."

"Why would you want him to know?"

"Because I'm going to back him into a corner, and I want to be sure he knows who's doing it."

They arrived at the entrance of the building with "Wholesale Traders" sign on the door. It was a long, low structure of wood weathered gray.

In a quiet voice Andre said, "I'm going inside to see if Norton is here. I want you to check around the outside. We are looking for somewhere they might be holding Mercedes. Meet me back here in fifteen minutes."

Bruno nodded and disappeared around the side of the building.

Andre opened the door, stepped inside, and looked around. He saw men working at the far end of the warehouse. One of the workers looked up at his entrance, broke away, and came toward him. He wiped his hands on a dirty neck cloth as he came.

"Hep you?" asked the man. He was dressed in brown homespun trousers and a dirty gray, collarless shirt. A ragged straw hat sat on his head.

"Yes, sir," Andre held out his hand. "I'm looking for someone who's interested in buying cotton."

"Name's Duffy," the man said as he offered his hand to Andre and winced at the grip. "We buy cotton, but the boss man ain't here today. Can you come back? It's just us fellas. We do all the backbreaking work. Boss man does the important stuff like buying." An easy smile crossed Duffy's face.

"Sure. I'll be in town for a few days. Do you have much work right now?" Andre asked.

"Always busy. Busiest in the harvest season although we do warehouse quite a bit."

"Who is the boss here?"

"Man's name is Norton, but he not here much. He travels. But y'all lucky. He's in town this week. His partner is a man name of Bragg, based in Galveston. He's in New Orleans, too, but don't expect either one today." The man gestured around the warehouse. "Y'all welcome to walk around. I get back to my chores if it's all the same."

" Don't mind if I do have a look. I'm interested in the quality of the cotton you're buying," Andre said. "Please tell your boss that Andre Lafitte stopped by and will be back to see him."

"Andre Lafitte?" said Duffy. "Sure, I tell him."

"One other question. Does your boss have his own ship or does he use outside shippers?"

"Oh, no sir. He don't own a ship. They ship mostly by steamer. Sailing ships on the longer hauls."

Andre thanked the man, who returned to his work. He walked though several aisles of cotton bales, then wandered to the side of the building where there were two doors and discreetly tried them. Locked. No signs indicated what might be inside. He listened at each door

Wings of the Wind

but heard nothing. After a while longer of pretending to examine cotton, Andre waved to Duffy and left.

Bruno was waiting for him.

"Find anything?" Andre asked.

Bruno shook his head. "Walls of windowless building to the rear. A few windows on the dock side. This is the only exit. How about you?"

"Bragg and Norton are partners in this operation, and they ship by steamer. We need to make sure we know when the next steamer leaves New Orleans. Two locked doors inside bear further investigation."

Bruno nodded, and they moved down the street toward the rendezvous point.

"We'll watch this building," Andre said to Bruno. "Bragg has to be somewhere nearby. Mercedes, too." He didn't want to think about how close she might be to Bragg.

As they approached the carriage, they saw Mickey squatting beside the carriage in animated conversation with an old Chinese man, who squatted with him. Both were gesturing wildly as they spoke.

The man with Mickey sported traditional Chinese garb, a small black cap, hair in a long queue, black pants, and a blousy jacket. He was passably clean except for dusty brown feet.

Mickey stood up as Andre and Bruno approached, and the other man followed his example. "Captain Lafitte. Here my friend Dickey Ho. Not see him many years."

Andre nodded a greeting.

"Much pleasure, Captain Lafitte," Dickey Ho said, bowing. "I hear many stories about you," he said in carefully enunciated English.

"You're thinking of Jean Lafitte," said Andre.

"No, Captain. I know Jean Lafitte. I cook for him

Marjorie Thelen

when he live in New Orleans. I never meet you, but I hear stories."

Andre frowned. "Sometime you'll have to tell me those stories but right now we've got urgent business."

He turned to Tito and Bruno who both stood with their arms crossed, legs widespread. "I want you two to keep watch on the Wholesale Traders Warehouse."

They nodded.

"Bruno says there's only one exit. I found two locked rooms. Mercedes might be in one of them."

"Tito, did you find anything?"

"No one saw the woman but some fellas think they saw Bragg here today."

"What about ships and steamers leaving today?"

"No sailing ships scheduled, mi Capitán. There is a steamer leaving this evening bound for Galveston."

The net was closing.

"Bragg will be on that steamer. We'll be there when she loads, if we don't find Mercedes before then."

Andre turned to Mickey. "I want you to stay around here and keep your eyes and ears open. Ask around to see if anyone has seen a big man with a woman in a white dress."

"Pardon me," said Dickey Ho, bowing. They all swiveled toward the sound of the voice.

"Such a couple went into warehouse earlier today."

They stared at the old man. He bowed again.

"Big man came out alone. Lady not with him."

"Are you sure?" asked Andre.

"Very sure. Old man Ho sweep dock outside warehouse when black carriage pull up. Lady not walk good. Old man Ho think that strange. Big man help her walk. Old man Ho think odd lady stay in warehouse."

Wings of the Wind

Mickey beamed at his friend. "Dickey Ho have good eyes for old man."

"Old man live long time because of good eyes. Eyes notice important things," he said, a grin crinkling his face.

Andre appraised the old man anew. "That's valuable information."

The old man bowed to Andre.

Seizing the opportunity, Mickey piped up, "Old man Dickey Ho need job, boss. Good cook. Maybe Bruno need help."

Andre shot a glance at Bruno, who shrugged and nodded his head.

"He's got a job," said Andre. "I need to know what time the steamer leaves for Galveston."

"Galveston steamer leave every evening 7:00 PM," Dickey Ho said.

"You sure about that?" asked Andre.

"Very sure," said Dickey Ho, bowing. "Old man Ho clean dock area after last steamer leave and last steamer is 7:00 PM to Galveston. Not always on time, but leaves everyday."

Andre clapped the old man on the shoulder. "You'll be a valuable asset on our ship. Thanks."

The old man's eyes crinkled again.

"Who has the time?"

Bruno pulled an enormous gold watch and chain from his vest pocket. "Six o'clock."

Andre looked back and studied the warehouse. "Let's pray she's in one of the locked rooms. We either try to take her here or at the steamer dock."

In answer to his prayer, a closed carriage, shiny black, rolled down the street to the warehouse. A high stepping, glossy, black horse pulled the rig.

Marjorie Thelen

"There the carriage," said the old man.

Andre made his decision. "We take her now. Mickey, ready our shore boat. Be prepared to shove off as soon as we come back with Mercedes. Tito and Bruno, come with me. Check your weapons."

Wings of the Wind

Chapter Fourteen

Julia wrapped packages of flour and corn meal for Mrs. Hellebush. She took the money and made change, handing it back with a smile and a thank you.

"I see you are doing well, Fraelein, with your cousin gone," said Mrs. Hellebush, German wife of the Lutheran minister and always one ready to offer an opinion when one wasn't required. "Are you worried? Have you word of them?" She enunciated each word precisely.

Even with the woman's careful pronunciation Julia had to listen closely because her accent was so thick. "No, we haven't, Mrs. Hellebush. I'm sure they're all right. It hasn't been that long." She forced a smile to hide the worry that weighed on her.

Julia knew that Mrs. Hellebush had broadcast Mercedes's absence all over Galveston Island, making it sound like an abduction, along with the news that Jamie had gone to sea with a pirate. Blast Sheriff McGreevy for his flapping mouth. In her daily visits to the store, Mrs. Hellebush fished for more grist to feed her gossip mill.

"It has been long enough. Are you not going to send someone to look for her? Are you not afraid for her person?"

"As I've told you, Mrs. Hellebush, we know where they are. They sailed with Captain Lafitte in his ship, *Wings of the Wind,* and he is bound for New Orleans. Mercedes has long wanted to visit New Orleans. She is always looking for new merchandise for the store, and this was her chance to see a little of the world, do some buying, and look after Jamie."

Julia felt a prick of conscience lying to the preacher's wife, but she couldn't confess that Mercedes had left in a barrel. That wouldn't help Mercedes' already tattered reputation. She couldn't confess her worry that Mercedes might not have made it safely aboard the ship, nor her worry that Mercedes would be mistreated by the Captain for having the audacity to stowaway on board his ship.

"I hope for your sake that everything works out for the best, Fraelein," Mrs. Hellebush said. "Lucky you have that nice man, Herr Carmichael, to help you out."

Julia knew Mrs. Hellebush had her fishing line out for information on Duncan, so she merely said, "Captain Lafitte sent him to help out while Mercedes was gone. Yes, he's been a great help."

Mrs. Hellebush eyed Julia suspiciously as if she didn't believe a word she said and that she wasn't fooled by Julia's smiles. "And your papa, how is he taking all this?"

"Taking all this?" Julia asked. It sounded like there had been a death in the family. She chose to ignore the implication of the question. "My father is quite well. He's in the garden weeding and fussing over the greens that he planted. The bugs seem to like greens as much as we do."

Julia gave Mrs. Hellebush an empty smile, hoping the insufferable woman would leave.

"Soap," said Mrs. Hellebush, who saw no humor in

Wings of the Wind

bugs. When she saw Julia's puzzled look, she added, "Soap and water. Mix a light solution of homemade soap and water and wash the greens right there in the garden patch. It gets the bugs off every time and keeps them from coming back. They do not like the taste of lye."

"Sure and thank you, Mrs. Hellebush. I will share that remedy with my father." Julia thought he probably knew every cure for bugs in south Texas, but maybe this was one he didn't know.

"I must be getting back to the preacher," Mrs. Hellebush declared, adjusting her black bonnet and picking up her packages. "If you need any help or have want of me, send Herr Carmichael over to the parsonage. I'm always glad to be of help. Auf Wiedersehen."

With that the Galveston Daily Bugle turned and made her way out of the Lavender Dry Goods Emporium, her packages tucked under her ample arm, her parasol filling in as a cane.

Julia sighed in relief and watched her customer's retreating back. She checked around the store for other customers. All was quiet and still. Too quiet and too still. No Jamie banging about the store. No Mercedes lighting up the day.

She leaned on the counter and thought about her cousins. Tears glistened in her eyes. She couldn't believe how much she missed them. She had to admit it was a help to have Duncan here. At least that rat of a captain had enough of a heart to leave help, but then he was protecting his own supposed interests, too.

She wondered again where they were and how they were doing. She hoped with all her heart that Mercedes had made it onto the ship and had not come to harm. Why-oh-why had she agreed to let Mercedes get into that barrel?

She could be all persuasion and charm when she wanted something, and she had wanted desperately to follow Jamie onto that ship.

Julia had aided and abetted the crime, and now chagrin and remorse were her constant companions. Anxiety consumed her and left her unable to eat. She heard footsteps and straightened quickly, passing a hand over her eyes to wipe away the tears. Better to keep a straight back and cheerful smile. No sense giving in to her fears.

Duncan approached and stood a few feet away, waiting for her to acknowledge his presence. His polite manners endeared him to her. He didn't ask questions and he didn't intrude. She liked his reserve. He had kept to the office since his sudden arrival, going over the books and preparing his reports for Captain Lafitte. She couldn't be of much help because the accounts had been Mercedes's realm.

She looked over her shoulder and put on her best smile.

"Hello, Mr. Carmichael. How is everything?"

He had taken the Captain's advice and, with her encouragement, had gotten rid of the heavy coat, vest, and hat he always wore. From the shop inventory he had bought a pair of the new ready-made trousers and a white, collarless cotton shirt. He had a broad chest and stocky build. Without all the clothing, the breadth of his shoulders was more noticeable, and he appeared less round.

He stood a few inches taller than Julia, so she had to look up to meet his eyes. She noticed how clear his eyes were. His hair had a sandy color to it. Since he wasn't overcome with heat, his face no longer was florid red, and his naturally rosy cheeks complimented the blue in his

Wings of the Wind

eyes.

"Miss Julia." He dipped his head in greeting. "Everything is fine. How are you?" He leaned closer. "You look tired, lass. I hope you are not ill."

Julia shook her head. "Not ill, just a bit tired." She lowered her eyes to hide the dark circles under them.

Duncan nodded his head in understanding. "You are overworked out front here. Now that I have the accounts reviewed, I'll be able to help out more. That's what I came to tell you."

"That's good news," said Julia, then she pursed her lips. "I hope everything balanced. There weren't any problems, were there?"

"Most certainly not," he said, affably. "Miss Mercedes has a good head for figures, and everything appears to be in order. I have prepared my reports for the Captain. I will send them off. Might you have some brown paper to wrap them and something leather, like a saddlebag? Might you have something like that?"

"Brown paper most certainly," Julia said. "We should wrap them securely and seal them since they are financial records." She reached for brown paper under the counter. "If you bring them out, I'll wrap them for you. Then you can address and seal them. I'll look see what we have in leather pouches."

"Thank you very much," he said. "That's awfully kind of you. I'll get them."

He trotted off down the hall, returning quickly with a stack of papers. Julia moved to the leather goods section of the shop, looking over the display of pouches and bags. She selected a large folder style with leather bands to secure the outside.

Duncan brought over the stack of papers, and Julia

wrapped the stack in the brown paper and inserted it in the pouch. They secured it with bands and buckles. Carmichael addressed a tag that read, "Captain Andre Lafitte, *Wings of the Wind*."

Julia frowned. "Is that all the address you'll be putting on? If it leaves with the post, they'll need a street address and city."

"I'm going to take it down to the wharf. It will go on one of the Captain's ships. I'll check which one leaves next for New Orleans. They'll drop it off at his office in New Orleans."

"Ship? He has more than one?" Julia looked perplexed.

Duncan cocked his head to one side and regarded her. "Captain Lafitte owns a regular shipping line that sails between here and New Orleans and other cities on the East Coast. He has several ships that haul freight between here and New Orleans. I'll walk over to the wharves to see which one is here."

Julia stared at him, trying to digest this revelation.

"Ships," she said again.

Duncan nodded and smiled. "Yes, the plural of ship."

"Forgive me, Mr. Carmichael, but I'm a bit confused. I didn't know Captain Lafitte had more than one ship. I don't believe Mercedes was aware of this either. She knows all the ships and who owns them and how often they sail and where they go. She and Jamie kept a chart with all the vessels and the important information on each. I know they never heard of Andre Lafitte until the day he sailed in here."

Duncan's face brightened to florid red. "There is much you don't know of Captain Lafitte."

Julia folded her arms, tilted her head, and stuck her

Wings of the Wind

face closer to his. He backed up a step.

"You wouldn't want to tell me more, would you?" Julia squinted at him. She saw the man's discomfort and that only added to her curiosity.

Duncan rubbed the tip of his nose then spread his hands before her. "I can tell you this. Captain Lafitte is a very private individual. He has different business interests, and they have different names. He is not usually listed as the owner, but he is always the money behind the enterprise. Those who work for him know who holds the power."

Julia let her breath out slowly. She guessed a pirate might be a private sort of individual. But this did sound like something more legitimate.

"I'd like to ask you something point blank," she said.

Duncan had not finished nodding before she blurted out, "Is he a pirate?"

The width of his clear, blue eyes told Julia this was a shocking question. Maybe Captain Lafitte didn't tell him everything. But surely he must know every last detail of the business since he did the books.

"No, lass." Duncan wagged his head vigorously. "You mustn't believe the rumors. He is a legitimate businessman. He doesn't believe in broadcasting the extent of his holdings. He's quite modest, I would say, and he's not a braggart or such like that. But he is successful, and he has a good touch for business and knows shipping and the sea better than anyone I ever met. He's a good employer, very fair. His crew on the *Wings of the Wind* is extremely loyal and wouldn't work for any other sea captain. He has a staff in Boston that handles the administrative part of his businesses." He offered up his hands in supplication. "I'm afraid I said more that I ought."

Marjorie Thelen

His look stopped Julia from asking anymore. "I am sorry I was so blunt and prying. It was not polite of me. Forgive me, but I was taken aback by the thought of his owning a ship let alone more than one."

Duncan tucked the pouch under his arm. "I best be off," he said, expressing with his eyes his gratitude for Julia's not pushing the subject any further. "You don't suppose I'll be needing a coat, do you?"

"In this heat? Gracious, no. Go as you are to the wharf. We aren't so formal here. This is Texas, you know."

Julia gave him a big Texas friendly grin. She liked the man, and she felt her heart warming. Like her father observed, it could have been a lot worse.

Duncan hurried off, calling back that he wouldn't be long and forgetting to take his hat.

Best to keep busy and keep her mind off her cousins. She pulled open the money drawer and began to count the change, intending to deposit the extra cash in the safe in the back room. But her mind kept wandering to Duncan's disclosure of the extent of Andre Lafitte's business enterprises. If Mercedes had known she would have told her. The man was private, indeed. To have hidden behind various business names so that not even Mercedes Lawless could ferret him out was an accomplishment of great magnitude.

She was still mulling over Duncan's revelations when a new customer came into the Lavender Dry Goods Emporium. She slipped the excess cash into the strong box and put it away under the counter. Julia walked to the front of the store to greet the customer. When he turned to her, she forgot her greeting, so startled was she by his eyes. They were lavender blue. Those were Mercedes eyes.

"How do you do?" said the stranger, bowing. "I'm

Wings of the Wind

looking for Miss Mercedes Lawless. The desk manager over at the Tremont Hotel told me I might find her here."

Julia gave a mental shake then remembered her manners and said, "Welcome to the Lavender Dry Goods Emporium. I'm sorry but Miss Lawless is not here at the moment. May I help you?"

Julia stared at the stranger, mesmerized. It was if she were looking at the male version of Mercedes. It was uncanny. The stranger took off his hat. Good grief, thought Julia, the hair is the same, mahogany tinged with red and curls. Same nose, same charming air. It was Mercedes twin. Could that be possible?

"I was hoping to see her. I've come quite a distance to find her."

"Find her?" Julia repeated. "Does she know you? I'm her cousin, Julia, and I know most of the people she knows. Galveston is a small town."

"How extraordinary. Please let me introduce myself. My name is Jeffrey Norton, and I'm Mercedes's uncle."

"That is not possible." Julia backed up a few paces. Her freckles disappeared into her pale face.

"Not possible? I am so sorry. I'm afraid I've shocked you. Please sit down. You don't look well." The stranger indicated a chair standing by the register counter.

Julia did as requested, trying to gather her wits. She gaped at him, trying to understand the reality of what was in front of her. Her tongue would not move.

The stranger broke the silence. "Did not my letter arrive? Perhaps Miss Lawless did not mention it to you?"

"Letter?"

"Yes, I wrote a letter, telling her about me and how I would be coming to meet her. I hoped not to shock her too much. I didn't know if she knew about me. I didn't know if her mother had told her she had an uncle. You see, the circumstances under which Mercedes's mother, Esther, left Boston were unfortunate. Our parents had quarreled with Esther. She was young, headstrong and in love. She wanted to marry a seaman, and our parents opposed the marriage. They thought she was marrying beneath her station in life." He paused as if waiting for comprehension to register.

Julia's complexion was coming back to pale pink. She couldn't think what to say. Mercedes was with Captain Lafitte right now looking for Jeffrey Norton in New Orleans. Could there be two of them? This one was a dead ringer for Mercedes. Then who was the other one? Who was the one who played cards on the ship with Captain Lafitte? This one knew Mercedes mother's name.

"Go on," she said at last. "Mercedes did receive a letter here from a Mr. Jeffrey Norton."

"Thank heaven," the stranger said. But then he knitted his brow. "If she received the letter, then it wouldn't be so shocking that I am here, would it?" He scratched his head.

"No, I mean, situations like this are always surprising." Julia stammered, trying to buy some time. She agonized over what to say. "It's one thing to get a letter. It's another to experience the real thing. Please do finish your story about Aunt Esther. She was my aunt, of sorts. At least we all called her Aunt Esther."

"Then you knew her, too." His face clouded. "I regret I shall never see her again."

He looked so crestfallen that Julia believed him. "Why don't we go into the parlor? It's to the back of the store. We can have tea. Or maybe you'd prefer something cool to drink. Lemonade?"

"Tea would be just the thing. Very accommodating of

you," he said, brightening. He followed her down the hallway to the back of the store.

Julia's mind raced as she made her way to the parlor. Thank goodness it was beginning to work again. Duncan would know. When he came back, he may or may not recognize this stranger. That would be the test.

Meanwhile, she didn't know how much to reveal to this man. For the present she was reluctant to tell him where Mercedes was and why she had gone there. She'd stick to the story that Mercedes went to New Orleans on a buying trip for the shop.

She invited the stranger to sit down, excused herself, and went out to the outside kitchen to find Maybelle, the servant who was helping out while Mercedes was gone, to ask her to fix them some tea and cakes.

Maybelle asked her if everything was all right, seeing as how Miss Julia looked mighty agitated. Julia owed that she had had shocking news but she would be a lot better with a good strong cup of tea. Julia smiled her thanks and went back to join her guest in the parlor. She sat opposite him on one of the lavender upholstered chairs, and they talked about the neutral topics of the weather in Galveston, when did he get in, how was his trip, was he enjoying his stay.

Maybelle appeared with tea and fixings and left them on the marble coffee table in front of Julia who poured and offered a cup to her guest. He accepted grateful thanks.

They stirred their tea, and Julia went back to the topic suspended between them. "Could you tell me more about Aunt Esther?"

Jeffrey Norton stared into his tea as if he found Esther's reflection there. A smile lit his face. "She was beautiful and kind. I'm told we looked much alike. Our

Marjorie Thelen

coloring, I suppose. I have no likeness of Esther."

He sipped his tea thoughtfully and set the cup down. "My parents never spoke of Esther. It seems so unfortunate. I longed to have a sister or a brother. I was lonely as a child. My parents were older and not in the best of health."

The unfolding story captivated Julia. Stirrings of sympathy for this man filled her. Maybe he was the real uncle.

"At any rate my father died some time ago, and in her old age my mother's heart softened. She died last year after a long illness. At the end she was delirious and kept calling the name that she had locked up all those years in her heart, Esther."

Jeffrey Norton closed his eyes as if remembering the scene. "When the solicitor read the will, to everyone's surprise my mother had equally divided the estate between son and daughter. That's why I had to find my sister, so I could tell her about the inheritance."

"But she's gone," he said in whisper. A cloud passed over the bright, hot Texas sun, and the room grew dark, adding to the sadness of the moment. Neither spoke for a long time.

Julia's hand covered her heart, but she uttered no sound, grief again washing over her for the loss of Aunt Esther, for all that would never be, for a family split apart by a young girl's passion.

Norton opened his eyes and gazed at Julia. "Then God in his great mercy revealed that Esther had two children in Galveston, Texas. What joy when I learned of that."

His joy turned to perplexity. "But I wrote all of this in the letter to Mercedes." He had lost interest in the tea, and the sugar cakes remained uneaten.

Wings of the Wind

Julia stared back at him in confusion. "You wrote all this in the letter? About the inheritance?" She wasn't sure she was going to have the strength to live through this day.

"Yes, I explained everything. I went to a lot of trouble to locate Esther. I hired a private investigator, who finally found the family here in Galveston. At least I have Mercedes and Jamie. I am anxious to see them." His words came out in a jumble, and his lavender blue eyes held a look of longing for that which had been denied him for a long time.

A long, low sigh escaped from Julia. Inheritance? Good grief.

"Mr. Norton," Julia said, "you said you wrote to her about this inheritance."

He nodded. "Did she mention it to you?"

Julia hesitated. "Not exactly." She thought back on the letter that Mercedes had showed her. It had not mentioned any inheritance. She decided partial truth would be best because she was reluctant to reveal her entire hand without knowing who the real Norton was. Duncan would know, and he would be back soon.

She made her decision. "Mr. Norton, I know you want to see them, but they've both sailed to New Orleans. Mercedes manages the Emporium, and she went on a buying trip. Jamie accompanied her. I'm not sure when they will be back, but I know they will want to meet you."

"I so hoped they would be here." He pressed his lips together. "I have come so far, and it's been such a long time."

Julia placed her hand on his arm. "There is another person that I would like you to meet. He helps out here but stepped out to arrange a shipment. He'll be back soon. Would you mind waiting?"

Marjorie Thelen

"No, not at all. My time here is to be totally dedicated to Mercedes and Jamie."

* * * * *

Back within the hour, Duncan was hardly inside the store before Julia tugged him into the office and shut the door.

"You better sit down," she said, and he obeyed because Julia looked about ready to explode.

"Duncan," she used his Christian name, she was so agitated, "a man is here to see Mercedes. You will never guess his name."

Duncan shook his head, baffled. He couldn't imagine what had Julia so flustered. He liked how she said his name though.

"Jeffrey Norton."

Duncan sat bolt upright. "He can't be here." He hesitated. "Can he?"

"That was my reaction. But this man looks like Mercedes. The weird thing is he sent her a letter that I don't think she got. There's an inheritance."

Duncan waited patiently for the rest of the story, wondering at the sight of the high color in Julia's cheeks.

"There was no inheritance mentioned in the letter Mercedes received. I saw the letter, and it only said he had taken over as her guardian."

Duncan tugged his lower lip. "That's the way I remember it from the Jeffrey Norton on our ship."

"You saw him, right?"

"Aye. We were on the same ship together for two weeks. Where is the man who just arrived?"

"He's in the garden. I took him there to enjoy Father's

flowers while he waited for you to return."

"Let's meet him then."

The stranger sat on a stone bench under a live oak tree on the west side of the garden, now in shadows. Elbows on his knees, he stared into the small goldfish pond in front of him. He raised his head when he heard them enter the garden.

He stood and came out of the shadows toward them. A smile brightened his face, and he held out his hand to Duncan.

"Jeffrey Norton at your service. I don't believe we've met."

Duncan shook his hand. "No, I don't believe we have."

Marjorie Thelen

Chapter Fifteen

Derek Bragg climbed down from the shiny black carriage, supremely satisfied with himself. He had his ladylove in hand. They would soon be on their way to Galveston. He'd have the use of Jack Lormand's private room on the steamer where he would enjoy Miss Mercedes Lawless. Small town Texas boy that he was, he was proud of having gained access to Jack Lormand's circle of influential friends. He loved being part of the elite in New Orleans. It made him feel good about himself. Maybe he should relocate to New Orleans. He had his intended. They would be married. They'd have a big family. He'd settle down to cotton and sugar brokering. It was a busy town, growing. There would be more opportunities for profit than in Galveston.

The driver closed the carriage door behind him and Bragg told him to wait, he would only be a few minutes. Then they would proceed to the wharf from whence the steamships departed. Bragg pulled out a huge key ring with a prodigious number of keys, selected the one for the entrance door to the Wholesale Traders Warehouse, and unlocked it. He walked in, fingering through the keys again until he found the small door key he sought.

The workers were gone for the day. A dusty silence had settled over the room. Bragg walked to the locked

Wings of the Wind

doors at the end of the room and slid the key into the lock of the first door. The door opened into darkness. The light from the exterior room lit a small figure propped up against the far wall. Mercedes Lawless squeezed her eyes shut against the sudden light. Her hands were tied behind her back and her feet, stretched out in front of her, were bound. A gag in her mouth, tied behind her head, completed her imprisonment.

Bragg smiled sweetly at his soon-to-be bride. He had not really wanted to tie her up, but he didn't trust his intended, given that she had gotten away from him once before. He stooped down and untied the gag and let it drop.

"You miserable jackass," Mercedes said, as soon as the gag was out of her mouth. "How dare you leave me tied up like a common criminal."

"Now, now my sweet thing, I told you I had errands to run. I didn't want you wandering off or warning the workers. You might have tried to escape from me again." Bragg smoothed her rumpled hair as if to smooth her rumpled spirit.

"Take your hands off me and untie me right now. I can't feel a thing in any of my limbs. I will hardly be a fit bride," she said, sarcastically, "if they have to amputate my arms and legs." She wriggled and squirmed to regain circulation in her extremities.

"I will, my sweet pet, but first we need to come to an understanding."

Mercedes stopped squirming and glared at him. "I can hardly wait to hear this."

He attempted another sweet smile. He was trying hard to charm this young woman. But she could be so vexing at times. Maybe she needed just a little cuff. The back of Bragg's hand swept across Mercedes' face. Her head snapped to the side with the impact of the blow. She looked back at him with pure, unadulterated hatred in her eyes. Blood welled up on her mouth from the cut in her lip.

Bragg narrowed his eyes at her, his voice hard. "My dear, you really must be more civil to your intended. You see, you don't have a say in the matter. You are mine now, and you will do as I say. Do you understand?"

The hatred in Mercedes eyes spoke volumes that even Bragg could understand. She looked away, as he raised his hand for another blow.

"Don't touch her," a low voice said from behind Bragg.

Startled, Bragg jerked around to look. A fist slammed into his face. He staggered back, crashing over a crate behind him, toppled backward over the crate, and ended up in a heap against the wall. He staggered to his feet and peered in the direction of the voice unable to see who he was fighting in the dimness of the room. He lunged toward his assailant, who nimbly stepped out of the way. A hand chopped down hard on the back of Bragg's neck, and he collapsed on the floor face down.

* * * * *

Andre Lafitte pulled Bragg to his feet and hit him again, this time in the stomach. Once. Twice. Bragg doubled over but was still on his feet. Blood dripped from his nose to the floor. He bent his head lower and plowed forward toward Andre, who stepped aside. Bragg went lumbering by. Andre gave him a kick in the rear end that sent him into the wall.

Bragg broke his fall with his arms and slid down the wall to the floor. He lay there panting.

Wings of the Wind

"Tough son-of-a-bitch, ain't he?" Bruno said from the doorway.

Andre stood with fingers hooked low on his hips, legs spread, breathing easily.

"More like mean son-of-a-bitch," said Andre. "That felt good." Massaging the backs of his knuckles, he walked over to Bragg. He stood towering over him.

"Who are you?" Bragg said between pants.

"Andre Lafitte."

Bragg wiped at his bloody lips and swore. "You're that murdering card sharp. You killed Jeffrey Norton."

Andre crossed his arms over his chest. "Not yet I haven't, but I might. I'm looking for him. I understand that you and he are partners. You wouldn't know where to find him, would you? We both know he's as alive as you are but it seems no one has seen him for awhile."

Bragg coughed and shifted to a sitting position. "He's not here. I don't know where he is."

"If he shows up tell him Andre Lafitte is looking for him. You can reach me through Jack Lormand."

"Jack Lormand?" Bragg said with a look of surprise on his bloody face.

"That's what I said." Andre turned and walked over to Mercedes, who sat with her head back against the wall, eyes closed.

He pulled her gently forward and cut the rope binding her hands behind her back. Her arms fell loosely by her sides. She shook and rubbed them to get rid of the pins and needles. Andre crouched and slit the ropes binding her legs then caressed her legs and arms to bring life back into them.

He was unprepared for the emotions that rushed through him upon seeing her. He was thankful she was alive. He was upset that she was hurt. He was glad he got there when he did. He hated Bragg and was glad he was a bleeding mess. He hoped that Mercedes had suffered nothing worse than a blackened eye although even that was too much. She might be trouble but she didn't deserve this.

Bragg tried to get to his feet. Andre looked over and tossed the rope to Bruno. "Tie him up. Gag him and make sure the ropes are good and tight."

Bruno caught the rope in one hand, walked over to Bragg, and started tying his legs. Bragg slumped back against the wall, coughing, his eyes unfocused.

Andre turned his attention back to Mercedes. His hand went under her chin and tilted it up. He turned her face to the side. "You're going to have a black eye." He wiped the blood from her puffy lips with his thumb.

She looked down but not before he noticed the tears glistening in her eyes.

He was unprepared for the tears. She looked so vulnerable, so helpless. She had been strong and pushy and hard to handle. But now she looked so defeated. His protective instincts welled up.

"Let's get you out of here," he said. "Do you think you can stand?"

She nodded mutely. Andre took her arms and helped her up. Her legs collapsed, and she fell against him.

"You aren't ready to walk yet."

He swept her up effortlessly in his arms. She encircled his neck with her arms and held on tightly, pushing her face into his neck.

He stepped over Bragg on his way to the door. Bruno was ready to put the gag on him.

"Wait a minute," said Bragg. "You're not going to leave me here like this, are you?" He struggled away from

Wings of the Wind

the scarf that Bruno held, the one that had gagged Mercedes. "This ain't right. This is my own warehouse. Nobody'll find me till morning."

"I hope not," Andre said on his way by.

Bruno deftly wedged the scarf in Bragg's mouth as he shouted, then tied it tight behind his head. Bragg struggled and bounced to no avail. They closed the door on his muffled rage.

"Lock the doors and toss the keys in the harbor," Andre said to Bruno.

"Aye, aye, Cap'n. With pleasure."

At the entrance door of the warehouse Andre paused and looked outside. The activity for the day had abated. The dockworkers were on their way home for supper or happily ensconced in the neighborhood taverns.

Tito sat in the driver's seat atop the carriage. The driver lay inside the warehouse door bound hand and foot, too scared to make a sound.

Tito jumped down when he saw Andre come out with Mercedes and opened the door of the carriage. Andre climbed inside and gently laid her back against the seat.

Bruno followed Andre out, closing and locking the door of the warehouse behind him. He tossed Bragg's ring of keys into the water not twenty feet from the warehouse door then joined Tito on the driver's bench atop the carriage. Tito slapped the shiny black horse with the reins, and they rolled down the street toward the mooring of their shore boat.

Inside the carriage Andre sat beside Mercedes, put his arm around her, and pulled her to him. Tears slid down her cheeks. She sat limply. He kissed the top of her head and ran his hand gently up and down her arm.

He thought about the hours she had spent with Bragg,

and he asked the question that he was afraid to ask. "What did he do to you?"

She sniffed and wiped her nose on her sleeve. She wiped the tears away with the tips of her fingers, sat up, and pulled away from him. She looked out the window, as if trying to remember.

"Someone hit me over the head by the patio fountain at the café," she began hoarsely. "Somehow they got me to the house next door. I only saw Bragg and one of his lackeys. He didn't hold me at the house long before he brought me here, tied me up, then left. He said he had to see some people before we left on the steamer tonight." She wiped away more tears. "He came back just before you arrived."

"Did he touch you?" He didn't know how to ask what the extent of the damage was. He placed his hand over hers.

She looked down at his hand. "He hit me once." She looked up then and into Andre's eyes.

"I think he was saving the good part for the steamer trip to Galveston." Her mouth twitched up into a crooked little smile.

Relief showed in Andre's eyes, in the way he caressed her hand, in how he gently wiped away more of her silent tears with his thumb.

Mercedes continued on. "He said we were going in Jack Lormand's private room. He brags a lot about his friendship with Lormand."

Andre swore. That bastard Lormand was playing both ends, tipping him off to Mercedes' whereabouts and aiding the abductor's escape. What was in this for him?

"Did he say anything else about Lormand?"

Mercedes tried to smooth the wrinkles from her dirt-streaked dress. She seemed not to hear him. Unsuccessful with the wrinkles, she pressed at the swelling on her check and lip. Andre took her hand down from her face.

"Mercedes," he said, softly. "Look at me."

Her eyes met his. The flesh around her eye was angry red and purple. Blood was caked on her lip. She murmured something.

Andre leaned closer to hear her.

"I'm going to get even with that jackass," she said in a determined whisper.

Andre smiled. The old Mercedes was coming back.

"Let me do the getting even," he said. "I think it's a more even match." He put his palm over her bruised cheek, and she closed her eyes.

She continued on in a whisper. "He said that Lormand controlled all the sugar and cotton trade out of New Orleans. He was the person to know." She slumped back against the seat. He knew she was tired from the strain of her captivity, weak with the relief that it was over.

"Did he say anything about Norton?" Andre asked.

Mercedes moved her head back and forth against the plush velvet of the seat, her eyes closed. "Nothing at all. Not one word. It's like the man doesn't even exist, and they are supposed to be partners."

"He might be dead, and I might be looking for a body and a murderer and a reason."

Mercedes eyes flew open. "We are looking," she said and sat up to look at him.

"We," she repeated. "We are in this together. She poked her finger in his chest and said, "You keep treating me like a piece of fluff." Her eyes were bright now, and her mouth was in a tight, puffy line. "You won't take me seriously. You leave me with Fabienne to keep me out of harms way and look what happens. I didn't take matters into my own hands and find my uncle and look what happens." She slapped the cushion of the seat. "Why won't you take me seriously?"

"It's obvious," Andre said, trying to keep the corners of his mouth from tipping up. He was glad to see the old Mercedes emerge once more. "You're a female, a member of the weaker sex, and you have to be protected."

"Sure, and that says it all." She clutched her head and winced. "This conversation is making my head ache worse." She blew out a breath of exasperation. "Captain Lafitte, I did not build one of the largest retail businesses in Galveston, Texas on recipes. I built it on good business sense and grit."

"Grit I agree with," said Andre, "and from what I see business sense had something to do with it, too." His mouth seemed determined to smile.

"This is not a laughing matter," she said, watching his smile. "Seldom have I seen you smile or anything close to a smile. Does my misfortune make you happy?"

Andre shook his head, grinning now. "I'm just glad to see your old spunk back."

"My spunk? Andre Lafitte, you are infuriating. I'm not a stupid person, but so far you have treated me like a stupid ninny. You wouldn't take me with you to New Orleans. I had to get myself on your ship in a very undignified manner but get myself on board I did. You wouldn't share any of the information you have on Norton, in whose whereabouts I have a vested interest since you say he handed over my assets to you. You dumped me with Fabienne to sightsee while you went off, and I got abducted. Now where are we?"

"Where?" asked Andre, who calmly watched Mt.

Wings of the Wind

Vesuvius erupting.

"You are so infuriating. I look like a bad excuse for two-bit actress, Norton is still missing, Lormand is working against us. Bragg will most certainly have a vendetta against us, and you aren't any closer to the bottom of this mess than you were the first day we met. You need my help. That's where we are."

The carriage had stopped. Bruno and Tito looked in spellbound, seeming to marvel at the volume emanating from the cab. Mercedes caught herself before she launched into her next round, looking startled to see the two men regarding her, their mouths agape. She snatched her finger away from the front of Andre's nose where it had been wagging with great vigor and worked at industriously smoothing her dress, reluctant to look at any of them.

"Excuse us, Captain," said Bruno, opening the carriage door. "But we've arrived. The boat is ready to leave for the ship whenever you say."

"Good," said Andre. "Shall we?" He indicated the open door to Mercedes, and she obliged by getting up unsteadily and making her way out the door with the help of Andre from behind and Bruno in front. Bruno supported her while Andre exited.

"Can you walk now?" Andre asked.

"Of course, I can walk," she said, indignantly, and took a step. Her legs gave out, and Andre, without ceremony, caught her as she went down and whisked her up in his arms.

"What should we do with the carriage?" asked Bruno.

"Leave it. The horse will find his way home. Lormand can figure out for himself why it returned without a thank you."

Mickey and Dickey were waiting in the boat. Tito

clambered down the dock ladder and turned to take Mercedes, as Andre handed her down. Bruno followed Andre into the boat, and they pushed off back to the *Wings of the Wind*. The unfinished conversation from the carriage hung in the air.

Chapter Sixteen

Andre personally strapped Mercedes into the landlubber chair and tugged on the ropes. "Heave away," he shouted up to the seamen on deck.

Mercedes held on tightly to the rope arms of the chair. She felt like a little girl on a swing under the tall live oak tree that graced the backyard at her home in Galveston in the days when she had a mother and a father, a home, and a brother. In the days before the world turned upside down.

As the chair inched up the smooth side of the *Wings of the Wind*, she again admired the grace of the ship as she looked down its sleek side to the stern. She savored the smell of the river that lapped against the clipper, the oak wood, the wet rope. Someday she vowed, she would own a ship like this beauty. She would ride on the wings of the wind, too.

Right now that was too much to think about. She longed to lie down and close her eyes. She needed to gather her strength. When she was weak and tired she made bad decisions. She couldn't afford any more bad decisions.

Tito reached out for her and pulled her delicately over the rail and onto the deck. Andre waited there. This time he didn't ask how her legs were. He scooped her up in his arms.

"Tito, take over," Andre said.

"Si, si, mi Capitán." He snapped a salute.

"Have the goods been loaded?"

Marjorie Thelen

"Si, mi Capitán, but we don't know where to go with everything. We don't know how we will make it to San Francisco with all this stuff.

"Mickey, help the men. I know you'll find space. Take Dickey with you and show him the galley so he can help Bruno. He can berth with you."

"Yes, boss," said Mickey, bowing. "This way, Dickey." Mickey motioned with a wave to the older Chinese man, who scurried after him.

"What are you staring at?" Andre scowled at Bruno.

Bruno lost his attempt to hide a grin. "I have never seen you barking orders with a beautiful woman in your arms."

"Aren't you needed in the galley?"

"Yep, you're right. Better get down there fast and see to feeding the men." He ambled off at an admirable speed for a man as big as a whale.

The crew, who had gathered round, got back to work, leaving Andre and Mercedes alone. Some had commented on how glad they were to see them back safely, and their concern touched Mercedes. She was beginning to feel a fondness for this unlikely bunch.

She looked at Andre, her face no more than a few inches from his. "I won't lecture anymore if that is what you are thinking."

Outside of a lock of hair that fell over his brow, he didn't look like he had been through a rescue ordeal. It impressed Mercedes how cool Andre stayed under pressure and how fast he could think on his feet. His arms held her securely. She wanted the moment to last forever.

"That would be kind, Miss Lawless. I'm not in the mood."

"Me, neither. I long to close my eyes for a little while."

Wings of the Wind

"That I can accommodate. I'll take you to your cabin and send in some water. You'll want a wash as well as a rest."

"I'd like that," she said, eyes heavy. She laid her head on his shoulder. "I can barely hold on anymore. I'm so tired."

They heard a yelling and scrambling, and Mercedes's head jerked up as Jamie appeared on deck, running toward them.

"I just heard you were back," he shouted. "Holy cow!" He skidded to a stop almost on top of them. "What happened to you?" He looked in horror at his sister's face.

"Accident," said Andre. "She's having trouble walking."

"I'm okay, Jamie," Mercedes said in a tired voice. "I need to rest, and then we'll talk."

"Jamie, fetch some water for your sister while I take her to her cabin."

"Aye, aye sir." Off he went in search of water.

"What a miraculous change in that boy." Mercedes wagged her head as much as comfort would allow. "Not long ago it was like pulling teeth to get him to pick up his room, and now he obeys your every command."

"He's a determined young man. He knows what he wants, and he understands the price he has to pay to get it."

With that he carried Mercedes down the stairs to her cabin. He shoved open the door with his boot and eased her onto the small bunk.

Jamie appeared behind him with a pitcher of water. He tried not to spill it, as the water sloshed precariously to and fro. Andre stepped out of the way, and Jamie deposited the pitcher on the bedside table.

"I'll be back in a second with basin, soap, and towel.

Bruno said he would send tea by in a few minutes."

Mercedes grabbed Jamie as he backed away and gave him a hug. "Thank you."

He looked at her face then hugged her back. "Boy, I'm glad to see you." He pulled away, looked up at Andre, backed out the room, and ran down the passageway.

Andre turned to leave, but Mercedes put her hand out and caught his. "I didn't thank you for rescuing me, and I'm sorry I lost my temper."

She regarded the hand she held, aware of the strength in that hand, of the calluses that spoke of hard work. "I meant it when I said we need to work together."

Andre turned her hand over palm up and studied the delicate lines of the fingers. He rubbed his thumb along her fingers as if he were savoring the smooth, soft feel of her skin.

"Rest," he said. "We'll talk later."

He bent, raised her palm to his lips, and kissed the tender mound of flesh below her thumb. She watched his lips meet her palm, felt the warmth of his breath, aware again of the tapestry he was weaving around her, and knew she was getting hopelessly lost in it.

* * * * *

Andre strode about the deck calling orders to his men, consulting on river conditions, the winds, looking over the sailing chart. He had a ship and cargo to sail to San Francisco, but he couldn't leave New Orleans without finding Norton, and he had to make another trip to Galveston to drop off Mercedes Lawless. He certainly didn't trust to put her on a steamship to Galveston, and he didn't want to. He wanted her with him. But there was a problem. He made a point of not letting personal stuff get in the way of business, and Mercedes was now personal stuff. It was interfering with business.

He had heard the call of the siren like Ulysses, a siren with a bad temper and bewitching lavender blue eyes. Was that siren going to lure him on the rocks and smash his ship, his dreams, his life? This particular siren threatened him more than any storm he had ever battled at sea.

There was a good possibility Norton was dead. Did he care? He didn't need to spend time looking for a murderer. He wasn't sure he wanted to open Pandora's box any further. The lid was up too far already, and nasty things were flying out.

There was the unsettled matter of the bet. There was the question of what Jack Lormand was up to. There was the idiot Bragg. There was the problem of Miss Mercedes Lawless and his feelings for her. Feelings. That was the real threat, and he didn't want to think about where that would lead him.

When things were well in hand on deck, he turned the command over to Tito and went below.

Mickey was behind him as he entered the cabin, carrying a tray with a bottle of Madeira and two glasses upon it. He set down the tray in its usual spot on the serving table. Andre glanced at the tray.

"Two glasses?"

"Yes, boss." Mickey grinned. "Maybe Missy Mercedes thirsty, too. Maybe she need something stronger than tea. Rough day. You want her come join you?"

Andre walked over to the table and poured himself a tall glass without looking at Mickey. "I need to do some thinking."

"What to think, boss? We can't leave till Missy

Mercedes know where uncle is. Maybe him dead."

Andre took a long drink and regarded Mickey. "I think he is dead, and I don't think he is her uncle. I'm not exactly sure what is going on and why. I'm not sure I want to know. We're scheduled to sail to San Francisco, and we're late."

"Dickey say Jack Lormand involved in opium trade from China. Nasty people involved in opium."

"I know," said Andre. "What I don't know is what motivates Lormand short of greed, which he has in long supply. He is king of New Orleans with his legitimate business interests. He has everything, but everything doesn't seem to be enough. Power and money become a game with people like Jack Lormand."

Andre ran a hand through his hair. He hoped he wouldn't turn out like Lormand.

"Fake uncle connected to Lormand. Maybe game get too hot and he back out." Mickey stood by the door, his hands tucked in his sleeves.

"Maybe." Andre shook his head and looked out the cabin window to someplace far away. "When I won the Lavender Emporium, I never thought it would come attached to a woman like Mercedes Lawless."

"Destiny call you to Galveston, boss," Mickey said with a twinkle in his eyes. "Destiny was wind blew you there. Destiny has many names. This one named Mercedes."

Andre gave a half smile. "Mickey the philosopher and oracle. What do you see in your crystal ball?"

"Crystal ball says two people meant for each other. Mickey has eyes that see these things. Eyes not so dim can't see. Written in your eyes, on your face. Hers, too."

Andre said nothing, uncomfortable with the direction of the conversation.

Wings of the Wind

"Besides, boss. You get old. Need to settle down, raise family."

"Old?" Andre walked over to the mirror and examined his face. No gray hair. A few wrinkles around the eyes from the sun. Two deep vertical lines between his eyes.

Mickey watched his boss peering into the mirror. "Old not have to do with wrinkles and gray hair. You act funny. Think you not satisfied with success. You not man need more success. You need woman now. Family."

"Family?" Andre walked over to his desk and sat down. "I'm not the family kind of man. I can't give up sailing. This is my life. I don't know anything else. A woman like Mercedes Lawless wouldn't be content with a man who's gone all the time. She's too beautiful. She would soon be looking elsewhere."

"Not every woman like your mother," Mickey said, softly.

The depth of Mickey Chinfatt's understanding of people amazed Andre once again. He had nothing to offer in response. Mickey was right. Andre's fear of commitment had everything to do with the beautiful mother who attached herself to whatever man was there with the most money. She was barely aware of two young sons who needed her love more than anything.

Mickey broke into his reverie once more. "Take Missy with you. She love travel and sea."

"How do you know?" Andre looked at Mickey suspiciously.

"Can see when she look at ship. When she walk deck. She tell me she long to get away from Galveston. See world."

Andre had seen that look in Mercedes's eyes. Taking Mercedes along hadn't occurred to him. Maybe she would like that. She was a businesswoman. She might be a help to him. Didn't she keep saying she could help him? He stopped his glass in mid-air. He was thinking of her as a partner. A business partner perhaps, certainly not a marriage partner. He shook his head to free himself of that thought. This was dangerous thinking.

Mickey watched Andre. "We sail? Or find Norton?"

Andre took long pull of his drink and gave his attention to Mickey's question. "I'll think it over. Better warm the water and bring in the bathtub so I can think better."

Mickey turned to go. Andre called after him. "Don't disturb the lady. She needs rest."

Mickey bowed and went off to fetch the Captain's bath.

Andre looked at the second glass on the table. His life so far had been one of a single glass on a tray. What would it be like to have two glasses? To have Mercedes' beautiful eyes looking back into his for the rest of his life? He didn't know if he were ready for that yet or if he ever would be.

* * * * *

Mercedes lay on her bunk drifting in and out of dreams laced with Andre Lafitte. She became aware of the sounds of the ship and listened. It was riding gently at anchor. With a start she realized they weren't moving. Did that mean they weren't sailing for Galveston? The cabin was dark. She didn't know how long she had slept, and she didn't know what time it was. She didn't hear activity on deck and decided to go up and have a look, if she could get her feet to move.

She gingerly pushed up on one elbow. Her head still

Wings of the Wind

ached. At least it wasn't pounding. She felt the cut on her lip with her tongue. She didn't taste blood and was glad for that. The swelling seemed to have gone down. She sat up, steadied herself with her hands, and waited for her head to come back into balance.

Before she lay down, she had bathed which had helped to restore her spirits. True to his word, Bruno had sent Jamie with a bracing pot of tea, which she had savored sip by sip. Jamie had not stayed to talk, saying he would be back in the morning to bring her breakfast.

She had managed to get out of her beautiful but soiled frock. She mourned its appearance. She hoped that with a bit of touch up and brush she could restore it to its original beauty. She sat in her linen shift. The night air was cool on her skin, a welcome relief from the oppressive heat of the day, a welcome relief from the entire day before.

She stood up slowly putting her hand on the wall for support. One leg up, then two. Standing on two legs, she tried a step then another. In that fashion she made her way to the door. Cool air slipped between the slats in the louvered door. It caressed her warm body. She paused by the door to steady herself, then opened the door a few inches and peeked out.

She saw no one in the passage, so she stepped out. Her feet and hands no longer felt like they were made of pins and needles. She was walking slowly, but she was walking. At the bottom of the stairs to the deck she paused, listening. She heard only the sighing of the breeze in the rigging.

Cautiously, she climbed the stairs putting first one foot then two to a step, holding tight to the rail. Then she was on deck, the feel of the wood smooth under her bare feet. She moved to the rail and looked out over dark water.

Marjorie Thelen

The stars extended down to the horizon, so clear was the night. Countless beautiful stars. Peace washed over Mercedes in waves, cleansing, calming waves. The wonder of the Creation touched her. She inhaled deeply and breathed out a long breath. She touched the rail, moved her hands across its smoothness. Everything about the ship was clean, trim, economical. Built for beauty and speed, *Wings of the Wind* lived up to all expectations.

Her shift moved in the breeze, and Mercedes enjoyed the freedom of the breeze cooling her body. She enjoyed the feeling of wearing only a shift, the cool air rising between her legs. She lifted her long curls and let the breeze cool the back of her neck. She shook out her hair and ran her fingers through it, freeing the tangled curls. She inhaled deeply again and breathed out slowly.

What would it be like to sail as far as San Francisco? They said that a clipper could do the trip in three months. Three months sailing further and further south night and day, then through the cold Straits of Magellan and up, up, up to San Francisco. It was far from Galveston, Texas. How she would love to go.

The breeze picked up her curls one by one and played with them, then let them drift down to her shoulders again. It molded the shift first to one side of her body then the other. Still she stood there, enjoying the night, the breeze, the sea, and her dreams. She felt life and strength flooding back into her body, into her spirit. She stretched out her arms to the heavens and gave thanks for her rescue.

Andre floated into her thoughts. Her feelings were more than a casual interest in a man. She was falling in love. It happened the first moment she stepped into his cabin and looked up to him standing there, eyes unreadable. He was someone she could hold on to and never let go. She needed to stop kidding herself. She was in love, and she never thought it would happen to her. She was the woman who was never going to marry. Did she want that now after meeting this man? He was someone she wouldn't mind seeing on the pillow next to her everyday for the rest of her life. What shocking thoughts. She delighted in them.

* * * * *

Andre stood on the deck above watching Mercedes. She was gazing out in the distance, her hands resting on the rail, leaning into it, the breeze playing with her garment, her hair. He had not been able to sleep. So he availed himself of the same lovely night, as had Mercedes. He watched, not wanting to interrupt, merely savoring the sight of her. His breath caught in his throat when she lifted her arms skyward. The freedom in that movement aroused him, made him want to press her to him.

Mercedes turned in his direction, looked up, and saw him. She didn't move. She didn't look away. He left his post, walked down the steps toward her, beckoned by the siren's call. He stopped several feet away. He saw her tremble and shiver as if the night has suddenly turned cold. He closed the distance between them and took her in his arms. He held her close, enveloped her like a cocoon. Gradually her trembling stopped. She rested her hands on his chest. He could feel her tenderness, her softness, the outline of her body through the thin shift, her soft breath on his chest.

When had it started he wondered. When had he started caring about this woman? When had he started thinking more about her than about himself? When had he started needing her?

He kissed the top of her head and caught the fragrance of lavender. She titled back her head, and he ran his thumb gently along her bruised cheek. He kissed the bruises around her eye, healing them. He kissed her puffy lip lightly, tenderly, healing it. He pulled her closer. She slid her arms up and around his neck. He lowered his lips and kissed her. She responded, and then they were lost in the kiss, in the sensation of their bodies touching.

Breathless she pulled away and lifted her hand to trace her fingers through his hair, touch his ear and trace its outline. Tentative, then with more assurance, she traced the strong line of his jaw. Her fingers slipped to his lips to trace the fullness of them. He caught her finger with his teeth, teased it with his lips, pulled on it gently with his mouth. With her other hand she pulled him to her and kissed him.

His hands glided down her back, over her hips, caressing them, savoring them. He pulled her into him. She pressed against him, moving with him, back and forth, tentative then harder, following the rhythm of his body, like a dance, the dance of love.

He swept her up into his arms and carried her to his cabin, his bare feet making no sound on the resting ship. He pushed open his cabin door with his shoulder, moved across the room to his bunk, stopping to lower her to the floor. He eased her white linen shift up over her head as he came up. She stood nude before him, unashamed, breathing deeply. He took in all of her. Her eyes were full and wide and trusting. He did not want to betray that trust.

He pulled off his shirt, and it dropped to the floor. Unbuttoning his britches, he let them drop. She took in his nakedness, and he saw admiration in her eyes. He pulled

Wings of the Wind

her into him their flesh pressed together, her arms around his waist. A moan of pleasure escaped her lips or was that his?

He lifted her chin, lowered his mouth to hers, and with kisses said with his mouth all the feeling that was in his heart. His lips left hers and traveled down her neck. The heat of her response and her longing drove him deeper into desire for her.

He picked her up and laid her on the bunk. She lay against the pillow, her body outlined against the white sheets. He eased himself on top of her, parting her legs with his knee and her thighs opened, welcoming him. She pulled his face to hers, and he surrendered to her, let her kiss him, love him. She caressed his hair, his face, his arms like there was no other moment. She shifted and gently pushed him back into the bunk as if she were aware of her power over him. He lay still, relishing her touch, letting them both drown in the moment. For a long time they explored and enjoyed each other until desire became unbearable. Arching against him, she joined his rhythm. A smile curved her lips. Their eyes opened, and they gazed into each other's souls. They didn't speak, as if to speak would unravel the tapestry that had woven around them during the night.

Marjorie Thelen

Chapter Seventeen

Andre awoke before dawn in a tangle of sheets, Mercedes' arm draped across him. He could hear activity on deck. He gazed upon the sleeping woman beside him. They had not spoken during the whole of their lovemaking, only when she called out his name. He wondered that he had been so open with such a woman as she was. Mercedes' smooth thigh was tangled in the sheets, and he saw faint smudges of blood on that lovely thigh. She breathed softly. Her lips were now swollen with the kisses of lovemaking. He moved, and her eyes fluttered open. She lay motionless watching him. Her hand reached for his cheek. He kissed it, and they began again, unaware that the rest of the world existed.

* * * * *

"This changes things," he said sometime later.

Mercedes nodded, unwilling to speak, looking deep into the warm softness in his eyes. Not trusting her voice, she said nothing. Her body had said it for her. She could not put into words her love for him. It seemed too fragile a thing.

They lay warm and relaxed together. "You didn't sail for Galveston," she said, softly.

Wings of the Wind

"No, we stay to find Norton today. I need to settle that mystery. Then I'll take you to Galveston and sail on for San Francisco."

Those words were like ice water thrown on Mercedes feelings for him. That was it. The words tore the beautiful tapestry that their lovemaking had woven. He had not included her in the voyage. There was no future for them. She was a fool to think there was.

She pushed off him, sat up, and grabbed for her shift on the floor. She noticed the smudges on her thigh and blushed for letting herself take the chance.

He caught the hand that fumbled with the shift. "Mercedes, I . . ."

"Don't say anything else," she said. "I knew what I was doing. It was a night of pleasure. I believe we both enjoyed it." She glared him to see if she were correct in her assessment.

"Is it just that easy to walk away?"

"It seems to be for you. You're going to sail out of my life." She bit her lip. She could not let him see how much she cared.

He cursed, threw off the sheets, and sat up. "I'm sorry I got you into this. I didn't expect to find anyone like you on the other end of that card game. It was a lark that I went to check on my winnings when we got to Galveston."

"So I am a lark?"

"No, of course not. I mean I just didn't expect this to happen." He gestured to the sheets, running his hand back through his tousled hair. "I mean I wanted it to happen, but . . ." He threw up his hands and looked at her. "You could be pregnant."

"Yes, I know," she said in a whisper. "Now is a good time to think about that, isn't it?"

"You didn't tell me you were a virgin."

"Was I supposed to put a sign on my forehead? It's your fault you listened to those lies about me."

She tugged her hand free and pulled the shift down over her head, glad for its protection. She looked around for the washstand.

"It's over there." Andre pointed to the washstand in the corner, his frustration etched in the taut lines of his face.

The reality of morning was upon them.

She moved to the stand, wet the cloth, and washed her face. She heard Andre pulling on his britches and shirt. She groaned. Her clothes were in her room. Now what was she going to do?

"I'll get your clothes," Andre said, reading her thoughts. He left the room without another word.

She fought back the tears that threatened to spill down her cheeks. "I can't breakdown. I'm not some ninny. I knew what I was doing," she said aloud. But her heart ached, a physical sensation in her chest, and she rubbed the spot between her breasts to ease the ache.

A small round mirror in a brass frame hung over the chest-of-drawers, fixed into the wall. She moved to the mirror and peered at herself. The face was the same except for the bruises, but the heart and body weren't. He was right, this changed things. It changed everything for her.

What was she to make of him? He cannonballs into her life with some wild story, won't let her help him, rebuffs her, treats her like a piece of fluff, rescues her, then makes love to her. Wasn't that what it was? Or maybe a man didn't make love. Maybe he just made lust.

She ran her hands through her curls, trying to tame them, but they were hopelessly tangled. She spied a brush lying atop the chest-of-drawers, took it in hand, and started brushing, wincing as she tried to brush out the tangles.

How could they spend such hours of bliss in lovemaking and then feel so miserable after a few spoken words? How could that beauty be destroyed so quickly? She wondered if she would ever understand a man. Last night had been magic. She had felt no hesitation. No holding back. She had at last found the man she could give herself to. But he didn't feel the same way for her. She had felt his caring, and she thought she felt his love, but she must have been mistaken.

She brushed and brushed the tangled hair taking her disappointment and frustration out on it. Andre came back into the room as she was braiding it.

He laid her dress and petticoats on the bed and then came over to stand behind her. He looked at her face in the mirror then turned her around to face him.

"I'm going ashore."

"I'm going with you."

"No, you are not," he said, enunciating each word carefully. "It's too dangerous. I can't be looking back over my shoulder trying to protect you and find out what is going on. You've been abducted once. Bragg will try again because now he is mad. I still don't know where Norton is."

"I can help you."

"You already were the bait and that didn't work. You can help me best by staying here so I don't have to worry about your safety. Do you understand? What do I have to say to get that through that beautiful head of yours? Don't make me tie you up."

Mercedes said nothing, her eyes downcast.

Andre's hands rested on her shoulders, and he bent down to bring his eyes level with hers so that she had to look at him.

"Trust me. In your world in Galveston you called the shots. This isn't your world. This is the world of men without scruples. They are bigger, stronger, and more ruthless. You've had only a taste of it. You don't know how to operate in such a world. I do."

Mercedes nodded, grudgingly.

"Does that mean you understand and that you won't try to follow me?"

She nodded again. She didn't like it. But he was right. She kept bungling things, making it worse for him.

"I'll stay here as you wish." She placed her hands on his waist. "But promise me one thing."

Andre looked at her. "Within reason."

"Be careful."

He smiled. "That I promise I will do." He gathered her into a close embrace. "Mercedes, I'm sorry about the argument. I'm not good with words sometimes."

"Me, too." She sighed a deep, heartfelt sigh.

"I've got to go. I'm taking Bruno. Mickey and Tito will stay here." He didn't say to guard you, but she knew that was what he was thinking. "Jamie will stay, too. I suggest you rest. You look like you could use it." He kissed her lightly on the lips. He got a tiny smile back from her.

Mercedes watched as he opened a drawer in the chest of drawers and selected a long, lethal looking knife from his collection. He strapped on a belt and put the knife in it. He pulled on a vest, slipped another knife inside. Her eyes widened.

"This is how I am careful," he said to answer the question in her eyes. He didn't answer the other unasked question in her eyes. What about us?

He slammed the drawer shut. "Mickey will bring you

tea. You can stay in my cabin today, if you'd like. With that he left, and he didn't look back.

* * * * *

Andre ran smack into Mickey, who was listening outside the door.

"You know to take her some tea then," he said to the small Chinaman.

"Yes, boss," Mickey grinned. "Right away."

Andre nodded and walked along the passage with Mickey on his heels.

"We sail today?"

"Maybe," said Andre. "My business in town might not take long at all."

"Yes, boss," said Mickey. "I take good care of Missy."

"Tea will be fine." Andre stopped and looked at him. "She needs to rest. She was through a lot yesterday."

Mickey grinned. "Yes, sir."

Andre narrowed his eyes.

"Boss look very chipper this morning."

A corner of Andre's mouth twisted up. "Get her the tea, will you, and something to eat." He walked off shaking his head. There were never any secrets on a ship.

"Tell Bruno to meet me up on deck." Andre called back over his shoulder. "We're going to town, just him and me."

On deck Andre sought out Tito who was on the upper deck talking to two of the seamen. Spike squatted calmly on his shoulder.

"Tito," called Andre.

"Si, si, mi Capitán," said Tito, coming over to stand before Andre, Spike bobbing beside his ear.

"Bruno and I will go ashore. You will make ready to sail. We'll be away as soon as we get back."

"Si, mi Capitán. I will tell Toadie to row you in."

"Good. He can guard the boat while we attend to business."

"Avast, buckaroos, avast," Spike screeched.

Mickey ran up with a mug of tea for the Captain. Jamie, wearing an unhappy face, was right behind him.

"Morning captain, sir," said Jamie, saluting. "Have you seen my sister, sir? Is she better? I went to see her this morning, but she wasn't in her cabin, sir."

"Morning, Jamie lad. Your sister is better. I told her she could rest in my cabin today since I won't be there. It will be more comfortable."

Andre knew the boy would learn soon enough where his sister had spent the night, but this was not the time to tell him. Besides he wasn't sure what to tell the teenage brother of the woman he had just seduced.

Jamie breathed an audible sigh of relief. "I was afraid something bad had happened to her."

Andre studied the boy. "She's all right." He'd like to think something good happened to her. "You might look in on her later, but I would recommend rest right now as the best curative. She had a tough day yesterday."

Jamie returned Andre's serious gaze. "Yes, sir. I'll do that."

Andre downed the tea as they lowered the shore boat. Bruno joined him, knives bristling.

Andre gave him a once over. "Maybe you should conceal some of the knives. You might give us away."

Bruno looked himself over. "I guess I over did it." He slid one or two deeper into their pockets. "I brought the pistols."

Wings of the Wind

"Give them to Toadie just in case," said Andre, handing the mug back to Mickey. "Let's go."

Bruno climbed down the ladder after Andre. "What's the plan?" he asked, as they settled into the boat. Toadie cast off, turning toward shore.

"Find Norton."

"So far we've not had a lot of luck."

Andre watched the distance lengthen as they drew away from the ship. "We call on Jack Lormand. He may be more helpful this time."

* * * * *

It was still early morning when Andre and Bruno climbed the ladder on the wharf. The workers were arriving to start another day of loading and unloading ships.

"Let's walk to Jackson Square," Andre said to Bruno. "We'll try Jack Lormand at his club first since that's his base of operation."

They moved through the throngs of men, coming to work at the docks. Wagons passed by loaded with crates, bales, bulging burlap bags, produce, squawking chickens, and other livestock.

They crossed Jackson Square, thankful for the shade of the live oaks. They bounded up the marble steps of Lormand's club. Andre again presented his card and asked for Lormand.

The doorman recognized Captain Lafitte. "Mr. Lormand is having breakfast in his private dining room. I'll announce you."

Andre and Bruno waited as the man walked off. He soon returned and indicated that they should follow him.

Marjorie Thelen

The doorman showed them to the same room where Andre had met Lormand before, but now there was a small table in the middle of the room set for breakfast. Lormand was breakfasting alone, reading the newspaper.

He rose as they came in. "Good to see you again Lafitte," he said and sounded as if he meant it.

Andre nodded. He gestured between Bruno and Lormand by way of introduction. Lormand acknowledged Bruno with a nod, looking him over.

"Will you join me for coffee and breakfast? I asked the doorman to bring more chairs."

"Coffee," said Andre.

The doorman arrived and placed two more chairs at the table. A waiter arrived with place settings and coffee. Andre and Bruno took the seats offered, and the waiter poured for them.

Lormand folded the newspaper and placed it on a side table. He looked at Andre. "You're out early this morning. Did you find Miss Lawless?" He took a sip of his coffee and sat back.

"We found her tied up in Jeffrey Norton's warehouse. She was in Derek Bragg's care."

Lormand raised his eyebrows.

"I understand Norton and Bragg work for you," Andre said, watching Lormand's face. Bruno sat to Andre's right facing the door.

Lormand assessed the younger man, as if he knew bluffing and stalling would not work with Andre Lafitte.

"That's right," Lormand said. "We're in business together, mostly cotton and sugar brokering."

"I heard it went further than that."

"What's your point?" asked Lormand, electing not to answer the question.

"I'm not real interested in what you're brokering. What I don't like is when innocent people get beat around."

"Miss Lawless?" Lormand asked.

Andre nodded once. "I have a problem with that. I'd appreciate if you would impress upon your man Bragg the importance of not trying to make a lady do something against her will. Tell him to stay away from her. He doesn't impress me as the brains in the outfit. He might listen to you."

"Maybe it wasn't against her will," Lormand suggested with a sly grin.

Andre's arm flashed across the table and grabbed Lormand's neck cloth. He yanked him up. "The lady was tied up," Andre said into Lormand's straining face. "That indicates to me that if she had had an option she would not have been there. She's got a swollen face this morning where the oaf hit her while she was tied up." He released Lormand with a shove that rocked him back into his chair.

Bruno looked back and forth between the two, placidly sipping his coffee. He reached into his vest and pulled out one of his blades, placing it in front of him on the table so that Lormand couldn't miss it.

Lormand straightened his neck cloth and smoothed back his hair. "I see. The picture is clearer to me now. I will speak to Bragg." He took a piece of toast and started buttering it, restoring his composure.

"What else?" Lormand asked when Andre made no attempt to leave.

"Where is Jeffrey Norton? He hasn't been seen in the last few days. Bragg didn't know where he was. I thought maybe you would."

Lormand toyed with the butter knife. "Let me ask you a question first."

"I'm listening."

"Have you thought over selling the Silver Slipper to me?"

Here it is, thought Andre, the price to be paid for information on Norton. "I've thought about it. I don't know if I'm ready to sell yet. I've been thinking about it."

"I heard you discussed the sale with your lawyer yesterday and were serious about selling."

Jack Lormand's New Orleans was like living on a ship. No secrets.

"This means that if I'm willing to sell to you, you know where Norton is and if I'm not, you don't. Is that it?" asked Andre, slouching back in his chair.

Lormand put down the butter knife and nodded once almost imperceptibly. "I know where he is, but I want to buy the Silver Slipper."

Andre assessed the older man across from him. Lormand didn't need one more successful business. This was a game to a man like Lormand. It was a power play, the kind of game Lormand liked best. If he had the Silver Slipper, he had access to the dirty secrets of some of the highest-ranking men in New Orleans society. But he probably had that already. Why did he want the Silver Slipper so badly? Andre wanted the answer to that question.

"Why the Silver Slipper? Why is it important to you? You don't need more money."

Lormand without hesitation said, "It's for Fabienne. I'm not getting any younger, and she needs security. She's a good business woman and would treat the girls decently." Lormand looked embarrassed to be admitting that he cared about anyone.

"I see. The wife and kids are all taken care of, so you

want to make sure your mistress is set. That's noble of you, Lormand. How do I know that Fabienne will benefit?"

"I will specify in our agreement that the establishment goes to Fabienne."

Andre thought that one over. "I'll have my lawyer draw up a letter of intent."

"When do you sail?"

"It depends when I find Norton."

"He's staying at the Silver Slipper. He knew you were in town, so he's laying low there." Lormand watched Andre's reaction.

"Son-of-a-bitch," Andre said, softly. He pounded his fist on the table. He was there yesterday. He pressed his lips together in a tight line. Some fur would fly when he found out who had helped Norton hide right under his nose.

Andre pushed himself up from the chair, inclined his head to Lormand. "I appreciate the information. I'll see to the letter of intent."

"Have it sent round before you leave, will you?"

Andre nodded his agreement.

"Captain Lafitte," said Lormand, "I trust the price will be reasonable."

"If it isn't?"

"I'll buy it anyway." A slow smile spread across Lormand's face.

A rueful one tugged at the Andre's mouth. "Thanks for the coffee. Come, Bruno. It's getting late."

Bruno slid his blade back into his vest and stood.

Andre hesitated then walked round the table to Lormand and offered his hand. Lormand stood and shook.

It was then that Andre detected Lormand's weak grip and the sallowness of his complexion. His eyes had a yellowish cast, and there were dark circles under them. Andre understood Lormand's need for the quick purchase of the Silver Slipper. He didn't expect to be around much longer.

Chapter Eighteen

The Silver Slipper occupied a large two-story house that sat at the end of a quiet street at the edge of the French Quarter. It was in good repair with bright yellow stucco walls and Napoleon blue shutters set in white trim. The shutters that faced the street were closed at this time of day. A black filigree ironwork balcony intertwined with bougainvillea adorned with bright fuchsia flowers graced the second floor and a matching gate secured the heavily curtained French doors of the main entrance on the first floor. Hanging baskets of feathery green ferns hung from the second floor balcony.

A narrow alleyway separated the Silver Slipper from the building next door, and it was into this alleyway that Andre and Bruno disappeared. Andre led them to a back entrance of the establishment, one he had used many times in his childhood. It opened into what used to be his mother's rooms, now his personal quarters, the ones he used when in town on business and that were off limits to the employees. His was the only key to the outside door.

He opened first the black iron filigree gate covering the entrance and then the door to the interior. He gestured Bruno inside.

Since it was an early hour of the day for such an establishment, the building and its inhabitants lay in slumber. Andre unlocked the desk positioned against one wall of the room. He sat down and pulled out paper and pen and scratched out a message to his lawyer about the sale of the Silver Slipper and delivery of a letter of intent to Lormand. He handed it to Bruno.

"Take this to my lawyer, Vincent St. Claire. He's on Jackson Square a few doors down from Lormand's club. St. Claire will be in by now. Don't waste any time.

"Got it," said Bruno. "Sure you don't need any help here?"

Andre shook his head. "When I find Norton, I'll find the person who has been hiding him. I don't see a problem."

"Aye, Captain," said Bruno. He handed Andre a pistol then disappeared out the door they had entered.

Andre turned back to the desk and pulled open a small drawer. He found the key he needed in the false floor of the drawer. Outside his quarters a narrow stairway led up to the upper floor and from there to the small attic chamber under the eaves that Andre occupied as a boy with his brother. Since it had been used for storage for years, or so he had assumed, he had failed to consider it as a hide-away. If his hunch were correct, it was in use again.

He crept up two flights of steps until he was outside the door to the attic room. He inserted the key quietly in the lock and turned. The door swung open to a dimly lit room.

The room, storage no longer, was simply furnished with an iron bed painted white standing against a red brick wall. A nightstand with pitcher and basin stood beside the bed along with a straight back chair with clothes heaped upon it. A dormer window on the wall to the side of the bed threw light on two forms lying entwined on the bed

Wings of the Wind

and covered with a white lace bed spread. Soft snores issued from beneath the spread.

Andre moved to within a few feet of the end of the bed. He pulled the pistol from his waistband and cocked it. The snoring stopped, and a hairy arm emerged from under the lace. A woman's sigh escaped from the smaller form.

"Don't go for the gun, Norton. You're a dead man if you do," Andre said and yanked hard on the lace spread.

A female scream pierced the room. A rosy derriere surfaced on the bed as the spread fell away.

Naked limbs flashed, scrambled, and grabbed for covering from the jumble of sheets on the bed. Andre kept his eyes on the hands of the man in the bed who seemed to be trying to cover his ladylove.

"Don't shoot. I'm not armed," said the man, sitting up in the sheets that barely covered his lower half. The lady in question pulled the sheet over her head but not before Andre saw the blond curls he suspected would be there.

"I'm glad you could come by and take advantage of my hospitality," said Andre with a look around the room. "Nice arrangement."

The man smiled a crooked grin. "Mind if I finish my cheroot?" he asked, reaching for a half-smoked stub on the nightstand.

"Don't let me stop you. Just don't do anything stupid," said Andre. "While you're doing that and only if it's not too much trouble, I'd appreciate your getting up and getting dressed. We're going on a trip."

"Oh?" said the man, lighting up the cheroot. "Where might that be?"

"To see your niece."

The man smiled another crooked grin. "Have you met her?"

"I have. She's a charming young woman. She didn't know she had an uncle."

The man laughed. "Of course not. Her mother never told her." He expelled a long plume of smoke.

"What's your real name?

"Norton."

"Right." Andre, in no mood for games, gestured to the heap of clothes. "Get into your clothes because we're leaving."

Norton nodded and pulled back the sheets. A whimper emanated from the other side of the bed.

"Goes for you, too, Tess," Andre said to the pile of sheets. "Get up and get your clothes on. Pack your bags, too. You need to look for a new job and a new place to live."

"No," screamed the banshee that emerged from the sheets, breasts modestly covered, hair flying.

Norton was out of bed pulling on trousers and shirt with his cheroot hanging from his lips, watching the show.

"You don't have any say in this place anymore," she said with a shriek. "Kitty will not hear of letting me go. You'll see. You aren't going to push me out like you did before."

"Kitty won't be the madam here anymore. Fabienne will be, and I don't recall her having any fondness for you." Andre heard footsteps clattering up the stairs and moved away from the door still holding the gun on Norton.

"What's going on here?" asked the full-figured woman in a bright blue floor length wrapper trimmed in matching boa feathers who burst into the room. "Who is screaming?"

She surveyed the room, the occupants, and the gun. Right behind her was a huge black man, taking in the same scene. She recognized the figure with the gun. "Captain

Wings of the Wind

Lafitte. How are you? What are you doing, holding a gun like that?"

"Hello, Kitty." Andre nodded in her direction. "I came by to give this gentleman a lift to my ship. It seems he took up residence here for a few days."

She looked at Norton, then at the woman in the bed. She narrowed her eyes. "What are you doing up here?" She cast her eyes about the room again. "Who fixed this up like this? Have you been turning tricks on the side again, not telling me?"

Kitty's hands were on her hips as she advanced toward the woman in the bed.

The woman in the bed shrank back. "You stay away from me. You don't come near me," she said and screamed, as Kitty grabbed a handful of hair and hauled her out of the bed. Woman and sheets tumbled to the floor in an ungracious pile.

"Get up," Kitty said. "Elijah, remove this bundle of trash from the room."

"Yes, ma'am," said the big black man. "Be my pleasure." He looked in Andre's direction and nodded.

"Elijah." Andre nodded back in acknowledgment. The man gave him a salute and an enormous grin.

"Yes, sir, Captain. Good to see you again."

"You, too. Help her pack then call a public carriage. Get her out of here and see she doesn't come back."

"Yes, sir."

"Have my carriage brought around, will you?"

"Yes, sir."

The black man scooped up the entire shrieking bundle and carried it from the room accompanied by screams of "Let me go. You can't do this to me. He didn't pay me."

Norton stood by the bed, dressed and finishing his

cheroot. He stumped it out in the washbasin. "I thought maybe if I laid low till you left town by the time I saw you again you might have cooled off."

Andre glanced at him. "I haven't cooled off. Your bad luck."

He turned to Kitty. "Tell me you didn't know about this little love nest up here."

She shook her head. "I knew something was wrong because revenue was off. But I couldn't put my finger on it. I don't know how long she's been using this room to conduct her own business." She nodded her head toward Norton. "Who's this?"

"A man I've been looking for ever since he lost a card game to me. Have you ever see him before?"

Kitty squinted at Norton. "I believe I have. He's a customer here sometimes. I didn't know he had this thing going with Tess." She looked at the Captain with clear, honest eyes. "Really I didn't know."

Andre studied her. "All right, I believe you. Fabienne will be taking over. Do you have any problem with that?"

"No, Captain, I don't. Fabienne's a good woman. We always got along well."

"Then you get to stay. I need to be going. You'll be hearing from Fabienne. Lead the way down the steps," he said to Kitty. She lost no time starting down the stairs.

He motioned with the gun to Norton. "Now you. I'll follow you down the stairs. If you feel like trying to escape this time, think twice. I'd just as soon shoot you as look at you. Since no one knows you are here, we could bury you in the basement. Nobody would be any the wiser."

Norton took to the stairs at once.

Andre pulled the door shut behind him. He would have to remember to tell Fabienne about the room upstairs,

Wings of the Wind

in case the other girls got any ideas.

Bruno was waiting in the main parlor watched by several ladies in various stages of undress, who peeked from the hallway. He was eyeing them appreciatively. He rose when Andre came into the room behind Norton.

"I see you got him," said Bruno.

Andre nodded. He saw the wide-eyed look of the girls focused on his gun, and he slipped it back into his waistband. "Let's go."

"The carriage is waiting in front," said Bruno, looking with longing at the girls.

Andre caught the look and shoved him gently toward the door. "Watch Norton, man. The girls will be waiting for you when we get back."

"Yeah, "said Bruno, "but that won't be till next year." He grabbed Norton by the upper arm and hauled him out of the room, grumbling about the unfairness of life.

Andre pulled the front door shut and looked round for Elijah, who was standing by the carriage, holding the door for Bruno and Norton. Andre motioned for Elijah to join him.

"Tell Fabienne what happened here. I won't get to see her because we're sailing. She knew I was looking for Norton. Tell her that Mercedes is safe with me. My lawyer will be contacting her about the Silver Slipper. She's going to take over. I know you'll appreciate that." He clapped his hand on the big man's shoulder.

Elijah nodded. "Consider it good as done, Captain, sir."

"You'll need to decide if you want to stay on with Fabienne. I'm sure she'll be glad to have you. The offer is still good for you to join us on our next voyage."

"Yes, sir. I think I'd like that."

Marjorie Thelen

Andre lowered his voice. "That attic room might be of use to help some of your friends get away on the Underground Railroad. Talk to Fabienne."

Elijah smiled his big, kind smile, acknowledging with a nod his understanding. "We'll see you then, Captain, long about this time next year."

"If not before. *Wings of the Wind* might set a record, if we ever get going." Andre held out his hand, and they shook.

"Take care of this place. Contact St. Claire, if you need something or need to get in contact with me."

"Aye, aye sir." Elijah saluted.

Andre bounded into the carriage and gave the signal for the driver to be off. The driver cracked his whip over the horse's head, and they sped off in the direction of the wharves.

The men rode without speaking inside the carriage until Norton broke the silence. "You know, Lafitte, some people might consider this kidnapping."

Andre, who sat looking out the window opposite Norton, flicked his eyes at him.

"Don't make me laugh," Andre said. "Let's call this an invitation to meet that niece that you've been wanting to get to know for so long. Since you need to supply some explanations, this is as good a time as any."

"What kind of explanations?" asked Norton with a face sublimely innocent.

"Like who you really are to start with."

"Like I told you, the name is Jeffrey Norton. I'm the uncle of Mercedes Lawless who lives in Galveston, and I was on my way to meet her."

"You seemed to have taken a detour on the trip."

"After our card game, it wasn't such an urgent visit as

Wings of the Wind

it was to begin with. I didn't want to tell my niece that I had lost her property."

"You're a little loose with other people's things."

Norton shrugged. "Easy come, easy go."

Andre studied Norton. The more he knew about the man, the less he liked him, and he hadn't had a liking for him to begin with. "You didn't mention you had business interests in New Orleans."

Norton shrugged. "Didn't seem to be necessary at the time."

"And Bragg?"

"What about him?"

"What's the connection?"

"Cotton brokering is the connection. We've been working together for several years. Lot of money to be made in cotton."

Andre knew he wasn't joking. It was getting so men would kill each other for cotton. Andre still hadn't figured out the angle on the two of them wanting Mercedes Lawless, but they had arrived at the wharf and the boat. Time for more questions later.

Toadie was waiting in the boat.

"Would you mind telling me where we're going?" asked Norton as he stepped from the carriage and looked down into the boat.

"Sure. We're sailing for Galveston. You wanted to meet your niece and nephew and that's exactly what you're going to do. See my ship out there?"

Norton didn't have to look. He knew the ship was out there. He nodded.

"Your niece and nephew are waiting for you on that ship. We will have time for a happy reunion while we all sail to Galveston to take Miss Lawless back to her store."

213

Marjorie Thelen

Norton sized up the situation and, looking like he saw no easy way of escape, he started down the ladder to the boat. "Let's not delay the reunion."

Chapter Nineteen

Andre was the first onto the ship, Norton followed, then Bruno. Tito was waiting for Andre, who gave the order for the men to weigh anchor and set sail. The sails lofted as they caught breeze off the river. The magnificence of *Wings of the Wind* unfurled.

"A sight to make your heart glad, eh, Capitán?" asked Tito.

Andre agreed, happy to feel the ship under him again. "It's great to be sailing, and it will be good to get back to the open sea."

Tito spied Norton. "Are you glad to be back?" he said by was of greeting.

"Can't say that I am. I like dry land myself." He pulled another cheroot from his pocket and tried to light it in the breeze without success.

Jamie stood at the edge of the group trying to see the newcomer.

Andre caught sight of him and called him over. "Jamie, lad, come meet your uncle."

Jamie squeezed between the big men in the group and went to stand beside Andre. He looked the stranger up and down.

The man held an unlit cheroot in his fingers. He was unshaven in a wrinkled jacket over a shirt open at the neck.

His uncombed hair reached over his collar.

"Hello, Jamie. I'm your uncle, Jeffrey Norton." He held out his hand. "It's a pleasure to meet you at last."

Jamie looked at the face of the man speaking then looked at the hand offered to him. He slowly extended his and shook.

"Pleased to make your acquaintance, sir," he said and hesitated. "Are you really my uncle?" Jamie looked from his unkempt hair to his unpolished shoes. "I guess you weren't expecting to meet us today."

Norton looked down at his clothes and started brushing his shoulders, tucking in his shirt, smoothing his hair. He felt his chin. "I didn't have time for a shave this morning." He glanced at Andre. "I had to rush to get here on time."

"Why don't we let Mr. Norton freshen up?" said Andre. "Jamie, would you like to show him to the cabin between Bruno and Tito? I'm sure he'll be most comfortable there."

"Aye, aye, sir," said Jamie, saluting. "This way please, Mr. Norton."

Norton stumbled off behind Jamie.

"Where's Mickey?" asked Andre, looking around.

"Here, boss." A slender hand shot out from behind the shoulders of the bigger men.

"How is Miss Lawless? Is she resting comfortably?"

"Yes, boss. She rest whole time you away. She still in your cabin."

"Thank you. Tito, let's go over our course."

"Si, si, mi Capitán."

Andre looked at the men eavesdropping on their conversation. Expectant faces peered back at him. "The rest of you back to your stations. Let's crack on." A cheer

Wings of the Wind

went up from the group, and they hurried to their tasks.

"Mickey, fix something to eat and bring it to my cabin, if you please."

"Yes, boss."

Andre and Tito made their way to the wheel, talking to the seaman as they went, checking sails, lines, and positions. Satisfied that his ship was in good order, Andre went below to his cabin.

He approached quietly and opened the door an inch. One look showed that the bunk was made. He inched the door open further, then further until he saw Mercedes sitting on the chair, mending a shirt of his. Such a scene of domestic tranquility he had not been privy to in his short acquaintance with Miss Lawless. He opened the door wide. Mercedes looked up.

She was neatly dressed, having done her best to clean her pretty white frock and smooth out the wrinkles. Her hair was dressed in coils of braids on the back of her head. The only disturbing feature in the scene of domestic tranquility was purple and yellow under her eye.

"Hello, Andre," she said. "I heard you were back." She got up and stood awkwardly, as if unsure of herself.

Andre covered the distance in an instant and took her in his arms. She sighed, and he rocked her back and forth.

"How are you feeling?" He looked down into her lavender blues. He kissed the bruise on her face and her puffy lips.

"A bit sore." She blushed. "I mean all over. My head doesn't hurt so much now. I was able to rest while you were gone. It's nice to have you back. I worried about you."

"Worried about me?

"Yes, about you."

"I can't recall that anyone has ever worried about me.

Marjorie Thelen

Or at least let on that they did."

He released her and held her at arm's length. "We found Norton."

Mercedes eyes lit up. "You did? Where is he?"

"Here on the ship."

"Excellent, Captain Lafitte. Well done. Now I know we can get this entire matter cleared up. I feel better already."

Andre smiled. "I'm glad I could do that for you."

"Where did you find him?"

"He was hiding at the Silver Slipper."

"The Silver Slipper?"

"It's a brothel," he said. There was no other way to put it. A brothel was a brothel.

Little frown lines knitted her brow.

"He was hiding there hoping to avoid running into me until we had cleared town."

"How did you know he was there?"

"Jack Lormand."

Mercedes eyes narrowed. "That man has a long reach. Tell me when I will meet Mr. Norton."

"He's cleaning up now. We had to leave in a hurry so he didn't have time to shave."

They heard a knock at the door. "That's Mickey," said Andre. "Enter."

Mickey came in balancing a tray heaped with fruit, cold meat, biscuits, and tea. "Thought you might be hungry, boss. Missy, too. Not eat much this morning."

"Thank you," said Andre.

Mickey set the tray on the table and set out two mugs. He poured hot tea into both.

"Tell Norton to join us when he is cleaned up."

"Yes, boss. Somesing else?"

"No, that's enough."

Mickey bowed and left the room with a grin on his face.

Andre walked to the table and indicated a seat for Mercedes. "Sit. Have something to eat."

She took a seat with more care than usual. She put three orange slices and a biscuit on a plate and stirred a generous helping of sugar into her tea. Andre joined her and speared some of the cold meat for his plate and helped himself to several biscuits.

"What are you going to say to Norton?" he asked.

Mercedes pursed her lips. "I've been thinking about that. I'm going to ask him a lot of family questions. I'm not convinced he's my relative. Did he meet Jamie?"

Andre nodded. "He did, briefly. Norton was rumpled looking, and Jamie made a remark about that." He smiled at the recollection.

"I hope he wasn't too rude. A boy that age can be painfully frank."

"Norton deserves it." They exchanged smiles, but the earlier question hung between them. Andre didn't know what to say about the night they spent together, about their argument, about their future. Avoiding conversation about it altogether was easiest.

Mercedes took a bite of orange slice, munching in silence. She pushed the plate aside. "Andre, what will you do about this bet? Are you going to pursue his claim to my Emporium?"

"Maybe it doesn't matter so much to me anymore," he said.

"Why not?"

"At first I was angry that he jumped ship and disappeared. Then I was curious to see what I had won when we docked in Galveston. Then I met you." Their eyes held in the way of new lovers.

Mercedes was the first to look away as if unsettled and unsure of herself. "As you said earlier, things have changed." She looked back to his waiting eyes.

This was dangerous ground they were treading and entirely new for him. He looked at her face, the bruised cheek. She was beautiful, and she was here in this room sitting right across from him. He wanted her now, again. This must be what it felt when a man said a woman drove him crazy. What was he going to do? The unspoken question of commitment hung in the air, and commitment was the hardest thing to ask of him.

A tap at the door made them both jump.

"It's probably Norton," Andre said, resenting the interruption of their interlude. "Are you ready to meet him or would you like more time?"

"I guess now is as good a time as any."

"Who is it?" called Andre.

"Mickey, boss. Mr. Norton resting. Say he see you later so he fresh to meet niece."

Andre smiled. "Fine with us." To Mercedes he said. "Do you want anything else?"

She shook her head.

"Thank you, Mickey. That will be all," Andre called.

"Yes, boss."

Andre took Mercedes's hand in his and rubbed his thumb over the smoothness of her skin. "I want you again." He looked into her eyes. "If you stay here, I might not be able to control myself."

She watched his thumb. "Where am I to go? Do I go back to my cabin to finish mending your shirt or to the galley to help with dinner? Or to Jamie to explain what I've been doing in the Captain's cabin?"

"We could go back to my bunk," Andre said in all seriousness.

Mercedes laughed, a joyous laugh, the kind of laugh a woman laughs when she is at ease with the company she's in.

"How do you feel about me?" he asked, smoothing the soft mound of her palm, studying her. He needed to know.

She sobered and said in a quiet voice, "I've never felt about a man the way I feel about you."

"You speak as if you are venturing out on a limb."

She looked into his eyes. The tapestry enveloped them once more. She inched out a little further on the limb. "I like you."

"That's an improvement from where we started in Galveston. So you like me?"

She seemed to cast about for the right words. "I wouldn't have been on the bunk with you last night if I didn't feel something for you."

Andre shifted his position on the chair. "A man doesn't have to feel anything for woman to get between the sheets with her."

"So I've heard. What has changed for you, Andre?"

He liked how she said Andre.

"You don't know much about me," he said, delaying his answer.

She shook her head.

"I don't get involved much. Not with people. Not with things. I don't get attached."

She waited for him to go on. There was something beautiful about the way she sat calmly listening to him. She had a quiet beauty that he liked. There was strength to it. She didn't titter and fawn the way some women did. He felt the pull of the Siren.

"But you and I are attached in some way," he said. This was new territory for him. He wasn't good at expressing feelings. "Beyond the body way, I mean. I've been with women before and have never felt attached. I don't know how to describe it. I feel an attachment between you and me."

She grasped his hand. He connected to its warmth and strength.

"I've had a feeling of something missing in my life," he said, creeping further out onto his limb. "It's as if I'm bored. Maybe it was curiosity that drew me to Galveston. My attraction to you started the day you showed up in my cabin with that outlandish proposition that you were going to help me find your uncle."

Her lips turned up into a quirky smile.

"You were so sure of yourself," Andre continued. "So brazen, so forward. Unlike any other woman I've met. Most are demure and lying. At least that's what my experience of women has been."

"Brazen." Mercedes sat up but she didn't look too upset. "Is that what you thought?"

"Yes, and I figured this was going to be some ride, and I wanted to be along."

"You scoundrel. You were just playing with me." But she was smiling. "Has it been worth it?"

"Every last inch so far. But you need to listen to me better," he said with that twitch at the corner of his mouth.

"I try, but I have this terrible stubborn streak and a pretty bad temper." Her look was almost apologetic.

He touched her bruised cheek. "I must do a better job of keeping you out of trouble."

Wings of the Wind

"I'm glad you got there when you did."

Andre caressed her cheek. Her skin was soft. Her complexion was clear and creamy, marred only by the bruise. Her eyes closed against his touch, and she leaned her cheek into his caress.

He wanted many more scenes like this with her in his life. He couldn't deny it.

A warm, charged silence stretched between them.

Reluctantly, he said, "You look tired, and I have a ship to sail. Do you want to go back to your cabin?"

She nodded. "I should. My reputation is already shot, but I should try to keep up appearances."

"I had heard that you had been with Bragg, but you weren't. I was your first man."

Mercedes flushed with what might have been embarrassment, but it came out as anger. "Bragg is a lying bastard with a mouth the size of Texas. He purposely tried to ruin me so I'd marry him. Over my dead body, believe me. The night he abducted me in Galveston he took me to the west end of the island. He has a house there, more like a shack. By the time we arrived he was plenty drunk, and I was furious. I managed to bash him in the face with an iron skillet in his own kitchen. I tied him up, too. I guess the ropes and his hitting me in the warehouse were his revenge. I left in the buckboard he brought me in and didn't get back to town till dawn. There you have it."

"You are a determined woman, and I'm glad for both of us that you are." Andre didn't want to think about how the scene would have played, if she hadn't been able to get away.

He held out his hand to help her up. "I'll escort you to your cabin. When Norton is rested, I'll send for you."

The unspoken question of their future together still

Marjorie Thelen

hovered between them.

* * * * *

It was late in the afternoon when Andre sent Mickey to rouse Norton and bring him to his cabin. Andre could feel a storm coming but as yet there was no sign of it. He instructed Tito to make the ship ready and went below. He wanted to talk to Norton alone before Mercedes joined them.

Norton was sitting in Andre's cabin smoking his endless cheroot, shaved, hair slicked back with water.

"Glad you could join me," said Andre. He walked over to where Norton sat.

"Sorry if I've been unsociable. I haven't got much sleep lately." Norton smiled a lazy grin. "Tess is a demanding woman."

"You're lucky you still got balls. She's been known to rip them right off a man." Andre leaned against the edge of his desk.

"I take it that is from personal experience."

"No, it isn't. It's complaints from the customers."

Norton guffawed. "You saved me then. I should thank you."

Andre shrugged. "We didn't finish our conversation on the carriage ride."

Norton squinted at him through the smoke from the cheroot. He waited for Andre to continue.

"You said that the connection between you and Bragg was cotton."

Norton nodded.

"What were you doing in Boston?"

"Brokering cotton. Like I told you, I'm from Boston.

Wings of the Wind

That's where I grew up. I keep a house there. Even before the folks died I got interested in cotton and started making trips south. I ended up in New Orleans what with one thing and another. Met Bragg through Jack Lormand."

"Was your name Norton in Boston?"

"What do you mean was my name Norton in Boston? Of course, it was," he said, sounding testy. "How many times do I have to tell you? I'm Mercedes' mother's brother. The family name is Norton."

Andre did not look convinced. "Was your given name Jeffrey?"

Norton squinted at him anew. "Where are you going with this?"

"There are lots of Nortons in Boston. Might be more than one Jeffrey Norton."

"My name is Jeffrey Norton. I don't know all the Nortons in Boston, but I'm the only Jeffrey that I know of."

"Just asking."

"You don't believe that I'm related to Mercedes Lawless, do you?"

Andre shook his head.

"Why not?"

"Some things don't fit."

"Such as?"

"Jack Lormand says he's known you more than a few years. He says you are from New Orleans."

"Lormand's information is wrong."

Andre shook his head again. "Jack Lormand knows everything that goes on in New Orleans. Lormand can twist the truth to fit his purpose, but I'd believe him before I'd believe you."

Norton shrugged. "Believe what you want."

"It bothers me that you could be from the same blood

225

as Jamie and Mercedes Lawless. No facts here, just a feeling I have. There's not a tiny resemblance physically, and morally there is no likeness at all. I find it hard to believe that a relation of Mercedes and Jamie would callously gamble away their living in a card game. Do you know what you bet when you bet the Lavender Dry Goods Emporium?"

Norton frowned. "Of course." He paused. "Well, I knew there was the store, but as I had not ever seen it, I assumed it was modest and of no consequence to them."

"No consequence?" Andre reached out, grabbed Norton by the shirt, and yanked him out of the chair. "That's how they live, you bastard," he said, shaking the man so hard his head snapped back and forth. "It supports the two of them and their uncle and cousin, and God knows how many charities in Galveston since Mercedes seems to be active in all of them. These people are hard workers and you know what? They are nice people. I don't put you in the same league with them." Andre gave a snort of disgust and pushed him away.

Norton stumbled backward then made a conspicuous show of straightening his shirt. "Maybe we came under different influences in our lives. Maybe not everyone is as blessed as they are." He narrowed his eyes. "You seem to be excessively fond of them. Are you compromising my niece?"

Andre folded his arms over his chest to keep his fists from smashing into Norton's face, and the look in his eyes said contempt. "If I were, you would be the last person to know."

"I consider myself responsible for her. I hope you are the gentleman when it comes to my niece."

"That's rich," said Andre. "This is from one gentleman

Wings of the Wind

to another, right?"

"That's right." Norton pulled himself up and glowered.

"Good imitation of a gentleman, Norton, but it needs some work," Andre said. "On the small matter of your right to their store, if you can't prove legal claim when we get to Galveston, and you don't settle your gambling debt, you go to jail."

Andre's smile was malicious. "Of course, you could offer some of your cotton brokering business as compensation. Now that I think of it, I like that better. Since there seems to be some question as to your right to the store to begin with, why don't you just pay me in cotton?"

Norton had a sudden fit of coughing then recovered. "I don't own cotton, I broker it."

"You must make money doing that. If you don't have any cotton, I'll take gold. Let's make things simple."

Norton had a more violent fit of coughing. "I'm a little short right now. But I could write you a note."

"Do I look stupid?"

Norton shook his head vigorously.

"It looks like jail for you."

"Wait, Captain, I'll arrange a deal with Bragg when we get to Galveston. He'll cover my debt, and I'll settle up with him later. Let's stop the jail talk."

"Bragg won't be in Galveston. Last time I saw him he was tied up in your warehouse in New Orleans."

"Well, that is inconvenient." Norton stuck a finger in his collar and pulled to loosen it, seeming to need more air. "Bragg has a lawyer in Galveston. We can make the necessary arrangements with him."

Andre narrowed his eyes. "All right but make sure I don't lose sight of you in Galveston. If I do, and I ever find

Marjorie Thelen

you again, you can kiss your sweet ass good-bye."

Norton cringed and nodded his understanding. "Now I'm rather keen to see my niece. Might we invite her in?"

Andre thought what sorry excuse for a human being this man was. He had a feeling that his hunch would prove right, that this man was in no way related to Mercedes and Jamie Lawless.

"Mickey!" he shouted.

Mickey peeked his head in the door. "Yes, boss, right here. I get Miss Mercedes. I bring Jamie, too?"

"No, just Mercedes."

"That man was standing right outside your door," said Norton when the door banged shut.

Andre shrugged. "That way I don't have to repeat myself a lot." He selected a cheroot from the humidor on his desk, and lit up. He needed something to take away the bad taste this man was leaving in his mouth.

"Whiskey?" he asked Norton, supposing he should be hospitable.

Norton nodded.

Andre walked over to the cupboard and opened a side panel. A large unmarked bottle of whiskey stood inside surrounded by heavy glasses. He poured two healthy portions and gave one to his guest.

They sipped the whiskey in silence, waiting for Mercedes to appear.

A soft tap sounded on the door.

"Enter."

The door opened, and Mercedes moved halfway in.

"Come in," said Andre, standing and motioning to Norton to do the same. "Your uncle is here and eager to meet you."

Mercedes looked from Andre to the man next to him.

Wings of the Wind

The look of surprise on her face said he wasn't what she expected. Norton stood slight and unremarkable beside Andre. She moved into the room but didn't advance any further toward her uncle. She studied him.

Her disbelief registered on her face because Andre said, "Yes, this is your uncle, Jeffrey Norton." He looked at Norton. "Forgetting your manners?"

"No." Norton recovered. "I'm terribly sorry. I was just taken aback by the sight of you after all the searching I've done."

Andre had to hand it to the man, he was one fine actor. He watched Mercedes and saw disbelief slide into disappointment.

Norton advanced to Mercedes. "Jeffrey Norton, at your service." He took her hand and kissed it.

Laying it on thick, thought Andre.

"My dear," said Norton. "You are a beauty, and you have the family eyes."

"I do?" said Mercedes, looking surprised.

"Yes, my dear. Everyone in Boston knows the family is famous for those lavender blue eyes. Yes, indeed. But what happened to your eye? Did you have an accident?" asked Norton, avoiding Andre's gaze.

"Yes, I met with an unfortunate accident at the hands of a man by the name of Derek Bragg. Do you know him?" asked Mercedes.

Norton looked thoughtful. "I'm afraid I do. We've done some business together. This is deplorable. I will speak to him on this matter."

Someone rapped on the door.

"Enter," said Andre.

Mickey's head popped in. "Boss, Tito say need you on deck. Storm come up."

Marjorie Thelen

"Be right there." He turned to Norton and Mercedes. "Please avail yourselves of my cabin. This storm will be a bad one. You'll want to move to your cabins soon. Do not venture on deck. We keep a full press of sails in a storm. We'll be moving fast."

Mercedes smiled a special smile for him then turned to Norton.

"I am eager to hear about our relatives in Boston", Andre heard her say as he left the room.

Chapter Twenty

Stormy weather drove them down the Mississippi, through the passes, and out into the open water of the Gulf of Mexico. The safety of the ship and its passengers demanded that the Captain be on deck as storm after storm came upon them. The storms did not allow the new lovers to weave any more length to the tapestry of their feeling for each other. The crew's exhilaration from the run of storms was evident in their shouts and laughter as they went about their tasks the first clear morning of the trip.

Andre walked the deck checking for storm damage as the sky in the east turned from pale to bright pink. The sun inched up over a cloudless horizon. In the west he could see the edge of land that would be the eastern end of Galveston Island. They had managed to hold their course throughout the stormy trip. The sole causality was one very sick Mr. Norton, who remained below.

He leaned on the railing, one booted foot on the bottom rail, looking toward the sunrise but not seeing the entrance of the new day. Mercedes Lawless crowded into his thoughts yet again. He wanted her more than he had ever wanted any woman. He knew she had made a commitment, but he didn't know what commitment he could make. Mistress would be satisfactory to him, but he knew it wouldn't be for her. She wasn't the mistress type.

His life was sailing. It was all he knew. The new ship was exciting, the trip to San Francisco a new adventure. But there was something missing that he couldn't put his finger on. Maybe it was a need not to be by himself anymore.

Marriage was out of the question. It astounded him that he even considered the institution. It would never work with him sailing as much as he did. A beautiful wife would develop eyes for other men, the first long voyage he'd go on, just like his mother had. When one man left, another would soon be on the doorstep. He knew what his physical needs were, and there were lots of women in every port that could fill them. How could a marriage work like that?

Tito and Spike joined him at the rail to enjoy the sunrise. "Mi Capitán is lost in thoughts, no?"

Andre nodded but didn't speak.

"I have come to report that we didn't suffer any great loss except one torn sail. It appears that is all the damage. What an exciting run that was, eh? I bet that is the best time any ship made from New Orleans to Galveston. How I love a good storm!"

Spike squawked and cackled his delight making little parrot whistles into Tito's ear.

"She handled beautifully," Andre said. "*Wings of the Wind* is everything we hoped for." He watched a line of dolphins playing on the horizon. "Look out there." He pointed to them.

Tito shaded his eyes, searching in the direction Andre pointed. "Aye, look at them leaping. This morning is fresh and sweet, no, mi Capitán? A good day to be alive."

Andre stretched and yawned. "Good day to be alive, after I've gotten some sleep. I haven't had much these last few days. I'm going below."

It had not only been storms that had interrupted his sleep. Desire for Mercedes and images jumbled into nightmares of ships wrecked upon gigantic rocks kept him tossing and turning when he did get a chance to bunk down.

"Take the ship in easy, Tito. After we drop anchor no one goes ashore until I give the order. That means no one." He gave Tito a hard look to make sure he understood.

"Si, si, mi Capitán."

"Avast, buckaroos, avast," Spike squawked and ended with a few whistles.

Andre went below to his cabin and bunk. He passed Mercedes's room and stopped. He should not open that door. His mind flashed warnings about sirens, ships, and gigantic rocks. His body longed for her touch. He wasn't sure about his heart.

He tapped lightly then opened the door just to look at her. She was asleep on the floor, her arms thrown out, a sheet wrapped loosely across her. Her hair tumbled around her shoulders. Her bosom rose and fell softly. He entered quietly, closed the door, and sat upon the bed gazing upon her. She stirred and opened her eyes maybe feeling his desire for her. She smiled and stretched out her arms to him.

He undressed and joined her in the love nest on the floor. The tapestry wove its gentle threads around them once again. Later, Andre left her sleeping and walked to his cabin. A mug of black tea sat on the nightstand. He collapsed face down on the bunk and shut his eyes, bypassing the tea. In the next instant he was asleep.

* * * * *

Bruno strolled over to Tito. Together they had watched Andre go below.

Bruno shook his head. "He's in love this time."

"I think you are right," Tito said.

"She's a real beauty."

"No question about that."

"Has a lot of spirit. I like that in a woman." Bruno clucked his tongue and winked an eye.

"Me, too. Looks like the Capitán does, too. Maybe he met his match."

"He has."

"What do you think he will do?" Tito glanced over at his mate.

"I think he'll marry her." Bruno's mouth moved into a smile.

"I sure would miss having him as the Capitán."

"He'll never leave the sea."

"It will be tough on a woman like that having him gone all the time."

"That won't be a problem. He'll bring her along. He just hasn't figured it out yet."

* * * * *

Mercedes appeared on deck in the lovely frock from Fabienne's shop she had cleaned as best she could. The breeze blew her skirts. The sun warmed her face.

Jamie caught up with her at the rail. They watched the crew polishing brass, touching up paint, climbing through the rigging.

"What a day!" Mercedes smiled at her brother.

"Weren't the storms magnificent?" said Jamie, his eyes aglow. "I got to help. The men tied a rope around me,

Wings of the Wind

so I wouldn't wash overboard. I helped Tito at the wheel. I couldn't sleep it was so exciting."

"I got some sleep toward morning," said Mercedes. She turned away from Jamie to hide the color that rose in her cheeks at the thought of the early morning visit from Andre. "They wouldn't let me on deck. I had to put my blanket on the floor since we were so far over most of the night that my bunk was upside."

"That was something," said Jamie. "By the way, how did our Uncle fare?"

"He's sick. He stayed in his cabin the entire trip. I haven't seen him this morning. I expect he's resting."

"What came of your talk with him?"

Mercedes frowned. "He spoke of our grandparents mostly. That would be what he knows. But he was vague. It was like he was reciting a story. Then the first storm started to blow in earnest, and he turned green and went to his cabin. I haven't seen him since."

"He sure wasn't what I expected of an uncle from a good family."

"Me, either," said Mercedes. "He's rather seedy looking. Maybe he will loosen up once we get to Galveston."

"Loosen up? He seems pretty loose now."

Mercedes straightened and pointed to the west.

"Look, Jamie is that land?"

"Sure is. It's Galveston."

"I wonder how Uncle Everett and Julia are doing, how business at the store is faring. It will be nice to see them again. But I dearly love this ship. She is a beauty, isn't she?"

"Yes, she is. You seem to like more than just this ship," he said, looking at her out of the corner of his eye.

Marjorie Thelen

Mercedes felt her face flush and kept her gaze on the horizon. What did one say to one's brother? What had he heard? She knew it couldn't be a secret that she had spent the night in Andre's cabin with Andre in it. She knew the crew took great delight in their Captain and what he did, down to what he ate and when. His spending the night with a woman on the ship would be big news.

Jamie tapped her shoulder. "Did you hear me? What about the Captain?"

She shrugged away, not knowing what to tell her brother. She guessed the truth would have to suffice. Albeit, not all of the truth.

"We have come to a new understanding."

"Are you sweet on him?"

"Sweet on him?" She was afraid the words were in love with him. "I like him more now than I did."

"Boy, that's saying a lot because you really didn't like him at first. Look at what you did with the sheriff."

"Do you have to keep bringing that up? I made an error in judgment. That's all. Everybody makes mistakes."

"Not you, Mercedes. You're usually right. Least ways that's what you always tell me."

"It was my first mistake," she said, daring to look at him. He regarded her with raised eyebrows, and they laughed. She ruffled his hair, and he pulled away.

"Stop doing that," he said.

They caught sight of Tito and Spike coming toward them.

"What goes on here?" Tito asked. "A fight, is it?"

"No, sir," said Jamie, "we were having a brother and sister discussion."

Spike squawked and flapped over to Jamie's shoulder.

"A fight it was then," he said, smiling at them. "Are

Wings of the Wind

you eager to get back to Galveston, Miss Mercedes?"

"Yes, I suppose I am. *Wings of the Wind* is nice though."

"You did not have problems with the storms?"

"Oh, no. They were wonderfully scary."

"You would make a good seaman."

"Do you think so?"

"Si, I can tell by your face how much you love the sea and sailing. You and your brother are cut from the same piece of cloth."

Sister and brother looked at one another. Mercedes wondered about that cloth. Her brother was free to go off on a ship like this, and her options were a store in Galveston and marriage to some dull but upright citizen. Then there was Andre.

"This is my first time on a clipper ship," said Mercedes. "I've been in small boats in the harbor, but this is my first time on the open sea. It's magnificent."

"I've been a seaman ever since I can remember. We're all like that on this ship. We don't know nothing else. I cannot imagine any other life."

"You're fortunate," said Mercedes, smiling up at him.

Tito nodded. "The Capitán turned in for a while. He gave us orders to stand off Galveston till he was ready. Then we'll take you in."

"We'll be ready," said Mercedes.

"I'm staying right here," said Jamie. "I'm not going ashore."

Mercedes looked at him in consternation. "Don't you want to say hello to Julia and Uncle Everett?"

"No, I just saw them. We haven't been gone that long. Nope, I'm staying right here. I'm not going to take any chance that this ship leaves without me."

Marjorie Thelen

Mercedes ruffled his hair again.

"Will you cut that out? I'm not some little kid anymore."

* * * * *

Andre awoke to the gentle sway of the ship as she rode at anchor. He sat up, shaking himself awake, and reached for the cold mug of tea on the stand. He downed it, grimacing at its bitterness, then sat and stared at the wall. The same thought was with him upon waking as he when had gone to sleep. Mercedes Lawless.

What was he going to do about her? He was going to have to make a choice. The thought put him in a bad mood.

He got up, walked to the basin, poured water, gave his face and head several healthy splashes, and toweled his face dry. He gave his long hair a few swift brushes and tied back its length with a strip of leather.

He glanced side-to-side in the mirror. He needed a shave. He worked up lather in the shaving mug, pulled out his straight edge, and started to scrape his face clean. While he shaved the thoughts battled on in his heart and his head. Desire and feeling battled reason and logic. Reason and logic demanded that he sail away and forget her. It was ludicrous to think that she would be the dutiful wife and placidly wait for him every time he went off on a trip. Desire and feeling wanted to stay by her and plan a life together. The lovemaking was good, but would the magic of it last a lifetime?

He stopped shaving and looked closely in the mirror.

"You're dreaming," he told his reflection. "How long do you think you would last? A day, a week, a month at the outside."

Wings of the Wind

He cleaned the razor and resumed shaving. No, he didn't think it could work. But then what if she were pregnant? He nicked himself and swore. Any other woman he would pay off. Mercedes was not just any woman. He dabbed at the cut and swore. Somehow the longer he lived the messier life got.

He splashed water on his face to be rid of the excess lather, checked the cut, and dried his face with the towel. He gazed again into the reflection in the mirror. It was the same face that looked back at him everyday. Why did he think that one woman was going to change the man that he was? He didn't want to change, not for her not for any woman. True, he felt an attachment for her, something special, but that would wear off. The intense desire would wear off, and then life would settle into a humdrum existence. He knew he could not take humdrum. He couldn't do it. He couldn't take the chance, couldn't make the commitment. No matter how beautiful she was, no matter how good the lovemaking was, no matter what the promise of life with her. He couldn't risk it. The thought of marriage made him shudder. It was too confining, too restrictive. He could not do it. He had to tell her now, before he changed his mind. He threw down the towel and strode from the room.

* * * * *

On deck the crew was profiting from the sun and breeze by washing and drying clothes. Some were at work mending the sail ripped in the storm. He nodded his greetings, calling each man by name. They nodded and called back their good mornings, winking to each other as he went by.

He joined Tito by the wheel. "How does it go?"

"Excelente, mi Capitán," he saluted and clicked his heels. "Fine day, fine day. Did you rest well?"

"I feel great," he said, looking around for Mercedes, not seeing her. "We'll put the lady and gentleman ashore. I'll go with them and take Bruno. I'm going to wrap up business today so that we can sail with the tide this evening. I don't anticipate any trouble on shore, but if anything unforeseen develops, I think Bruno and I will be able to handle it." Andre paused. "If for some strange reason we aren't back by dark, come looking for us. Bring several of the men and weapons."

Tito nodded his understanding with a grin. "Si, si, mi Capitán."

"Where are our guests at the moment?"

"Norton is still in his cabin, sick. Miss Mercedes is with Toadie's group mending clothes." He indicated the group with the direction of his head.

Andre stared at another perfect picture of domesticity. He liked the setting on the deck better than in front of a fireplace in some snug little house. He liked her better under him with no clothes on.

Get on with it, he told himself. Get it over. Tell her.

"Will you ask her to join me?"

"Si, mi Capitán."

Tito bounced down the stairs two at a time.

Andre watched as Mercedes put down her mending and came aft. She wore a smile and walked with arms swinging lightly, toes dancing across the deck.

This was a happy woman, he thought. So light, so carefree.

He liked to think their morning interlude was the cause. She didn't look like she had suffered much from the

Wings of the Wind

trip. Rather she looked like it had invigorated her. He knew he was about to ruin her day. Tell her and get it over.

"Good morning," she greeted him as she came up the stairs. "I hope you rested comfortably. You look well." She stopped an arm's length from him, smiling, her eyes bright.

"You do, too. You look like you are enjoying the morning. I trust last night's storm did not overly frighten you." Nor your early morning visitor. "The storms are worse in the Gulf then on the river."

"Oh, no," she said shaking her head. "It was exciting, and I didn't get sick."

"Good. Are you ready to return to Galveston? I thought I would take you and Norton in now. I'm sure your cousin and uncle must be worried about you." He turned toward the shore. "There seems to be a small party gathered on the wharf, no doubt waiting for you."

Mercedes looked toward the wharf. "Yes, I see them. It will be good to be with them again." She hesitated. "What about settling the legal matter of the bet?"

Andre studied the group on the wharf. "Norton and I have come to an agreement. He is going to make good on the bet, and it will not involve anything of yours. He says that Bragg will cover the bet. He and I will take care of that after I have seen you safely home."

She studied her hands not looking at him. "And after that?" she said, softly.

"I sail for San Francisco." He didn't need to look to see the disappointment in her eyes.

"I see," she said, still studying her hands.

There was an awkward silence.

She squared her shoulders and took a deep breath. "Then I'm ready." She turned to go.

"Mercedes."

She paused but did not look back.

"I thought about it ten ways till Sunday and back, and it won't work for us. My mistress is the sea, and this ship marries me to her. I can't live without the sea. It's part of my being."

She whirled around and came so close he could feel the heat of anger radiating out from her. She looked straight into his eyes and, carefully enunciating each word, said, "You can keep your blasted ship for all I care. I am perfectly happy where I am. I am successful. I love my family, friends, and Galveston. I don't need you to make me happy." She backed up a step. "I am more than ready to leave you and your ship. Will you please take me in?"

He bowed in response. "I'd be delighted, my dear."

* * * * *

As the shore boat rowed closer, Mercedes saw that the party on the wharf was made up of Julia, Uncle Everett, Sheriff McGreevy, and a well-dressed gentleman in a top hat. She didn't know the stranger but she was worried about the sheriff. What was he doing here? She hoped this did not mean trouble and ventured a discreet glance at Andre. His face revealed nothing but his eyes were on the sheriff. She saw him glance at Bruno and saw Bruno nod his head. No one spoke.

She looked at Norton, who had finally dragged himself onto the deck right before their departure. Now he sat slumped, eyes downcast with an unlit cheroot in hand, swaying slightly back and forth to the rhythm of the rowing. He was a poor excuse for an uncle.

She sat ramrod stiff, still smarting from Andre's

Wings of the Wind

rejection. After the wonderful moments they had shared together it was over just like that. He was going to sail away just like a man. She wasn't going to think of the consequences. She would know the outcome soon enough, and she would worry if and when the time came. Right now she wanted to be far away from the sight of him.

Yet somewhere inside a little voice was weeping, crying it wasn't fair, it wasn't fair. Finally she found a man she liked and thought she could make a life with, and he would have to be in love with the sea and not her.

Damnation, she thought, better to get him out of sight so she could start forgetting. She blew out a great sigh, and the rest of the boat's inhabitants looked at her. She felt their stares but chose not to acknowledge them. Instead she sat straighter and clenched her teeth. She wasn't going to let anyone see she was upset.

She watched the party on the wharf. Julia jumped up and down waving at them with a handkerchief. Uncle Everett stood hat in hand, grinning from ear to ear. Sheriff McGreevy had his hands on his guns. What in God's great creation was he doing?

"Hold up, Toadie, don't go in any further," Andre told his man in a low voice, watching the sheriff and his guns.

Toadie stopped rowing and back pulled to hold them steady.

Mercedes judged they were out of firing range of the guns.

"Would you like to tell us what the sheriff is doing here?" shouted Andre, his hand alongside his mouth.

"He's part of the welcoming party," Julia shouted back. She looked over at the Sheriff and saw where he had his hands. She nudged her uncle who looked down at the Sheriff. Everett tapped on the Sheriff's shoulder and pointed to his hands. The Sheriff smiled sheepishly, took off his gun belt, and gave it to Uncle Everett.

"Thank you," called Andre. "Anyone else with weapons?"

Four heads wagged side to side.

"Toadie, take her in now." Andre glanced at Bruno. "I don't have a good feeling about the sheriff. Keep you eyes open and your weapon handy. You go first. I'll help Mercedes up, then Norton. I'll bring up the rear."

Bruno acknowledged the order with a nod without taking his eyes from the group.

Mercedes climbed the ladder from the boat to the dock with as much grace as a woman could clad in a dress and petticoats, exiting from a bouncing boat.

"Be careful," Julia called out.

Uncle Everett reached for Mercedes and helped her up the last rungs.

As soon as she cleared the ladder, Julia grabbed and hugged Mercedes so tight she squeaked. They hugged and laughed turning round and round. Uncle Everett thumped them both on the back.

Julia said, "I am so glad you are safe. I can't tell you how I have worried. But what's this?" She turned Mercedes' face and assessed her black eye. "How did this happen?"

"Bragg," Mercedes said under her breath. "I'll tell you later. Right now I want you to meet Jeffrey Norton. Andre found him in New Orleans."

"Wait!" Julia pulled Mercedes off to the side, as the men climbed onto the dock. Julia wrung her hands and lowered her voice. "My dear, I have to tell you . . . "

But just then out of the corner of her eye Mercedes saw the Sheriff pull a gun from his waistband at the small

Wings of the Wind

of his back and aim it at Andre, who had just made it up onto the dock.

"Stop right there," said the Sheriff with a growl. "We have unfinished business, Captain Lafitte. Don't let your man near me, ya hear? I know you both have weapons so you better drop them right now."

Andre stopped and hooked his thumbs on the knife belt on his hips, legs apart. He made no move to relinquish the knife.

Before Andre could say anything, Julia shoved her way over to stand in front of the Sheriff, oblivious to the gun he pointed.

"Whatever are you doing, Jeremiah? What do you think this is? We told these folks we had no weapons, and you lied." She poked his chest for emphasis. Her color was up.

"Now calm down, Julia," said the Sheriff, not taking his gaze from Andre. "Of course I lied what with varmints like these around. You know I have to uphold law and order in this town, and these two are a threat to law and order. Derek Bragg told me if I ever laid eyes on this here Captain again to put him behind bars. Now out of my way." He moved her aside with a sweep of his arm.

Jeffrey Norton, still with his unlit cheroot, came alive and stepped up. "I have to agree with you, Sheriff. Derek Bragg is my business partner and a man of good sense. If he says these men should be in jail, you better take them in."

The sheriff screwed up his face but kept the gun and his gaze on Andre. "What'd you say your name was, Mister?"

"Jeffrey Norton, uncle of Jamie and Mercedes Lawless, at your service," he said with a bow.

245

"Hold on now." The Sheriff grimaced. "There's something fishy going on. I thought you was dead. This here Captain murdered you."

"No, no, no, no!" said Mercedes, stepping in front of the sheriff. "He's not dead. He's right here." She indicated the man with the cheroot. "There has been no murder. There is nothing to charge Captain Lafitte with. We should all go home. Please, Sheriff, put this gun away!" She pushed it gingerly away from her chest.

The man in the top hat, who had been hovering at the edge of the group, elbowed his way in and came to stand in front of the man with the cheroot.

"You can't be Jeffrey Norton," the top hat said to the cheroot.

The man with the cheroot cocked an eyebrow at the new face. "Oh, yeah and why not?" He took a second look at the man in the top hat and scrunched up his face like he was trying to remember something.

"Because I am," said the top hat. "I'm their uncle. You, sir, are an impostor."

"Now hold on just a minute." The sheriff turned to Julia. "I thought you introduced him as Mr. Horton." He pointed to the man in the top hat with his gun then lowered it to his side.

"I said Norton," said Julia, loudly. "I said his name was Norton. With an N."

The sheriff tugged on his ear like he had a hearing problem.

Andre stood on the periphery of the unfolding melodrama, wagging his head, obviously feeling no compunction to get involved.

Mercedes kept glancing from one Norton to the other, speechless, an unusual state for her. Her eyes were almost as wide as her mouth.

"Mercedes, that's what I started to tell you," Julia said, throwing her hands in the air. "This man is your uncle," she said, gesturing to the man in the top hat. "I don't know who the man is you found in New Orleans."

Chapter Twenty-One

The two Nortons sized each other up. The one in the top hat examined the face before him and pursed his lips. "Don't I know you?" He squinted his eyes and tapped his chin. "I've seen you before." He peered at the man's rumpled attire. "You were better dressed the last time I saw you. You're man to whom I gave the letter in Boston to deliver to my niece because you were sailing for Galveston."

Mercedes recovered her voice. "Who are you?" she asked the man speaking, curiosity putting all good manners and convention aside.

The man doffed his hat. "Allow me to introduce myself." He bowed. I am Jeffrey Norton, your real uncle, and you would be my niece, Mercedes. I would know those eyes anywhere. I cannot tell you what a great pleasure it is to meet you at last." He took her hand in his and kissed it.

Mercedes stared at the man standing before her with his top hat off. Without the shadow from the hat brim she saw that his eyes looked like hers. They were the same color, same shape, same arching eyebrows. Even his nose resembled hers, long and straight.

If this gentleman was her uncle, then who did they bring from New Orleans? She said a little prayer the New Orleans man wasn't related and that this man in front of her was. She would rather have this nice looking gentleman as her uncle.

"Sorry, I didn't mean to stare," she said. "I'm Mercedes Lawless. We do resemble each other, don't we?" She glanced at Julia. "Then you've met my cousin, Julia, and my Uncle Everett?"

"Most assuredly."

"When did you arrive?"

"Just after you left. I stayed on at the Tremont Hotel, waiting for you to come back."

"All the saints be praised," Mercedes said, studying the two uncles. She turned and looked at Andre, who watched her, as if waiting to see what she would do. She looked at Julia, at Uncle Everett, at the Sheriff.

"Will somebody tell me what's going on here and why there are two Jeffrey Nortons?" Her outstretched arms pleaded for mercy.

Andre stepped forward, finally deciding to enter the fray.

"Hold on just a minute there, you varmint." The Sheriff's gun pointed again at Andre.

"Jeremiah McGreevy, will you please put that gun down?" said Mercedes. "You're making me mad." She clenched her fists in agitation.

Bruno, standing slightly back from the Sheriff, reached out and snapped the gun from the sheriff's hand in one deft movement. He checked the bullet chamber. It was empty. He stuck the gun in his waistband.

The Sheriff blushed. "Shucks." He cuffed his toe in the dirt not able to meet anyone's gaze. "See, it wasn't even loaded. I wasn't going to shoot anybody."

A small crowd had begun to gather around the curious group.

Andre said, "Shouldn't we conduct our reunion in a less public place? What do you think, Miss Lawless?"

Mercedes gave him a curt nod, joined Julia, and tucked her arm in hers.

"Julia, we are forgetting our manners," Mercedes said. "Shall we repair to the Lavender Dry Goods Emporium to sort this matter out?"

Everyone in their immediate group nodded agreement except for the man with the cheroot, who looked like he'd prefer a place under a rock. Bruno grasped his upper arm, encouraging him to join them in their walk to the Lavender Dry Goods Emporium.

Mercedes and Julia led the way, and the rest followed. The little parade wove along the street the short distance to the Emporium.

Julia leaned closer to her cousin and asked, "Where is Jamie?"

"He wouldn't get off the boat," Mercedes said, picking her way through the crowded street and holding up her skirts.

"What?"

"He's afraid of being left behind so he wouldn't come ashore. I think he was afraid that I might tie him up so he couldn't get back to the ship." She lifted one shoulder. "I'm afraid I've lost control over him." She gave a little smile of apology. "He said to say hello."

"Well, I never," said Julia. "The little scamp." She frowned in concern. "He'll be all right, won't he?"

"All right? My dear cousin, you never saw a happier young man than our Jamie on that beautiful clipper ship. I will never entice him away."

Mercedes looked around to see how close the entourage was to them and satisfied they would not be

Wings of the Wind

overheard, she continued. "Julia, please tell me what you know of the man with the top hat. He certainly presents a good figure."

"Doesn't he? He showed up shortly after you left. When I saw him, before I knew who he was, I nearly fainted. He looks so much like you."

"It is uncanny, isn't it?"

"Duncan said the same thing."

"Duncan, is it?" Mercedes said with the lift of her brow. The way Julia said his name suggested more than a friendly interest. "Where is he, by the way?"

"He's minding the store. He's working out real well, Mercedes. He's smart and very good with the books." Julia kept her gaze straight ahead, but Mercedes caught the rosy hue in her cheeks.

"I am glad to hear that," she said with a smile. "Now, tell me why you think the man in the top hat is my real uncle."

"Mercedes, you won't believe this, but he sent you a letter you never received. Apparently, he gave it to that sleazy man from New Orleans, instructing him to deliver it to you when he arrived in Galveston, but that never happened. That man from New Orleans is an impostor. Your real uncle showed us a copy of the letter he wrote. It says nothing about his assuming control of your store."

"It doesn't?" said Mercedes, as they started up the steps to the Emporium. She stopped at the entrance to the store, her face aglow. Her heart filled with joy. Her dear, beloved store she would never give up. Not for anyone.

The rest of the group caught up and, happily, Mercedes led the way into the welcoming coolness of the Lavender Dry Goods Emporium, where she stopped a few feet inside the door.

Marjorie Thelen

It was a beautiful sight. The lavender fragrance that washed over her soothed her troubled spirit. Nothing had changed at the Lavender Dry Goods Emporium, even though so much had happened since she left.

She felt a pang in her bosom and realized in that moment how much the Emporium meant to her, how much her life in Galveston meant to her. To think not long ago she was ready to throw it all away and chase after that worthless captain. Live and learn, she thought, trying to ignore the ache in her heart. For now she would get this uncle business cleared up.

The Sheriff came over and offered his excuses. Since he wasn't needed any longer he would be moseying along back to the jail, allowing as how there didn't seem to be any murder committed. If she needed any help, not to hesitate to send for him. He was sorry if he gave anybody a fright. It was all in the line of duty.

Mercedes thanked him and breathed a sigh of relief, as he swaggered out the store. He paused before Bruno to retrieve his gun. Bruno shook his head, eyes not acknowledging the hand outstretched before him. The Sheriff pulled his hat further down over his head and stomped out.

Several lady customers were in the store. When they recognized Mercedes in the group by the door, they rushed over, calling out greetings to her. How was she? It was good to have her back. Would she be at the church supper tonight? Oh dear, what happened to her eye?

Mercedes now regretted coming in the front door of the Emporium. Still in a state of shock over her uncles, she wasn't doing much coherent thinking.

Julia came to the rescue. "Ladies," she smiled and held out her hands, "Mercedes is fine. We won't make the

Wings of the Wind

church supper tonight. She's tired from traveling. Stop by tomorrow, and she'll be able to visit. She needs a good night's rest." She herded them toward the door in the manner of the best sheep herding dog.

A sea of bonnets and skirts swirled round Andre and Bruno, standing inside the door, as Julia hustled the ladies out. She returned in an instant and approached the two Nortons.

"Let me invite you to our parlor and offer you some refreshment, gentlemen. Please come with me."

They duly tagged after Julia, the cheroot looking around the store with great interest as he went by the displays.

Andre, Bruno, and Mercedes watched the group travel down the hall.

"Will you join us?" Mercedes asked Andre in a voice laced with icicles. It was the first she spoke to him since their argument. She didn't meet his eyes. She couldn't, it was too painful. She could feel his eyes upon her, but she would not give him the satisfaction of returning his gaze.

"Briefly," Andre said. "I'll haul the Norton from New Orleans off to settle our bet. Then we leave."

Mercedes bristled, stung again by his resolve to dump her. "Aren't you curious to know who the real uncle is? I guess you're only interested in settling the bet."

"It's obvious who the real one is," he said. "Whoever the impostor is, isn't important to me, as long as he settles up on our wager."

Andre's indifference pierced Mercedes to the core.

Julia appeared and interrupted their conversation. "Mercedes, are you coming?"

The tension in the air warned Julia stay her distance. Bruno moved back a few steps to stay clear of the line of fire.

"Yes, of course." Mercedes gathered up her skirts with dignity. "Excuse me, gentlemen. I must join my guests and become better acquainted with my new uncle." She followed after Julia without a backward glance.

* * * * *

"Someone's disappointed." Bruno ventured his opinion as they watched the two ladies walk away.

Andre cut him a sharp look. "What do you mean?"

"I mean someone is not happy about the new arrangements."

"What new arrangements?"

"You going off to San Francisco."

"Nothing new about that. We were always going to San Francisco."

"True, but not without Miss Mercedes."

Andre looked down the hall where the two ladies had disappeared.

"It's impossible for her to go. It would never work out." His face was hard, all angles and planes.

"What ever you say, Captain. Whatever you say." Bruno knew when to change the subject. "How are you going to get New Orleans Norton to pay up on his bet?"

"I'll talk to Carmichael about that. Somehow settling that debt has lost its urgency." Andre's glanced around. "I wonder where Carmichael is. He has to be here. He was the one looking after the store when everyone was down on the dock."

Andre walked toward the back of the store, looking around displays and counters.

Duncan stuck his head up from behind a counter filled

Wings of the Wind

with three different styles of seaman's hats. An ear-to-ear smile spread quickly across his face.

"Captain Lafitte, how good to see you. I thought I heard some commotion but I didn't think that you would be here. Usually the commotion is a bunch of ladies excited over some new frippery. I've learned to tune it out."

"Smart man, catches on fast," said Bruno, coming up behind Andre. Bruno gave Duncan the once over, noticing his new trousers and shirt. He looked a different man than the one they had left behind. "How do you like being on dry land?"

"I like it. Nice town. Nice people. I'm getting accustomed to the weather. I took off some clothes, like the Captain suggested."

All three of them laughed.

Duncan continued. "Julia's father has a marvelous garden in the back. Miss Julia and I sit out there in the evening." His face took on a deeper shade of red. "The work is pleasant. Julia manages the store and house well. She's a good cook. I could stay on here, I believe," he said, his voice drifting off at the end.

Bruno looked at Andre. "Did you hear that, Captain? Man says the lady is a good cook. What do you say to that?"

"I didn't know he liked red heads," said Andre. He considered Duncan. "He looks different, more domesticated or something and look at those fine new clothes he's wearing. He looks more the frontier man now."

Duncan's color deepened even more, and he picked up a fan to wave it in front of him. "I guess I have changed some." He hesitated, seeming to gather his courage, then blurted out, "Miss Julia's a fine woman, and I believe it's time I should be settling down. I haven't spoken to her father yet, but I have hopes the lady would have me."

Andre smiled and extended his hand. "My congratulations. I hope for your sake, she'll accept. She's a fine looking woman."

Bruno laughed and clapped Duncan on the shoulder. "You work fast, man. I should take lessons from you, not that I'm looking for anything permanent."

Duncan grinned then peered uncertainly at Andre. "I hope you don't mind my leaving your employ, Captain Lafitte."

"You're a good man, Carmichael, but under the circumstances, I'd say you made a good choice." Andre smiled at him, then his brows knit together. "I do have one final request of you."

"What would that be, Captain?"

"I take it you know about the two Nortons."

Duncan nodded. "That I do. It was a shock the day the real uncle walked in. At first, we couldn't figure out what was going on."

"It turns out the New Orleans Norton is the impostor, but he owes me. He says that he'll get Derek Bragg to cover the debt. Will you press him on that since you'll be staying on here? You can write me of the outcome. As soon as that party breaks up in there, corner the man. We already know he's slippery, so you'll need to stay on him before he disappears again. He may be part of an extortion ring. You should give the Sheriff that information. I'm not sure about the Sheriff's abilities but . . ." Andre shrugged by way of finishing the thought.

"That I will, sir. I'll be glad to look into it."

"Thank you. We'll be in touch." Andre turned to Bruno. "Let's say our good-byes and be off. I've spent enough time tangled up in this mess. I'm anxious get back

Wings of the Wind

onto the high seas."

Bruno glanced at Andre and shook his head. "I never figured you for obtuse but obtuse you are."

"What?" said Andre.

Duncan watched them with interest.

"Nothing, Captain," said Bruno. "Nothing at all. Let's say good-bye."

Andre regarded Bruno like he had two heads then strode down the corridor toward the parlor.

Bruno shrugged, noticed Duncan's puzzled face and said, "The man got a good thing going, and he can't see it. It's time he settled down."

Duncan's eyebrows went up. "You mean the Captain and Miss Mercedes?"

"Yeah. They been sniffing around each other ever since she showed up on the decks of *Wings of the Wind* here in Galveston. But you know how love is. They can't see it when it's looking right at them. The crew is making bets how long it's gonna take them to tie the knot."

Duncan grinned. "It is unnerving, I have to admit. When you've never been in love, it's kind of hard to figure what's wrong with you. It feels like a fever, an affliction. I couldn't take my eyes off Miss Julia, and I wanted to be everywhere she was. When you aren't used to that, it takes awhile to figure out."

"Didn't take you long."

"Miss Julia was the one to point it out. I was following her around like a puppy. I'm not a forward guy, but I reached for her hand the first night we sat out there in the garden. My hand just reached over and grabbed hers, like it had a life of its own. There wasn't much thinking involved."

Bruno thumped Duncan on the back. "I wish you the

best. I better go in and see how things are going."

* * * * *

In the parlor, Andre encountered consternation and confusion.

"Where could he have gone?" Mercedes asked.

"He was just here," said Julia. "I only stepped out to see if you were coming and when I got back he was gone. Father, you mean you didn't see him leave?"

"No, me and Mr. Norton here, we were talking what varieties of tomatoes to plant in a sub tropical climate, and I guess we were standing with our backs to the man. Is that right, Mr. Norton?"

"Quite right. We turned to look out to the garden, and, when we were turned back, Julia was gone and so was the other gentleman. I assumed he went with you, Miss Julia."

"No, he wasn't with me. I went to see what was keeping Mercedes."

Mercedes fumed in frustration. "Now he's gone again. After all the chasing we did, he slipped through our fingers."

"It may be good riddance," said Andre from the doorway. Everyone turned to stare at him.

Mercedes recovered first. "The Norton from New Orleans has disappeared."

"I heard." Andre examined the parlor exits. "He probably went out the back and over the wall in the garden. I doubt we'll see him again."

"Aren't you going to go after him?" asked Mercedes.

"No, I'm not going after him. Duncan will check around for me."

"What about your bet?"

Wings of the Wind

"I might have to kiss it good-bye. I've already wasted far too much time on that weasel. It looks like you have the right uncle here." Andre nodded and advanced in the direction of the man standing by Uncle Everett.

"I do believe I am the real uncle," the man chuckled and held out his hand to Andre. "Jeffrey Norton at your service, Captain Lafitte. Quite delighted to meet you. I recall now who that other man is. His name is Reginald Ross. I met him at my club in Boston, and we played cards together. He was well dressed, charming, and knowledgeable about the cotton business. He was in town on business and came to the club with a friend. In the course of the evening, one of my associates at the card table asked me how my efforts were going to find my niece. The private investigator I had enlisted had just given me Mercedes' address in Galveston."

He looked in her direction. Her heart opened like a flower to this man who looked so much like her. He was her real uncle, her mother's real brother. It was a dream come true. He smiled the kindest smile and advanced toward her.

"This man expressed quite an interest in the details of my search for you, and now that I think of it, I suppose I was too free with my information. I told him about finding you had a store, the Lavender Dry Goods Emporium, and how proud I was you had the Norton business sense. He said he was enroute to Galveston and could take a letter if I so desired."

Mercedes studied her uncle. "A letter did arrive but it arrived by post, not through him."

Her uncle nodded. "I gave him the letter, he apparently rewrote it, then posted it along the way. I didn't think about the encounter until today. The man seemed honest enough.

He played a decent hand of cards, very civilized. He mentioned that he was going to book passage to New Orleans and Galveston, and I mentioned that one of our ships was leaving soon for New Orleans, and maybe he would want to talk to the Captain about sailing with him. There usually are a few cabins on a clipper, but I didn't know if they were available since I don't pay much attention to that end of our business. I gave him the letter for you, and I never saw him again until today."

"Our ship?" asked Andre. "What ship would that be?"

"Why *Wings of the Wind,* Captain Lafitte," said Uncle Jeffrey.

Shocked silence ensued.

Uncle Jeffrey gazed from one pair of wide eyes to the other. His settled on Mercedes. "I didn't know, my dear, you had left for New Orleans on *Wings of the Wind*. In our conversations, Julia didn't mention the ship or the captain. I assumed you had gone over on the steamer to shop in New Orleans. Miss Julia said that you had left on a buying trip for the Emporium."

Julia sneaked a peak at Mercedes. "I didn't know what to tell him, Mercedes. The circumstances of your leaving were rather unusual."

Mercedes let out a long, unladylike sigh, nodding her head. "I best sit down," she said and collapsed on the settee.

Julia sat beside her and took her hand. "He has more to tell you, my dear. It's about your grandmother and the inheritance."

"My grandmother?" It was such a strange word to Mercedes's tongue. She had not thought of having a grandmother.

"Are you one of the partners in World Shipping?" said

Andre, cutting into the conversation and directing his question to Jeffrey Norton.

"Yes, we own a large share," Jeffrey said to Andre, "but we're silent partners, operating under the name of Back Bay, Ltd. We are merely investors and are not involved in the day-to-day operation. Our main business interests are in railroads. We've sold off much of the other businesses and have consolidated our investments in railroads and ships. I took over as head of the business after Father passed on sometime back."

Uncle Jeffrey directed his remarks to Mercedes. "Your grandmother died repenting of her estrangement with her daughter. She left half of the inheritance and business to me and the other half to Esther. That is why it was imperative that I find my sister."

"And now that your sister is gone?" asked Andre.

"Mercedes and Jamie inherit equally."

Mercedes peered thunderstruck at her uncle. "That means that I am a part owner of the *Wings of the Wind*." The full impact of what he said about an inheritance was lost on her. *Wings of the Wind* mattered most.

"That's right," said her uncle, smiling at her. "It's a fine ship, isn't it, Captain Lafitte? We are proud of her and feel fortunate to have Captain Lafitte take her on her maiden voyage to San Francisco. I've only heard of Captain Lafitte, but long I've wanted to meet him, and here we are." He beamed at Andre.

Mercedes looked at Andre, who was wearing his poker face. She could not read what was going through his mind. But a smile spread across her face. "So if I'm an owner then I could sail with *Wings of the Wind* to San Francisco, couldn't I, Uncle?"

He looked perplexed. "Why would you want to do

that? You have this nice shop. We've just met, and I thought that maybe you might want to go back with me to Boston. We have relatives that want to meet you. Perhaps that you might even consider moving there to live closer to me and the family business. You could help out."

"I've never been to San Francisco, but I've wanted to go for some time." Mercedes watched Andre, hoping for some sign that he was relenting. "My brother Jamie is sailing with Captain Lafitte as his ship's clerk. Won't he be delighted?"

Andre assessed Mercedes with a shake of his head. "You have the most amazing luck, Miss Lawless."

With a whoop she was on her feet and dancing around the floor with Uncle Jeffrey. "Don't you see, Uncle? I've always wanted my own shipping line, and now I have it. I've been saving to invest in a ship, and I've already got one."

"My dear, you have more than one," he said, trying to keep up with her crazy steps. "I'm not sure at the moment how many we've invested in. I'm not surprised that your grandfather's business acumen flows in your veins. Did you know he got his start with a retail shop?"

Mercedes stopped. "He didn't."

"He did. He did." Uncle Jeffrey sobered. "I tell you it was such a disappointment when your mother ran off. Your grandfather was so angry. He always said she had thrown her life away. Of course, there was the disgrace of her running away with a seaman. Your grandfather was a strict, God fearing man. Women in his world didn't act like your mother. He was kind to your grandmother, but he ruled the roost. Over the years she wanted to try to find your mother, but he would hear none of it."

"How kind of you to search for us. I mean, you could

Wings of the Wind

have chosen to keep everything for yourself," said Mercedes.

"There is plenty to go around. I really wanted family. It gets lonely being a bachelor. I should have looked for a wife, but I've been too involved with the business."

Mercedes turned to Andre who stood regarding her with crossed arms. "Captain Lafitte, what do you say to having me as a passenger?" It was if only the two of them were in the room, and time stood still. Mercedes searched the hard lines of Andre's face for some softening, some sign that he cared.

The set of Andre's jaw remained firm, unmoving. "Miss Lawless, if this is true, as an owner you can do as you wish, but you will have to look for another captain. I resign my position as of this moment." Their eyes locked, and Mercedes knew she had lost the battle.

"You can't do that, Captain Lafitte, you signed a contract with us to take this clipper to San Francisco," said Uncle Jeffrey.

"I can break the contract. There's a penalty to be paid, but I'll pay it. I'll speak to the crew. I hand picked them, but I'm sure they'll stay on. I might be able to find you another captain."

Silence once again reigned in the room, an unsettled, unhappy silence.

Mercedes walked to the window that overlooked the garden and looked out. She didn't want anyone to see the hurt and anger rage across her face. Even in her pain, the businesswoman in her was smart enough to know that they needed Captain Andre Lafitte to take the clipper to San Francisco. She wasn't good in the business of the heart, but the business of money she understood.

She allowed the loveliness of the garden to ease her

heart. The white and pink of the oleander flowers, the lantana in bright pink, yellows and golds, bougainvillea in fuchsia and yellow draping the wall. She had lost him. He didn't want her. It wouldn't work. She wanted to leave the room, get away from him, away from the confusion and disappointment.

She turned back to the group in the room. Everyone was watching her. She kept her eyes averted and struggled to keep her face composed. "I won't go." She bit her lip, picked up her skirts, and pushed her way past Andre then Bruno, who stood in the doorway.

Uncle Everett watched her go, his hands in his back pockets. Uncle Jeffrey looked at Andre in puzzlement. Julia picked up her skirts to follow Mercedes.

"Gentlemen," she said to the group. "Mercedes is tired. She's been through a lot. I'll see what I can do for her. There'll be no cooked dinner today at the Lavender Dry Goods Emporium. Uncle Jeffrey, would you invite our guests to have dinner with you at the Tremont?"

"Quite," said Uncle Jeffrey, recovering himself. "Quite so, gentlemen. Capital idea. Why don't we all go to the Tremont for a bit of refreshment? We can talk this whole thing over there. The ladies can take the situation in hand."

"Thank you." Julia bobbed a curtsey and hurried from the parlor.

"I'll stay here, gentlemen," said Uncle Everett. "I've have work to do in the garden, and I think I'll get to it." He gave them a wave and left to find solace in the garden.

"Captain Lafitte," said Uncle Jeffrey. "Shall we?" He indicated the door. "Let's go to the Tremont and relax with a whiskey."

Andre followed Uncle Jeffrey from the room in stony

silence. Bruno brought up the rear wagging his head.

Marjorie Thelen

Chapter Twenty-Two

Andre stood, fingers hooked on his hips, on the porch of the Lavender Dry Goods Emporium, wondering how the hell things had gotten so complicated. He squinted into the blazing sun, watched the horses and carriages in the street. He was in no mood to sit in some fancy hotel with this top hatted gentleman. Where he wanted to be was on his beautiful, sleek clipper ship, *Wings of the Wind*, away from land, out on the vast, glorious ocean. But here he was sweating in the muggy heat of a Galveston summer day, having just resigned his position on his beautiful, sleek clipper, all because of Mercedes Lawless.

What infernal luck the woman had, and as it was turning out, what infernal bad luck he had when the impostor, Reginald Ross, or whatever his name was, signed onto his ship. That's when all of this had started. No, even before that when her real uncle had told the impostor to sign on to *Wings of the Wind*.

What Mercedes and Uncle Jeffrey did not know was that Andre owned controlling interest in World Shipping Line. It made him downright irritable that this preposterous misadventure was costing him money. It served him right for being greedy to claim what was now an insignificant wager.

Bruno nudged his elbow. "Captain, you going to stand

here all day in this heat? Let's go have a drink. You look like you could use two or three. Maybe a bottle."

"Right you are. Where's Norton?"

"Right here, Captain Lafitte." Uncle Jeffrey came up behind them. "Shall we go? I'm sure we can work something out about the ship."

"I know we can," Andre said, not looking around. "Let's go to the Salty Alligator. I like the atmosphere better there."

Andre and Bruno strode down the steps with Uncle Jeffrey hurrying behind to keep up. The Salty Alligator Saloon was on a pier, the next street over from the Emporium.

Andre pushed through the swinging doors into the bedlam and sweat of a seaman's bar. He elbowed his way to the long mahogany bar with brass foot railing and ordered a bottle and three glasses. He flipped a coin on the bar for the bartender and took bottle and glasses over to the table that Bruno cleared for them.

"Interesting crowd," said Jeffrey, gazing about. He set his top hat on the table, took a seat, and thanked Andre for the tall tumbler of whiskey pushed his way.

"My kind of people," Andre said, as he poured for Bruno and himself. They both sat facing the door. Andre took a long draw on his whisky and surveyed the tables where groups of four and five seaman in various stages of inebriation played cards.

Uncle Jeffrey cleared his throat. "Captain Lafitte, shall we talk about your resignation or forget you ever brought it up?"

"The latter." Andre sipped his whiskey, considering whether to say anything else. He added, "Miss Lawless isn't going, so I'll take the ship."

Marjorie Thelen

"Glad to hear you will." Jeffrey looked thoughtful. "I see that I will have to get accustomed to my niece. She seems a bit forward and likes to take command of the situation. She's just like my father. If he hadn't been so bull-headed, we never would have had Esther's estrangement from the family."

He glanced at Andre, who had finished his first tumbler of whiskey and was helping himself to another. "I recall hearing that the Captain of *Wings of the Wind* was an owner in World Shipping."

Andre cocked any eyebrow. "Where did you hear that?"

"At my club, playing cards."

Andre gave an internal headshake. Where would they all be without cards? "I'm an owner."

Uncle Jeffrey held his hand out to Andre, who shook it. "So we are partners, Captain Lafitte. It is you who has controlling interest in the company, is it not?"

Andre nodded once.

"As I suspected. You really weren't serious when you resigned."

"I would have been serious if Miss Lawless had insisted on going."

"What do you have against my niece, Captain?"

Andre didn't answer right away, preferring to let a few more sips of the whiskey slide down his throat. He didn't have anything against his niece that a few nights in bed with her would go a long way to curing. Maybe it would take a week. Maybe a month. By that time they'd be almost to the Straits of Magellan, and he wouldn't have shown his face for a month on deck being shacked up with the lady. What a disaster that would be. A little voice said, maybe it would take a lifetime. Bah, he said to the voice. He didn't want to think about lifetime.

Add to his lust for her the simple fact that thoughts of her were now driving him to the edge of sanity. Not that he would admit it to anyone. A long sea voyage away from her would be the perfect thing to drive every last lewd and licentious thought he had of her from his head.

So Andre said, "I have nothing against your niece. She is a lovely woman and quite accomplished. I don't take women passengers on my ships. I explained that to Miss Lawless."

Bruno sniggered softly into his glass that earned him a withering look from Andre.

Without warning, Bruno sat up straighter and nudged Andre. "Look who's sitting at the table playing cards at the far end of the room last table on the right, almost hidden by the piano."

Andre and Jeffrey peered through the smoky haze to the section of the room Bruno indicated.

"I say, isn't that the fellow who claimed he was me?" Jeffrey squinted his eyes like that would help them focus better.

"That's him all right," Andre said.

Bruno polished off his drink. "Haven't you got unfinished business with that guy?"

Andre ran his tongue over his teeth and made a sucking sound. "He still owes me." He sat considering. "Does the man ever do any useful work? I've seen him playing cards, in bed at a whorehouse, and here in a saloon playing cards again. No wonder he has to dream up scams to relieve upstanding citizens of their money. I'll go over and invite him outside." Andre finished off his second tumbler and put his hands on the table to rise.

Bruno put his hand on Andre's arm to check his

progress. "Hold on a second, Captain, look who just came through the door."

Andre eased back into his seat and stared toward the door. "I wonder how Bragg made it out of the ropes and to Galveston that fast. Steamer service must be better that I thought. Let's have another round and see what happens."

Andre divided the rest of the bottle of whiskey evenly between the three of them. They sat back to see what would happen next.

"Excuse me, Captain, but who is the man to whom Bruno was referring? Are we talking about the big, husky looking chap with his back to us at the bar?" Jeffrey gestured toward the general direction of the bar.

Andre's mouth tugged on one corner. "That's one of Miss Lawless's suitors. He's tried twice to get her to marry him, but the lady isn't willing. Last time we saw him he was tied up in a cotton warehouse in New Orleans."

"My niece's suitor? Good grief. He doesn't look the gentleman. That's another good reason to take my niece back to Boston with me."

"He isn't a gentleman. He's supposed to be partners with the man you called Reginald Ross. Whatever they're partners in, most of it isn't legal. I like your idea of taking Miss Lawless to Boston. I'll hold you to that." It would save Andre the worry of Mercedes being stalked by Bragg without him here to protect her.

"Come Bruno, let's see if we can get into that card game." Andre tossed back the last of his drink, rose, and stretched.

Bruno jerked his head toward the big, beefy guy at the bar. "What we going to do about him?"

Andre shrugged. "See what he does when he finds Ross at the card table. Maybe he's here to meet up with

Wings of the Wind

him."

Bruno shoved back his chair and got up, flexing his huge, muscular arms.

Jeffrey tried the same and flopped right back down in the seat. "My-oh-my. That whiskey was rather strong," he said to his two standing companions. "I think I'll just lay my head on the table and take a little ssnap," he said with a slur and clonked over face down on the table.

Bruno glanced at Andre, who shrugged his shoulders. "Leave him here. We'll take him back to the hotel when the card game is over."

They left Jeffrey and strolled to the back of the saloon, past the bar two and three deep in seaman, past the piano where an enthusiastic player was pounding out an off key tune, to a table covered with glasses, bottles, coins, and cards. They stopped behind the three men who sat at the table. One chair went unoccupied.

"Mind if we join you?" asked Andre.

The three men looked up at the two tall men who stood by their table.

"Got any money?" asked the skinny one with an unkempt beard.

"This man here owes me," said Andre. "Maybe he could put some up for me. Isn't that right, Ross?"

Reginald Ross, still in the same rumpled clothes with a smoking cheroot hanging out his mouth, cocked his head. "If it ain't Captain Lafitte." He smiled his lazy grin. "Sit down, sit down. Let's find a chair for your friend. Boys, get this man a chair."

"Get it yourself," the skinny guy said, curling his lip.

Someone shoved a chair up to the table.

"How 'bout this one?" The chair came with a big, beefy hand attached. "Captain Lafitte, is it? Imagine meeting you here," said Derek Bragg.

Andre tugged at his chin. "Where did I see you last? Was it in a warehouse in New Orleans?"

"You got that right," Bragg said and let go with a punch intended for Andre.

Bruno, standing a shade to the side of Andre, blocked the punch and delivered one himself direct to Bragg's belly. It sent him lurching into the skinny guy's lap.

"Hey," said the skinny guy. "Get out of my lap."

Bragg obliged as the force of his fall carried him the whole way to the floor between the chairs and the table. The table, being a mite unsteady itself with only two good legs out of four, let go and tilted its contents onto the floor with a crash of glass and tinkle of coins. The three card players sprang to their feet, as other occupants of the room rushed over to check out the action.

Bragg hauled himself up from the table debris and lunged for Bruno who stepped aside enough to allow Bragg to hit the guy behind him. Three men jumped on Bragg, and then there was pandemonium, as arms swung from all directions.

Andre searched the room for Ross, but he had disappeared in the sea of swinging arms. He led Bruno through the melee toward the door. They pulled Jeffrey off the table and out of his chair, and the three of them stumbled into the street.

The sun was setting over Galveston Bay by the time they got Uncle Jeffrey back to the Tremont Hotel and into his bed, out cold.

Andre and Bruno left the hotel and strode down the street toward the wharf.

"Let's get back to the ship," Andre said, "because Tito may show up anytime. I told him to come looking if we hadn't made it back by dark."

"So we're going to sail, eh, Captain?" Bruno said. "Not going to take your new business partner with you?"

"Who? Norton?"

"You know who I mean."

Andre studied water of Galveston Bay, stretching out to the horizon. He shook his head. "I can't serve two mistresses, and the sea is the one I choose."

* * * * *

Julia looked in on Mercedes early the next morning. She found her cousin wide-awake, lying in bed. By the tousled look of the sheets and her hair and the dark circles under her eyes, she knew Mercedes had not rested well.

"Good morning." Julia went over to stand by the narrow bed. "How do you feel?"

Mercedes gave a faint smile and sat up. She had only one question, but she already knew the answer. "Did they sail?"

Julia gave a sad smile and faint nod of the head. "Last night with the tide." She sat on the edge of the bed and took her cousin's hand. "I'm sorry."

Mercedes softly blew out a breath of resignation. "Don't be sorry on my account.

"You're in love with him." Julia didn't even try to make it into a question.

Mercedes gazed out the window. "As much as any person can be in love with the wind." She turned back to her cousin. "He's right. It wouldn't work." But that wasn't what her heart said. "The bad part is Jamie is with him. If I could make a clean break and never hear about him again, it would be better. But hearing from Jamie, I'll be hearing about the wonders of Captain Lafitte. Besides that, now we're partners in the shipping business. At some point in my life, I'll run across him. I hope by then I'm over him."

But she knew in her heart she would never get over Andre Lafitte. She was a one-man woman, and she had found her man. She was not the type to keep looking. She knew what she wanted, and if he didn't want her, she would remain alone. If she saw him again, she hoped that the pain she felt in her heart would be healed, and she would be able to look at him without regret.

Mercedes pulled off the sheet, looking around her small room. Over the last weeks she had lost track of the season and the rhythm of her daily life, but here she was back in her own familiar world that wasn't as comforting as it once was.

They sat in silence. Julia tried to look cheerful and changed the subject. "How does it feel to be an heiress?"

Heiress. The thought had swirled through her mind during her sleepless night. "It hasn't sunk in. I feel like I'm in a dream, like none of this is real. That if I got dressed and went below, Jamie would be unpacking boxes, I would have only one uncle, New Orleans would be only a name, and I would never have met Andre Lafitte."

"Everything has changed," said Julia with a bittersweet smile for her cousin. "It's been too much for you to handle with so many changes in so short a time." She paused. "I have some good news for you."

Mercedes' face lit up. "What?"

"Duncan has asked Father for my hand. We're to be married." Julia let go with the biggest smile Mercedes had ever seen on her face.

"That's wonderful." She embraced her cousin and held her tight. "He's a good man. I'm happy for you. When will you tie the knot?"

"In a week or two as soon as we can organize a little party. I thought maybe you would help me. It might take your mind off things." Her smile held a question in it.

"Of course, I'd love to. Thank you for including me." Mercedes gave her cousin a kiss on the cheek then leaned back on the wall. She studied Julia.

"Julia," she began slowly, "now that Duncan will be staying on, how would you feel about the two of you taking over the store?"

Julia flashed her a wide-eyed look. "That would be perfect for us. I'm sure Duncan would be pleased."

"Good, that settles it. The store shall be my wedding gift to you both."

"Mercedes, how very kind of you! But what will you do?" She stopped. "I'm forgetting. You have other business interests to look after now."

Mercedes nodded. "Lying in bed this morning, I thought about New Orleans. I liked it. I thought I might take a house there for a while, after I come back from New England. I've decided to take my uncle up on his invitation of visiting Boston. It's a comfort to know that I have family on my mother's side."

Tears glistened in her eyes, and she felt the old grief for her mother. But she also rejoiced in her newfound uncle, and she looked forward to spending more time with him.

She wiped her eyes with the tips of her fingers. "Jamie's gone so I don't have that responsibility. I guess I'm a free woman." Her smile was ironic. "Besides, I want to get away from Galveston. That boor Bragg might be back to bother me, and I don't want to have to hire a bodyguard."

Marjorie Thelen

* * * * *

Mercedes and Jeffrey stayed in Galveston until Julia and Duncan married. Mercedes showed him around the town and the island and, as they passed the time together, they realized how much they thought alike.

Jeffrey Norton had an enlightened mind, a product of the winds of change blowing through the United States of America, where ideas were heady things. He read widely, enjoyed the theater, believed in the railroads and what they would do for the expansion of the country and had become involved in the anti-slavery movement. It troubled him to see the slaves on the island. He discovered in his niece a ready audience, good conversationalist, and a thirst for knowledge to match his own.

On a Saturday afternoon Duncan and Julia married in a modest ceremony in Trinity Episcopal Church. They held a small reception after the wedding in Uncle Everett's garden, ablaze in floral color. Mercedes gave a recital for them on her new pianoforte, and no one passed out from nerves or heat exhaustion.

Uncle and niece left for Boston on the evening steamer the day after the wedding. In New Orleans they boarded a sailing ship bound for Boston. It wasn't a clipper, and it wasn't the *Wings of the Wind*. Nothing would ever come close to that ship.

The whirl of the wedding preparations and then the trip to Boston and the newness of it kept Mercedes preoccupied and busy. She fit in easily to the pace of the New England town and the days filled with meeting relatives, getting acquainted with the family business and endless social engagements and cultural events.

The weather had started to cool into fall when one

morning Mercedes awoke in her suite of rooms in the Norton house with a queasy stomach. She barely made it to the chamber pot before she threw up. Each morning for the next few weeks the same routine continued. She got tired earlier in the evenings. She had not had her monthly courses since she had been with Andre. Her maid, Antoinette, helped her find a discreet doctor who confirmed her suspicions. She was expecting a child.

She stayed with Jeffrey through the Christmas holidays, Antoinette helping to alter her dresses to disguise her rounding figure. Then she decided it was time to take up her plan to retire to a house in New Orleans. Besides, the New England winter wasn't to her taste.

With sad protestations from her uncle, promises to return in the spring, and a tearful parting from her relatives, she took passage on one of her own sailing vessels and went back to her corner of the world.

Marjorie Thelen

Chapter Twenty-Three

"How does the Captain seem to you?" Bruno asked Tito as they watched the longshoremen unloading the cargo from the *Wings of the Wind*. The fog was so heavy they could barely make out the buildings of San Francisco in front of them.

"More restless than usual. A night in town will do him good."

"I don't think it's that," said Bruno. "He still has that little shopkeeper in Galveston under his skin."

"Could be but he will not tell us if he does or not."

They both nodded, watching the cargo going ashore.

Bruno pulled out a splinter of wood and worked at one of his teeth with it. "That Jamie is something, isn't he? He's become the Captain's shadow. Has the makings of a fine seaman."

Tito nodded in agreement. "It is nice to see the way the Captain treats him, like a brother."

"If the Captain thought this trip was going to make him forget that girl, it didn't work." Bruno gave Tito a sideways glance. "Hard to forget a woman like that."

"Si, but you didn't win the bet that he'd bring her with him on this trip." Tito gave his mate a shove with his arm. "I think you are in love with her."

"Maybe I am," said Bruno. "She is mighty fine,

Wings of the Wind

mighty fine. I'd give up a life at sea for her. Maybe I'll look her up when we get back."

"If the Captain doesn't beat you to it. Besides what would a pretty girl like her want with an ugly, old bastard like you?"

* * * * *

"I've heard a lot about you," Blaze said to Andre as she showed him into the parlor of her private rooms.

"I'm pretty far from where I call home. I can't believe I'm a legend yet."

"You're getting there. We hear a lot of tales in my establishment with all the seaman that come in. I heard you have your own brothel in New Orleans." She poured a healthy glass of whisky and handed it to him.

Andre gave a soft snort in reply before he took a good swig of the drink. "It's not mine anymore. I sold it for a goodly sum." It never failed to amaze him how small the sailing world was.

"I know your trip here had to make you a tidy sum. Your sailing time was right up there with the records so far. Everyone is talking about the *Wings of the Wind*."

Andre nodded. The trip had made him even more money than he already had, his ship had performed flawlessly, his crew was in great shape, his new ship's clerk worked out well. But for all his success he was unfulfilled, unsatisfied, restless. Maybe Blaze could help him out. He looked at her standing in the candlelight, her head tilted waiting for a response for him.

Her cleavage alone begged attention. The candlelight picked up the gold highlights in her hair and the sparkle in her blue eyes. Any other time he would have made his move by now. But she smelled of lavender and the fragrance brought into his heart the image of Mercedes. The thought of her had been his constant companion the entire voyage. Every night he lay down on his bunk with her image, the taste of her, the feel of her still fresh in his senses.

He shook his head as if trying to clear it, and Blaze gave him a questioning look. "Do you have a girlfriend back home?"

He gave a short laugh. Women like Blaze had wisdom beyond their years. "I didn't think I did. Or at least I was trying not to but there is a girl I can't get out of my thoughts."

Blaze nodded her head in understanding. "I've seen it before. Men come in here and think that a night with one of our girls will cure that illness. But it doesn't." She smiled. "If it did, I'd be a very wealthy woman."

She indicated the sofa. "Sit down and tell me about her. It won't be the first time I've listened to this story."

Andre told Blaze, a woman he had never met, the story of Mercedes Lawless. Blaze listened without interruption and then asked, "What is it you want out of life?"

Andre frowned. "I have it. Money, success, a life at sea."

"But here you sit on a couch with a whore, telling her about another woman when you should be enjoying the whore considering the money you've paid. Now why aren't you?"

Andre thought about it. "I guess it feels like it would be a betrayal to touch another woman."

Blaze nodded her head knowingly. "Well then you don't have everything because the woman you want isn't with you, isn't here tonight to warm your bed and your heart. You can sail around the world and not escape your heart."

Andre gazed unseeing into the fire on the hearth. "I know that now."

"We all learn our lessons in our own way."

Andre smiled over at Blaze. "Thank you. I think I'll be on my way. I have a long trip back to Mercedes."

* * * * *

Mercedes took a modest two-story house in New Orleans in the French Quarter on Dumaine Street. The house sat back from the street and had a small, enclosed garden to the rear. Rumor had that the plantation style house beside hers was the former residence of one of Jean Lafitte's lieutenants, when the band of pirates lived in New Orleans in the early part if the century. Tall shade trees lined the quiet street. Her maid Antoinette, of whom she had grown fond, had returned with her.

Fabienne Beluche and Claudette came to visit soon after their arrival. "I heard you were in town, ma cherie. I hope you don't mind my calling on you."

"Of course not, it's good to see you," said Mercedes with a smile. "You look marvelous." They exchanged kisses in the French style.

Mercedes bent to greet Claudette in the same fashion and asked her how she was. The child smiled shyly up to her, dropped a polite curtsey and answered, "Very well, mademoiselle."

"I see I have moved to a small world," said Mercedes.

Fabienne laughed with a sparkle. "It is not such a small world, so much as I have a very great nose."

Mercedes joined in her laughter, leading them into a parlor decorated in the latest rococo revival style and indicated a seat for each.

"Why would I mind your calling on me?"

"After our last adventure, I was not sure if you would want to see me again. Now I am the madam of the Silver Slipper so I am not very respectable company for you."

Mercedes smiled ruefully when she thought of their last adventure. "That seems long ago for me, does it for you?"

"Yes, it does."

"I didn't know about the Silver Slipper. Didn't Captain Lafitte own it?" She could talk about Andre now. She could smile about the bubble of life she could feel awakening in her.

"He did. But before he left New Orleans the last time, he sold it to Jack Lormand. Before he died, Jack gave it to me."

Mercedes raised her eyebrows. "Jack Lormand is dead? That must be sad for you, Fabienne."

"I miss him, of course. Jack took good care of me. He knew he was dying, and he wanted to make sure I had something to tide me over in my old age. I will stay with it a few more years, then sell and retire. Maybe I will go to Paris to live, who knows?" Fabienne made a wry face. "No one liked Jack much besides me and his wife, and Andre's mother, of course, when she lived."

"Andre's mother?"

"Mais, oui. Andre's mother owned the Silver Slipper. He inherited it from her. That's where he and his brother grew up."

"Andre's mother was a . . . " Mercedes stopped, realizing what she was about to say.

Fabienne nodded. "Andre's mother was a lovely, beautiful woman but not a good mother. Are you shocked? He said that he had not told you. I thought it was time, now that he is gone and cannot so easily strangle me."

"I didn't know." Mercedes even smiled, couldn't help smiling with Fabienne who was so gay and carefree. "I guess that's all part of who Andre is."

Not ready to talk freely about Andre, Mercedes brought up another subject that was on her mind. "Are you still making dresses, Fabienne? The one you have on is striking. Green must be your favorite color because the last time we were together you were in green silk. I ask because I need to have some new ones made."

Fabienne assessed Mercedes' sitting figure. "I still have the shop, and three good women who run it for me. Green is the only color I wear as I think you prefer lavender, no? It sets off your eyes the best. I think you have gained weight since last I saw you. You will need something a bit fuller around the middle."

Mercedes' blush highlighted the lavender in her eyes. "Yes, I will need something fuller around the middle. Maybe you could create a new style for me."

Fabienne laughed. "With these styles now, they are so full, no one will notice. Your new condition agrees with you. Your eyes glow, and your skin is clear and rosy."

"Thank you, Fabienne. I feel quite well though I don't plan to go about much in the next few months."

"Do you have a good doctor here?"

When Mercedes shook her head, Fabienne said, "I have an excellent one, and I will give you the name. You will have no problems."

"Thank you, Fabienne. You are kind to help me."

"We business women need to stick together," said

Fabienne. She picked at the folds in her dress. "I have a favor to ask of you."

"Of course, how can I be of help?"

"It's Claudette." Fabienne gazed lovingly at the beautiful child sitting on the chair with her hands folded in her lap. "Where we live now it is not such a good environment for a little girl. Might she come to live with you? I know I am being bold to ask this of you, but I think you would be good for her, and she for you."

"With me? Claudette?" Mercedes raised her hand to her heart. She hesitated but an instant and decided. "What a lovely idea. It will be nice to have company. Would you like that, Claudette?"

Silky blond curls danced around the child's head, as she nodded her agreement.

"It's done then. You'll come to stay with me." Mercedes leaned over, took the little girl's hand and gave it a squeeze. "I have a lovely garden here where we can spend the afternoons in the shade. I could help you with your lessons, too."

"Perfect," said Fabienne. "She needs a tutor. I have been helping her, but with my new responsibilities my time is limited."

Mercedes face clouded for a moment. "I don't know how long I will stay, Fabienne. It depends what happens in the next several months. I may be going back to Boston in the spring, but we can talk then."

"Yes, of course. This means so much to me. I cannot thank you enough," she said, blinking back tears. "Is there anything I can help you with while you stay in our lovely city?"

Mercedes worried her lower lip. "Yes, there is. I need a manservant, like a butler, someone who would guard the house. I would feel safer. This is an unfamiliar city for me."

Fabienne got up and paced back and forth. "I could get you someone, but he would not be a slave. I know someone who is a free person of color. There are many of us in New Orleans. I don't deal in slaves, do you understand? The people I employ are free. Sometimes it is hard to keep them that way."

Mercedes watched Fabienne pace. "I've not ever had slaves. I find slavery abhorrent."

"I thought as much. The man is called Elijah. He has worked at the Silver Slipper for many years. He is older and needs a situation less demanding, should I say? I think he would be perfect here. I will talk to him. He is a favorite of Andre's."

Their eyes met at the mention of Andre.

"Have you heard from him?" asked Fabienne, softly.

Mercedes gave Fabienne a sad smile. "Not from him, only news of him through my brother, Jamie, who adores him. Jamie doesn't write often, but, when he does, there are always glowing statements about Captain Lafitte. They made it to San Francisco in 95 days, almost a record. They are on their way back."

"Will they come here?"

"Jamie writes that they go to Boston first. They apparently have cargo they are bringing back for customers in the Boston area."

"What will you do?" Fabienne walked over and sat down on settee next to Mercedes.

Mercedes gazed straight ahead toward the garden windows where the afternoon sun slanted in. "I live one day at a time and try not to think of Andre. It's difficult though," she said, patting her tummy.

Marjorie Thelen

Fabienne pulled her into a hug, and they rocked together for a long while.

* * * * *

The yellow blooms on the Carolina Jasmine came and went along with the magnolia and azalea blossoms. The days in New Orleans were gently slipping into summer.

Fabienne Beluche sat at the desk in her office in the Silver Slipper, the French doors opened to the alleyway, when a shadow fell across the door. She glanced up and started, and then jumped up and into Andre Lafitte's embrace. She laughed and hugged him.

"Andre, Andre, how good to see you. How are you? When did you get back? Thank you for the Silver Slipper. Have you been to see Mercedes?"

"Hold on, wait a minute." Andre smiled. "I can't answer all those questions at once. First, let me look at you."

He held her at arm's length. Their faces wore the smiles of friends long standing.

"Beautiful as ever." Andre glanced around. "It looks like the place suits you. How do you like it?"

"It's good for me. The girls are happy. Business is steady. What more could an old whore want?" She laughed. "You look the same. Let me see you."

She looked him over with a practiced eye. "You are the only man I know who looks perpetually good in a simple pair of dark brown britches and a loose fitting, white cotton shirt. You have the look of the sea about you, all tan and sun bleached hair. How was the voyage?"

"Beyond expectation," said Andre, the success of the trip lighting up his eyes. "*Wings of the Wind* handled incredibly. We made a handsome profit on everything we took to California. I could have sold the ship, if I had wanted to. I had an offer to take her to China to pick up tea. But I stuck to the schedule on the return run and did the planned stops in South America. I dropped off everything in Boston."

"What brings you to New Orleans?"

Andre's hesitated only a moment. "The regular run. I dropped Jamie off with his Uncle in Boston to visit. I'll do the East Coast to New Orleans run for a while."

"Have you seen Mercedes? She's here, you know."

"Jamie told me. I haven't seen her."

"You are going to see her, aren't you?" Fabienne narrowed her eyes at him.

"She's the reason I came to New Orleans." He returned her gaze, his eyes clear and steady.

"You need to marry that girl, Andre Lafitte."

"It's crossed my mind, but she might not want me. We didn't part on the best of terms, and what will she say when she finds out I'm the son of a whore? She comes from a good Boston family. They might turn her out like they turned her mother out."

"Do you think that matters to her? I told her about your mother."

Andre's eyebrows shot up. "You did?"

"Don't strangle me. She wasn't horror struck. We are talking about an intelligent, compassionate, and, do I need to add, beautiful woman."

The corners of his mouth curled up into a smile. "I see we have another Mercedes Lawless fan. You and her brother. It was hard to forget her with him around. Lord knows I tried." He gave a heartfelt sigh.

Andre peered behind Fabienne as if searching for

someone. "Where is Claudette? She is still with you, isn't she?"

"She lives with Mercedes now, and it's working out well. I don't think I will be able to take her away from Mercedes. They are inseparable."

"I can see both of them in the same visit."

No, Fabienne thought, you will be seeing all three of them in the same visit.

* * * * *

A thunderstorm came up just after dark. It poured buckets, straight down. The French doors to the back garden stood ajar, and rain splattered hard on the bricks outside. Mercedes sat beside the bassinet in the parlor, adjusting a lace coverlet over the sleeping baby. Claudette had gone upstairs with Antoinette to bathe and prepare for bed.

Mercedes rose to adjust the doors, so that the rain would not splash in, when she heard a carriage pull up in front of the house. Her brows knit together, as she wondered who would be calling at this hour of the night.

She walked to the window beside the entrance door to peer out. Through the rain and the darkness she tried to see who was alighting from the carriage. The figure was tall, and she feared at first it might be Derek Bragg. Thank goodness Elijah was in the stable to the rear of the house, bedding the horses down for the night.

The light changed as the figure drew closer, and then she recognized the familiar outline of the person walking up to the door. She inhaled deeply to calm her nerves, exhaled carefully, and opened the door.

Andre stepped into the pool of light from the

Wings of the Wind

entranceway.

"It didn't work," he said. "I thought if I got away from you the sea and the sun and the wind would wash you out of my head. But you were stuck in my heart. It didn't work."

She grasped his forearm and pulled him in out of the rain. Water dripped from his dark hair, and his shirt was wet. But he was smiling, and he looked wonderful.

He reached out with his hand and caressed her cheek. She closed her eyes and leaned into the caress, taking his hand in both of hers.

She opened her eyes and offered a faint smile. "You're wet."

"It's raining," he said, his eyes glowing. "I don't mind. I'm here with you, and that's what's important. I found what was missing in my life on the trip to San Francisco. It was you."

"I didn't know if you would ever be back, but I hoped you would. You will never know how much I prayed that you would return to me."

He pulled her to him and wrapped his arms around her. "Mercedes?"

"Yes?" She sank into his warmth, embracing his strength. She would never let him go again.

"I'm sorry. Will you forgive me for leaving you?"

"I'm sorry, too, for being so unreasonable and head strong. I've given our relationship a lot of thought over these last months. You are back and that's what is important."

"Then, will you marry me?"

She pulled back and gazed up into his eyes. "What about the man who will never be around and won't take females on his ship?"

"I'm going to change my policies." He grinned down at her, but the smile drifted away.

He searched her eyes. "You need to know one thing about me."

She put her finger to his lips. "I already know about your mother. Fabienne told me."

"Did she tell you Jack Lormand was my father?"

Mercedes eyes opened wider. "No, that she didn't. Do you know he passed away?"

Andre nodded. "His lawyer got in touch with me. Jack Lormand left me some of his empire. Some of the legal part of it, which I thought was real considerate of him."

"He gave Fabienne the Silver Slipper," Mercedes said. "He was the kind of man that took care of his own."

"I wished I had known he was my father while he lived. It might have been different between us."

He pulled on one of the curls aside of her face and twirled it around his finger. "Now you know I'm not the son of a pirate. I hope that puts your fears to rest."

Mercedes laughed softly. "I believe you."

"But there's something else." He took her face into his hands and looked deep into her eyes. "I am a pirate of sorts. I'm involved in smuggling, and it is illegal. You need to consider what I tell you before you decide to marry me. It could make life uncomfortable, even dangerous for you."

She searched his face for clues, but she knew that nothing he could tell her would change the feelings in her heart.

He seemed to struggle over how to tell her. "There is network of people in the South," he began, "that help slaves escape to the North. I smuggle one or two at a time to the North on my ship. Folks here don't look kindly on people who help runaway slaves. They say it's stealing

Wings of the Wind

another man's property. I don't believe in slavery and that's why I help smuggle them out. Fabienne and Elijah help, too. Fabienne told me Elijah works for you now. You are at risk by employing Elijah and by marrying me, if we are ever found out. That's why you must consider carefully before you marry me. Do you understand?"

Mercedes gazed into the eyes of the tall, broad shouldered man holding her in his embrace. He was not only the man of her dreams and of her heart, he was a man of courage and conviction. She hoped that she would be his equal as a lifelong partner.

"I don't believe in slavery either. I support what you are doing."

He bent and kissed her lips. "Then you will marry me?"

"Yes, I will," she said, and they kissed again, longer, sweeter. They kissed and kissed and kissed until they were breathless with longing and desire for one another.

"When?" she asked between kisses.

"Tomorrow?"

She laughed into his kisses. "Andre Lafitte, every time I think I'll never be surprised by you, you come up with something new. I think the sooner we get married the better because I have a surprise for you."

"I already know that Claudette is here with you."

"It's another surprise. Come." She took his hand and led him to the parlor.

He spied the bassinet and froze. "Great God in Heaven, what's this?"

"It's little Andre."

He walked to the bassinet and bent down to peek in. He looked up at her and pointed in. "It's a baby."

Mercedes nodded and looked into the bassinet, her

face lit with pride for the wee babe they had made together.

"I think he looks like you, don't you think?" she asked, gazing at the baby still sleeping, fists curled beside his head.

Andre reached for her and pulled her close. "Why didn't you tell me?"

"We were trying to forget each other, remember? You didn't leave Galveston throwing me kisses from the deck of the *Wings of the Wind*."

"I'm sorry, Mercedes. I didn't know," he whispered into her hair.

"I'm sorry, too. We're both pretty headstrong."

"I hope the little guy in there doesn't inherit a double dose of headstrong, or we're in trouble." Andre looked again at the baby. "This will take some getting used to." He cocked his head. "He's cute though, isn't he?" He stooped down and leaned closer. "He smells nice, like lavender. May I hold him?"

"Of course." Mercedes reached into the bassinet and lifted the baby into Andre's arms.

He gazed at him and touched his nose. The little boy giggled back at him.

"This is wonderful," he said. "Can we make more of these?"

"I think we should wait until we're married."

"Until tomorrow night then. After that we all sail together to Boston on the *Wings of the Wind*."

THE END

By Way of Acknowledgement

I started in romance in Washington DC with the Washington Romance Writers. I must first thank the writers in that group for their encouragement and support. I learned character development by writing romance. When I moved to west, I got better at plot and found new materials for the mysteries I started to write. By then I had joined the Harney Basin Writers of Eastern Oregon, who I thank for their support and encouragement over these last ten years. I have advance readers who tell me if the book works or not, and to them I extend my gratitude and appreciation. A special thank you goes to Lorna Cagle, fellow author, for her unending support of all my novels and for her encouraging me to publish this one. My appreciation extends to all the librarians who helped me gather the historical data I needed to write this book. I so love books and libraries and hope we never lose the bricks and mortar buildings that house them. A big round of gratefulness goes to my loyal readers, who keep coming back. Last, as always my love and blessings go to my dear husband John, who likes my books and keeps cheering me on.

Marjorie Thelen

About the Author

Marjorie Thelen lives and writes novels on a tiny ranch on the Oregon frontier twenty miles from the small town of Burns. She enjoys writing stories that entertain her and, hopefully, her readers. She writes light-hearted mystery, utopian science fiction, and historical romance. She has been known to occasionally produce an essay or poem. All her books in Kindle and print are available on Amazon.com. Visit her web site: www.MarjorieThelen.com